Other Novels by Mildred Walker
Available in Bison Books Editions

MILDRED WALKER

IF
A
LION
COULD
TALK

Introduction to the Bison Books Edition
by James Welch

University of Nebraska Press
Lincoln and London

❂ The paper in this book meets the minimum requirements of
American National Standard for Information Sciences—Perma-
nence of Paper for Printed Library Materials, ANSI Z39.48-1984.

First Bison Books printing: 1995
Most recent printing indicated by the last digit below:
10   9   8   7   6   5   4   3   2   1

Library of Congress Cataloging-in-Publication Data
Walker, Mildred, 1905–
If a lion could talk / Mildred Walker.
p.   cm.
"Introduction to the Bison books edition by James Welch."
ISBN 0-8032-9778-5 (pbk.: alk. paper)
I. Title.
PS3545.A524I36   1995
813'.52—dc20
95-10946   CIP

Reprinted by arrangement with Mildred Walker Schemm.
Reprinted from the original 1970 edition by Harcourt Brace
Jovanovich, Inc., New York.

For Aequanimitas and the Tupa Tribe

AUTHOR'S NOTE

The characters and situation of this novel were suggested by actual persons who lived in historical time, but my treatment and interpretation of them are entirely fictional.

I am grateful to Professor Allan R. Taylor for his help with the Blackfoot terms and names used; and to Professor Howard N. Doughty for his biography of Francis Parkman and the insight it gives into the reaction to the Wilderness of a young New Englander in the early nineteenth century. I am also indebted to Mrs. Anne McDonnell, of the Montana Historical Library, who furnished me with rich background material.

INTRODUCTION

James Welch

It's difficult today to imagine Montana as the wilderness it once was. True, there are vast high plains; mountains that loom blue-black on the western and southern horizons; rivers deep and slow or fast and flashing; animals, such as grizzly, wolverine, elk, and wolf, not commonly found in other areas. And there are wilderness areas, carefully delineated roadless areas, traversed only by foot or horseback. But there are also freeways, fences, power lines, small cities, jet trails across the sky, the roar of snowmobiles in the backwoods. There are vast mining operations, endless miles of strip-farming, logging operations that have left whole mountainsides bare and ruined. Where once the wild buffalo roamed, there are herds of patient hereford and black angus cattle.

Yet, the Montana territory was a wilderness when a young Baptist minister left his comfortable New England town and church in the mid-nineteenth century to save "savage" souls on the upper Missouri River. These souls belonged to the Blackfeet Indians, or the Pikunis (hide scrapers), as they called themselves.

If a Lion Could Talk is the story of Mark Ryegate's failure to convert the Indians to Christianity through his almost legendary eloquence. Mark was not alone in his arrogance—missionaries of all denominations were spreading throughout the West at that time, each bringing his (they were all male) message of salvation to the Indians.

Mark did not last long in the wilderness, perhaps because his "call" was a single sentence in the Bible, from Isaiah: "The voice of him that crieth in the wilderness, Prepare ye the way of the Lord, make straight in the desert a highway for our God." At the risk of being disrespectful, a single sentence from the Bible, no matter how powerful, does not cut it in the wilderness. What does work in the wilderness is commitment, patience, perseverance, the willingness to listen, to acquire knowledge of the natives' way of life and religious beliefs. Unlike many of his Catholic counterparts in that region, Mark is sadly lacking in these virtues. Consequently, after only four months, he goes back down the river to his home and church thinking of himself as a failure. This is where *If a Lion Could Talk* begins (the enigmatic title comes from the Austrian philosopher Ludwig Wittgenstein: "If a lion could talk, we could not understand him"). Mark and his wife, Harriet, are first seen returning from the wilderness to their small New England town in the middle of the night, tired, dazed, feeling greatly dislocated in their familiar house.

Mildred Walker has chosen to tell this story of the young minister and his wife in an interesting style of flashbacks, letters, and diary entries, as well as straightforward narrative. The combination of such literary techniques is risky and can often lead to confusion, flatness, and unevenness in pace and tone. But Walker has given us a story that needed to be told about this period of clashing cultures and those individuals who are attracted to and repulsed by a people unlike themselves. And she writes in a consistently brilliant style, as only an author in control of her material can.

As if to emphasize his calling to the wilderness, Mark has left his wife of one year to journey west—to the shock of the deacons and the church wives. But Harriet, the daughter of one of the town's leading citizens (now deceased), relies less on religious zeal and more on love for her man and her determination to be with him. After a couple of months, she decides to join him in the wilderness, making the arduous journey to St. Louis, then by boat up to Fort Benton, the trading post where Mark is attempting his conversions. Mark almost wishes she hadn't come but nevertheless welcomes her with amorous embraces on a buffalo-skin rug.

Harriet, who has come to the wilderness in good faith, becomes a willing pawn in Mark's desire to return home. She becomes pregnant, thereby giving Mark an excuse. Even though the journey home, undertaken at the onset of winter, will be much more difficult than staying at the fort to have the baby, he convinces himself and her that she will be better served by her own doctor back east. And so the novel opens with their late night return to their home in the fictional town of Woollett, Massachusetts.

This is Mildred Walker's last published novel and perhaps her most interesting from a psychological standpoint. If you're looking for an action-packed frontier adventure, you'd better look to the rowdy dudes who write that kind of stuff. Walker is much more interested in matters of the mind and spirit, the struggles within as well as without. Mark and Harriet, the two major characters in *If a Lion Could Talk,* are haunted by a third character, the wife of the factor of the trading post at Fort Benton, Montana. Her name is Eenisskim and she is a Blood Indian from Canada. By the time Mark and Harriet reach the wilderness, Eenisskim has been married to Major Phillips for fourteen years, even though she is still a relatively young woman.

Eenisskim is a powerful and beautiful woman who has helped her husband become the principal trader among the Blackfeet Indians. Even though she has taken to wearing fancy gowns and a gold cross around her neck, she is highly respected by them; she is also a persuasive businesswoman, and so the Indians bring their pelts and hides to Major Phillips' trading post. Through her marriage to Major Phillips, Eenisskim has learned the English language. It is clear that she understands it and can—but rarely, if ever—speak it.

As soon as he meets her, Mark becomes obsessed with the notion that if she would act as his go-between and translator, he could reach vast numbers of Indians who would see the light and reason of Christianity. Without her, Mark's mission is a dreadful failure. He rarely gets to use his eloquence to more than a handful of Indians and then they laugh at him. Pierre, a French Canadian clerk at the fort, serves as his translator, and Mark is convinced that Pierre does not do his fine words justice. It is probably true, but in a nice stroke of comedy, Pierre explains: "But what you tell them sometimes is crazy to them, *mon père.* One time you tell 'em God is fisher of men. They laugh to think of Indian jerked up out of river! And they don't know what the hell is shepherd. Better when you say God is burning bush."

To add insult to injury, Pierre tells Mark that a Catholic

priest a little while back had great luck converting Indians. When the priest left by boat, a hundred Indians followed down the riverbank for three miles, seeking a final blessing. When Mark leaves, only one Indian woman, a cut-nose (adulterous women often were mutilated by having their noses cut off), weeps and waves to him.

Mark does bring something back with him from the wilderness: a vision. One late afternoon, after he and the Major have spent the day on horseback searching for a suitable site for a church that would never be built, Mark, exhausted, lies down on the riverbank for a nap. He feels a drop of water, then another, and he awakens, but his arm is slung over his face, and he does not see the source of the drops. Finally he looks and sees a wide spread of feathers, wings and breast. Then the wings lift, and Mark believes them to be eagle wings, and he feels himself rising with them. "He felt light of body, weightless, translated out of his own lame flesh, up, up . . . infinitely free." Then he hears laughter, "high and sharp as a bird's cry," and it turns out to be Eenisskim, holding a wet duck over him. Later, at dinner, as a kind of final humiliation, she serves the duck. But Mark still feels, even after his return from the wilderness, that the vision of the bird lifting him is a valid sign from God, even if the circumstances were a bit absurd.

One other thing happens in the wilderness that will create most of the tension between Mark and Harriet for the rest of the book. Eenisskim loses her son by drowning and mourns in the Indian way—she cuts her hair ragged, slashes her arms, covers herself with ashes, and wails and shrieks in grief. Mark feels that it is his duty to comfort her and follows her to a distant butte, where she mourns for three days and nights. Mark is aghast at how primitive and animal-like she becomes. Her screams and moans are "sub-human." Then, miraculously, Mark realizes that he loves this woman as God loves all his creatures. He goes to her and puts his arm around her, feeling that "the love God had poured into my heart must reach her, but she was too lost in the depths of her pagan despair." She ignores him, and Mark is torn between his feeling of love for this woman and his failure to comfort her.

Mark does not tell Harriet about his encounter when he returns to the fort. She learns of it several months later when Mark relates this story, instead of a traditional Christ sermon, to his New England congregation on Easter Sunday. Of course, they are totally shocked at the idea of his physical contact with the pagan woman—and of his seeming acceptance of the sensuality of the moment. Harriet is shocked too, but even more than that, she experiences a feeling of betrayal.

Mark's career as a minister goes downhill after that. People stop coming to church. The deacons decide he is not the right man for them. And Harriet begins to lose her trust in him.

The rest of the novel is the story of their growing estrangement, the back and forth of love and trust, the sacrifices they should make for each other but can't. Frankly, at this point, the reader begins to recognize a feeling that has been nagging since the Ryegates' return from the wilderness: Mark is not a very likeable man. He is self-absorbed as only a man with a message can be; he is manipulative; he is in love with his oratorical powers. He feels that he is special because he has been to the wilderness. On the other hand, he is occasionally filled with self-loathing, doubt, and a sense of failure in most things. His eloquence, so effective when he preaches traditional sermons to his traditional flock, at times seems a mockery of what he perceives as his true calling—to go into the wilderness and bring the wilderness back to civilization. He can't understand why his parishioners display nothing more than a greedy curiosity about the frontier and its savages.

Harriet, for her part, feels a confusing distance from this husband, who only a few months previously she had followed into the wilderness. Her diary entries and her thoughts record her belief that Eenisskim has "bewitched" Mark. Of course, nothing of the kind has happened; Eenisskim has not played that active a role; it has all been in Mark's obsessive mind. But in a few well-done brush-strokes, the author makes us see that the Indian woman becomes an obsession with Harriet, too.

Mark does land on his feet after losing his church by becoming involved in the abolition movement. He throws himself headlong into the antislavery fight, to the exclusion of his wife and newborn daughter. In one telling scene of his self-absorption, Harriet holds the baby up for Mark to see: "Isn't she lovely, Mark!" "Can't tell yet," he teased; then he asked abruptly, "I wonder what she'll make of her father when she grows up?"

As a result of his involvement with the abolitionist movement, Mark goes to Kansas where the slavery and antislavery forces are going at it hammer and tongs. Mark becomes something of a celebrity for his thunderous sermons and speeches. Kansas is a violent place to be and Mark eventually ends up with a rope around his neck. He survives, but the tightness of the rope has damaged his vocal cords, perhaps permanently. And so, in the grand irony of the book, the orator is reduced to speaking in a harsh whisper.

Meanwhile, the estrangement of the couple goes on (they do not sign their letters with "love" anymore) and both end up blaming each other for it.

The book could probably end here, with Mark having gotten his just desserts in a simplistic way and Harriet becoming increasingly, necessarily independent, but Mildred Walker is too canny an author to allow that to happen. In a denouement that combines all of her stylistic gifts, she brings together the wilderness and civilization in a startling, but inevitable, manner.

If a Lion Could Talk is based loosely on historical fact. There was a Fort Benton (still is), there was a Major Culbertson and his Blood wife, Natawista. By all accounts, Natawista was a beautiful, intriguing woman. She could ride with the buffalo hunters, swim like a fish, preside over her husband's dinner table in her regal gowns, and enrapture the men. Audubon makes a trip to the fort and is impressed with her: "how amazed would have been any European lady or some of our modern belles who boast their equestrian skill, at seeing the magnificent riding of the Indian princess . . . [her] magnificent black hair floating like a banner behind her." But he is a bit taken aback when, after a buffalo hunt, she has a brave split open a buffalo skull so that she can enjoy the raw brains.

Mildred Walker wrote an article about Natawista in *The Montana Magazine of History* in 1952, almost twenty years before *If a Lion Could Talk* was published. In the article, she included descriptions of the Indian woman by important visitors to the fort, such as Audubon, Governor Stevens of Washington Territory, and a Swiss artist. Almost all of their accounts used the words "refined" and "regal." One of the accounts was that of a not-so-important visitor. Walker writes: "The young minister, Reverend Elkanah Mackey, who was discouraged before he began his task of making good Presbyterians out of the Indians, wrote gravely in a letter to his Board in 1856: 'I think she (Mrs. Culbertson) is a very remarkable woman ... her influence on Mr. Culbertson seems to be of the most favorable kind.'"

Could this unsuccessful young minister be the model for Mark? Probably. In any case, Mildred Walker, whose own father had been a minister back east, chooses to get inside the head of a minister who has come to the wilderness and failed. Eenisskim (Natawista), Major Phillips (Culbertson), and the wilderness are simply catalysts for a story of faith, aspiration, failure, and psychological analysis of a most tortured kind.

If a lion could talk, we could not understand him.

LUDWIG WITTGENSTEIN

In silence we must wrap much of our life, because it is too fine for speech, because also we cannot explain it to others, and because somewhat we cannot yet understand.

RALPH WALDO EMERSON

Part One

THE RETURN

Chapter One

THEY came up the walk to their own house in the dark, like fugitives. Behind them, the cab they had been lucky to get at such an hour retreated over the cobblestone street, the hoof-beats of the horse and the creak of the wheels lightly muffled in a thin layer of snow. When Mark turned the big brass key in the lock, the door still held, bolted on the inside.

"I never thought of the bolt!" Harriet murmured.

"Isn't Hannah here?" Mark started to lift the knocker.

"There was no reason for her to stay when we expected to be gone so long."

He put the knocker down without letting it sound, as though he didn't want to disturb the silence of the street. "You wait here, Harriet. I think I can get in through the study window, or if I can't, I'll find some way to break in."

But to stand outside their own door in the chilling dark, with a bag at her feet, to have Mark climb in through a window like a thief in the night made her feel stealthy. This was her home; she had been born here, had lived all her life in this house. Now she looked over her shoulder down a street that had become suddenly unfamiliar, almost hostile in the dark. The houses reared up tall, with sharp pointed roofs, and the trees crowded close. She shivered and drew her fur cape more tightly around her; yet she had been far colder on the way. On either side, the houses were dark. What would Miss Dinwiddie or the Allens think when they saw that she and

Mark were back? What would the Church think, for that matter?

She remembered how eagerly she had gone out of this door,
leaving Hannah to close it and wave a tearful good-bye. Never
before in her life, except of course when she married Mark,
had she felt so sure of what she was doing; for how could she
not follow her husband into the Wilderness? But now he was
back. And she was with him.

It seemed a long wait before she saw, through the glass
panes on either side of the door, a small flame moving through
the house. Mark set the kerosine lamp down on the little table
beside the card tray, not stopping to light the gas jet, and shot
the bolt back with a grating sound. The door stuck as he pulled
it open and reached out to draw her in. A powder of snow came,
too, on the hem of her skirt. Then he brought in the bag. Of all
they had taken—the melodeon, the four trunks, the boxes of
books and beads, the rolls of cotton flannel and calico and
the patterns for underwear for the Indian children that she
had never unfolded, the religious tracts and the colored Bible
pictures—a single carpetbag was little to bring back.

Major Phillips had said he would send their trunks on the
first boat down river in the spring, but she knew very well
that his wife would dress up in her clothes and promenade in
front of the giggling squaws. Harriet stepped into the parlor,
away from the remembered sound of squaw laughter, feeling
rather than seeing the heavy furniture and the great square
piano assembled there in the dark.

She watched Mark hanging his fur cap and heavy skin coat
on the hatrack, which creaked under its strange burden. He
looked foreign to this hall in his elkskin shirt and trousers,
with his ruddy face and his beard.

An odd silence had fallen on them both for an instant, as
though they couldn't quite realize where they were; then Mark
came to her. "We're home, Harriet," he said solemnly. "The
Lord has brought us through all the dangers of the Wilderness." He put his arm around her, but his voice had a for-

mal sound in the stillness of the cold, dimly lit room. She was afraid he was going to kneel in prayer.

Her own "yes" came out small and inadequate to the occasion, she felt. That time when the river was blocked by ice, and in the blizzard, she hadn't been sure they would ever reach home. It wasn't that she was not grateful to the Lord, but she was suddenly too tired to kneel or try to pray. The clock in the church tower struck one, startling her. She had forgotten how town clocks sounded.

"Mark, the clock!"

"What, dear?"

"The clock," she managed to repeat.

"Oh, yes." Mark seemed to bring his thought from a long way off. "We're back in civilization. Come, Harriet, you need to get to bed."

She watched their shadows climb with them up the staircase, her hand on the mahogany rail that had been polished until it was smoother than her own palm. The white wallpaper was patterned in red and blue flowers, like the beaded pattern on Mrs. Phillips' white elkskin dress, the one that had become all spotted with blood when she ate the raw buffalo brains. Against the wall Mark's shadow, with his long hair and beard, seemed to belong to some trapper; but her own shadow, in bonnet and cape, looked strange to her, too.

Their bedroom was enormous, and cold. The head of the bed lost itself in the shadows of the high ceiling, and the marble top of the dresser gleamed like gray ice and grated beneath the lamp Mark set on it while he lighted the gas light. It seemed to take him a long time, and the first match didn't catch. Then the yellow light flared out with a low hissing sound.

Harriet stood in front of the dresser, taking off her bonnet. That thin woman in the mirror, with the wind-reddened face between lank loops of light hair, was herself. Behind her she saw Mark, just standing there, looking around the room. No, his hair and beard gave him the look of a prophet, not a mountain man. Getting here seemed to have taken all their strength; they seemed unable to go about the motions of undressing or the effort of talking. Then she felt Mark's hands taking off her cape.

"Are you all right, Harriet? The terrible trip hasn't hurt you?"

"No. I'm all right, only so tired." Her words came out with an unexpected quaver. Mark lifted her up and laid her on the bed. She closed her eyes, hardly aware that he was unhooking her jacket, covering her with a quilt, murmuring comforting things to her about building a fire . . . warm in a minute. His voice drew farther and farther away. She fell asleep before she could get any words out to protest.

The buffalo skin was warm beneath them, rough-haired and yet not rough. The hide had a sharp, raw smell, so different from the lavender-scented sheets at home. Animal feet ran on the roof—were they squirrels or rats? Outside, in the black dark, was the Wilderness, where savages roamed, and animals, wild animals, lurked. But she didn't care. She had made the long trip by herself to be with Mark, and now she lay in his arms, naked on the fur skin. At home they had never lain naked together. Mark lifted his mouth from hers to whisper, "You should never have come, my darling, but you don't know how I wanted you."

The walls were thin between the rooms. Curses in a hard voice burst through the cracks, words she did not understand, had never even heard. Mark drew the blanket up over their heads. "This is no place for you, Harriet, but I'm thankful the Major's wife is a lady."

The Major's wife's eyes were shining and black. Now her face was bending over Harriet instead of Mark's. The gold cross she wore on her red silk bodice swung on its leather thong, just above Harriet's eyes. But she didn't speak.

"Why won't you speak for Mark, Mrs. Phillips? He wants

you to interpret for him." The Major's wife's black bright eyes only smiled.

Mark sat on the bed with his face in his hands. "She wouldn't speak to me, Harriet."

"Don't mind, Mark. Maybe she listened."

But Mark just shook his head. His face was drawn; there were smudges of black and white paint on it, like the paint on Mrs. Phillips' face. He didn't look like Mark; he looked terrible. "Harriet, can't you see? I failed."

She put her hands up to his face to draw him to her, but it wasn't Mark's face. A mutilated, masklike, horrible face leered down at her. The face was Aapaaki's. The black eyes on either side of the holes of her nose stared at Harriet. Harriet tried to scream, but no one came. Where was Mark? Why did Aapaaki follow Mark around all the time? Harriet tried to drive her away. She had a big stick in her hand, but Aapaaki ran off after Mark.

Mark was holding a service at the end of the big room in the Fort. He was reading from the Bible: "He that is without sin among you, let him first cut off her nose." But the young braves who cut off Aapaaki's nose weren't there; only some squaws, and the Major's wife.

Now it was time for the hymn, and she was playing the melodeon, but only she and Mark were singing. The Indian children kept up a crazy yah-yah-yah. "Stop it!" She swung around from the melodeon, waving her big stick, but Mrs. Phillips was laughing at her.

"But why won't she listen to me, Harriet? Why?" Mark kept asking.

"What do you want to say to her, Mark?"

"I want to say 'loved.' 'God so loved. . . .' "

"But she knows all that; she's a Christian already. The Catholic priest converted her; don't you know that? She wears a gold cross around her neck."

Mark was walking away, down by the bank of the river.

She saw him lifted up into the air by a great bird, and Mrs. Phillips was with him, holding his hand. They were going up and up into that enormous sky, beyond the cliff of rock, where she could never find them. And she was standing on the ground, calling. Aapaaki was beside her, holding her there, so she couldn't run after them. Harriet couldn't bear to watch, and hid her face in the big pillow of goose down, plump in its cold linen case, and soft. . . .

She dropped down into a sleep too deep for dreaming.

Mark stared into the dark of the furniture-filled bedroom. They were home and safe in their own bed. Harriet had kept turning and tossing, moaning in her sleep out of sheer exhaustion, but now she was sleeping quietly. Why couldn't he sleep instead of lying as rigid as though he were squeezed into that Mackinaw boat, close to the icy water, feeling the current under them? That was the closest thing to being in the belly of a whale he could think of. Might as well have been; he felt like Jonah. He hadn't refused to go to Nineveh, but he had refused to stay there long enough to accomplish the Lord's work. . . . But would he have accomplished it if he had stayed?

He got out of bed and went down through the cold house to his study, feeling his way. He had paced the study floor often enough to cross to his desk in the dark, and he managed to light the green-shaded lamps. He picked up the afghan that lay as it always had on the couch, pulled it around him like an Indian blanket, and sat down in his high-backed leather armchair.

Almost reluctantly, his eyes reached up to the high shelves where the books marched rank on rank in stern array. The gold word "Exegesis" leaped from the backs of one row, broken by a gap where he had taken two volumes out when he left. No one at the Fort would ever try to read them; they would be tossed into the fire some bitter cold night, along with those tracts and the colored Bible pictures for the children.

His eyes came back to his desk. Twin circles of yellow light spread over the blotter pad that he had left bare when he went away; blotted into its surface was his own confident handwriting, perhaps from one of his many letters to the Mission Board, perhaps from his last sermon here at Calvary Church. He spread his cold hands in the light to warm them, and saw the scrap of paper folded under the inkwell—some quotation or idea he had scribbled down. He pulled it out, curious because it belonged to that other time, before he went away. "What I must do is all that concerns me, not what the people think." Emerson, of course. Emerson had said so many things he had taken unto himself.

But it hadn't been Emerson that had sent him to the Wilderness; it had been that single sentence in Isaiah: "The voice of him that crieth in the wilderness, Prepare ye the way of the Lord, make straight in the desert a highway for our God." He remembered his excitement, sitting here at this desk. He had read it plenty of times before and never thought of it as directed at him. He had even looked with a slight curiosity at classmates in the seminary who were going to the mission field. But that day he had thought of John the Baptist preaching in the wilderness. And then he had thought of himself there.

The next Sunday, when he stood in his pulpit and looked down at the placid faces framed in their bonnets, and the faces above the beards and high white collars and cravats— almost anonymous in their similarity—he had felt a powerful urge to go to the Wilderness, to preach to ignorant heathen who had never heard the Word. He had felt called of God. Or had he put it that way to himself? He was sick of questioning.

He had been convinced of his call, even though he had been at Calvary Church so short a time and it would mean leaving Harriet until the next year, perhaps longer. He had told himself that a man called of God must make sacrifices and endure hardships, that surely the experience in the Wilderness would be a period of growth in power for himself, power he would use in the work of the Lord.

How little he had known, or the Mission Board either, of what such a mission would be! The ignorant savages had not been eager to hear him, and he knew now what a fool he had been to think he could make them listen to him, let alone understand him, unless he spoke their tongue. He had sat here at this desk and imagined himself with redskins thronging around him!

There had never been any throngs, except for the one time seventy lodges had come to the Fort to see the Major. The Major, Ephraim Phillips, had introduced him to them as their white brother who had come to bring them "good medicine," and he had stepped forth into that great circle of dark faces, feeling stirred as never before, full of a sense of his power to bring them to God.

But after that there had not even been crowds. He had preached to a handful of children, half a dozen braves at best —usually old ones—a dozen or more squaws, and the Major's wife. The Major was always too busy to come.

How stupid he had been not to know it would be difficult to preach through an interpreter. Pierre, that conceited little French Canuck clerk, translated his evangel into some kind of Indian dialect that sometimes set them laughing. He had accused Pierre of adding comments of his own, but Pierre swore he only repeated what Mark preached. "But what you tell them sometimes is crazy to them, *mon père*. One time you tell 'em God is fisher of men. They laugh to think of Indian jerked up out of river! And they don't know what the hell is shepherd. Better when you say God is burning bush."

"I said God appeared to Moses *in* a burning bush," he had pleaded with him hopelessly.

That next Sunday he had begun so simply: "God is a mighty hunter, the mightiest and bravest of all hunters. His arrow is more swift and sure than the arrow of the greatest Indian brave." Then he had to wait for Pierre to turn the words into an unintelligible chain of t's, k's, and s's. He was always relieved when Pierre came to a stop, but startled.

"It is the arrow of truth," he would begin again. . . . If Mrs. Phillips had only translated for him, it could have been so different. He still believed he might have reached them through her, but she would never even try.

Mark jerked his body up straight in the chair to pull his mind out of its memory. He lifted the silver top of the cut-glass inkwell and saw that the ink had dried and the nibs of the pens on the tray were crusted with dry ink. He pulled open the left drawer and saw the sermons he had written, each one folded three times. He raised one and looked at the inscription on the back as though someone else had written it.

CALVARY BAPTIST CHURCH

WOOLLETT, MASS.

The Foundations of Faith

He dropped it back in its place without unfolding it; without, in fact, having any sense of recognition that he had ever conceived and composed it.

Yet, though Mrs. Phillips had never tried to speak to him, and had never translated for him, he had always to remember that it was through her that his vision had come. If it was a vision.

He had been over it a hundred times, resorting to the Scriptures to prove the importance of visions. "Your young men shall see visions." And the inverse statement: "Night shall be unto you that ye shall not have a vision; it shall be dark unto you." Now he would look at the incident coldly, under the light of his own study lamps, and determine whether or not he had had a vision.

That day, the very first week at the Fort, he had ridden from sunup until late afternoon with the Major, hunting a site for the church that never got built. He had been so lame and hot when he came back that he had thrown himself down on the bank above the river and fallen asleep, even as Jacob had been asleep when his vision came. Mark covered his face with his hands, giving himself up to the memory, almost fearfully.

A drop of water fell cold on his face, waking him instantly, but he lay still, not moving the arm that covered his eyes. His skin crawled with fear, and he had trouble keeping his breathing even. There was no sound. Another drop hit his face, then another. Someone was close to him . . . above him. Human breathing.

A cold drop struck lower down, on his neck, and he had an impulse to jump up and confront that breathing presence hovering over him, but he held himself rigid. Pretending that he was stirring restlessly in his sleep, he moved his arm ever so slightly, trying to see beneath it.

Something was coming down; he felt it just above his face. It blocked the light that seeped under his sleeve. Still trying to imitate the unconscious movements of sleep, he threw back his arm and found himself gazing up into a wide spread of feathers.

The wings came closer. The soft, downy feathers of a great bird's breast brushed against his face with coolness. He could have thrust out at it with his arm, but he lay still, staring up, blinking as a cold drop of water fell from the wings into his eye.

The wings were lifting! He felt himself rising with them. Now he could see the interlacing feathers, edged with color, white-shafted, and the strong bony joinings of the wide-spread wings. Eagle wings . . . infinitely strong, infinitely soft. He felt light of body, weightless, translated out of his own lame flesh, up, up . . . infinitely free.

"I bare you on eagles' wings, and brought you unto myself."

The wings lowered again, touching lightly, coolly against his face, then lifted, drawing him with them.

Mark let out his tight-held breath in a sigh, and opened his eyes. He hadn't lost it. Even back here in his own study that incredible sense of weightlessness, of holiness, returned. He lifted his hand and let it fall on the desk in triumph. The vision was all he had brought back from the Wilderness, really. But wasn't it enough? Just once in a lifetime to feel caught up far beyond ordinary human experience!

He tried to stop his mind there, but that laugh, high and sharp as a bird's cry, still sounded in his brain. His head had bumped against the wings as he sat up, and the bird fell heavily onto his knees. Mrs. Phillips was standing in front of him, bending double with laughter, her heavy black hair, which had come unbraided, falling over her face. Her elkskin dress was dark with water, and water ran from it onto the ground, even onto his Testament, which had slipped out of his pocket. She had pointed at him, speaking some Indian word that sent her off again into swoops of laughter.

When he picked up the bird, the head wobbled forward; its eyes stared blindly. It was a duck, black with green feathers.

He remembered asking where it had come from; and without a word she had slid down the steep bank. Just as he got to his feet, still holding the dripping duck, she disappeared under water.

Where the current slackened into smooth water, ducks moved back and forth, flashing the sun from their wings in nets of sudden light. Even now he could see that whole stretch of river. Some bird shrilled ceaselessly on the sand bar, but there was no sign of Mrs. Phillips. While his eyes searched for her one of the ducks bobbed out of sight, then rose again, feet first, in a human hand, and Mrs. Phillips' laughing face appeared for a moment before she swam back, this time half out of water, the bird cutting the ripple ahead of her as she held it in her hand. He had left the duck on the ground, picked up his Testament, and gone back into his room at the Fort. It had been dark after the light outside, he remembered, as dark as his own angry disillusionment.

He had told himself then that there had been no vision.

He was only confused by being wakened so suddenly with that cold drop of water and the sense of fright. It had been some kind of Indian trick to scare him to death. Maybe just a prank, as Harriet had said.

Yet how could he not have had a vision when he had felt himself drawn up by those wings? The duck's wingspread could not have been more than twelve to fifteen inches. How could he possibly have thought the interlacing feathers stretched far out beyond the reach of his eyes unless the illusion *was* a vision? Those drops of cool water had touched his hot eyelids like some heavenly ichor, and he had had an incredible sense of nearness to God. Not incredible; he had known it.

Nor did it matter that at dinner that night Mrs. Phillips was again the Major's lady, in a black silk dress, with gold earrings and the gold cross around her neck. Her hair was brushed smooth and polished with grease, a braid down over each shoulder. He had met her eyes once as she dropped them to the table for the grace he asked, but they gave no sign. The kettle of stew that sometimes reeked nauseatingly of wild meat gave off a savory aroma, and he spoke of the good smell. Mrs. Phillips, who seldom spoke to the Major during the meal, said something to him in her own tongue, and the Major told him she wanted him to know that the stew was made from a couple of ducks she had caught that day. "Then I should thank you," he had said, not sure she would detect the sarcasm in his tone. He remembered the way she inclined her head so that half her face was shadowed and only the smooth brow shone between those tight-drawn bands of hair; she lifted her face and her eyes met his. They were alive with laughter.

But there was her other face, painted black and white with green lines across the forehead, a hideous mask of horror; the eyes dull and staring as blindly as the dead duck's. And her hair standing up in ragged clumps, chopped off all over her head.

He sat a long time, lifting the top of the inkwell with one of the dry pens and letting it fall closed. Then he flung the pen down on the desk. He could never tell anyone about that time on the butte; neither could he ever get it out of his mind. That monotonous, inhuman cry of despair—like a voice out of hell, or some woman wailing for her demon lover in the mad kingdom of Kubla Khan. She had seemed beyond human power to reach, and no divine power was given him. Even his faith had failed him.

He hadn't been able to tell Harriet how it had been, except that he had failed. But it was the night after he came back, as though she might not have spoken of it so soon otherwise, that Harriet told him about the child. And that, too, his tired mind must go back over. He had seemed to get nothing settled on the long trip back; he had been too much on edge. Here in his study, where he had once been so confident, he could think about what they had done. He had to look squarely tonight at all that had happened to him, for tomorrow he would have to announce himself and explain why they had returned so soon.

They had wanted a child, and had prayed for one; yet when Harriet told him, he had turned around from his table and sat dumb and half incredulous—the way Joseph must have felt, he thought now, with a sense of not irreverent amusement. He had looked at Harriet speaking so calmly over there on the bed. He couldn't remember what he had said, if anything. Their eyes held in the wonder of it, and they were drawn so close together that he had no need to go to her. Then his mind had leaped at the thought of the coming child as a reason for leaving the Wilderness. And, almost at the same instant, Harriet had said perhaps they should try to go back home, as though their eyes, looking into each other's, had propagated the same thought.

It would be terrible to be there in winter, she had said. She could only stay huddled up inside most of the time. Pierre had told them there weren't many Indians at the Fort then, only coming and going; mostly the *engagés* who worked at the Fort, and Mark knew how little they came to the services. He could only say a prayer over them if one got stabbed in a drunken fight.

Of course that was true enough, but it startled him to have Harriet speak so cynically. He had listened, half wondering if she was saying these things or if they were his own thoughts.

Could he accomplish very much during the winter, really? Ever since she had heard that the Phillipses were making the trip all the way to St. Louis, she had been thinking . . . Maybe he should talk to the Major.

He remembered how he had gone over to sit beside her. "You want terribly to go, don't you, Harriet?" he had asked. She was slow in answering, not looking at him. It all depended on him; he would have to decide, she said finally. She would have the baby there if he thought they should stay.

And he had said that of course it would be better for her to be at home; he would be relieved to have her under Dr. Fothergill's care. But the trip would be dangerous. It might be too rugged in her condition, and if she should lose the baby . . . She had said she was sure she could stand the trip. Hadn't she come up all alone? She knew what it would be like. That was quite another thing, he had said, although it had taken plenty of courage, and she should never have tried it. But this time it would be in October and November.

If she hadn't come, she had started to say, but he had said quickly that he could come back up with the first boat in the spring, because there was no use going into that. He could spend the winter working with the Mission Board—studying the language, he had said vaguely; or it might be that Calvary hadn't settled on a permanent pastor, though he doubted that. It did seem, with the baby coming and the Phillipses leaving just then, so they could go with them, as though Providence . . . Another name for God, but at one remove, he always thought. He had used the term when he wrote the Mission Board.

Then the thought had struck him, as it should have in the very beginning. He had asked her point-blank whether she was suggesting their going just to give him an excuse for leaving, because of his—and it had been hard, suddenly, to say it, but they were speaking so clearly and honestly together—because of his *failure*.

For answer she had put her arms around his neck and brought his face down to hers. "Oh, Mark, I love you," she had said. "If you hadn't asked that, I would have minded. I don't care if you tell the Major that I want to go home to have the baby; you can even say that I'm afraid to have it without a doctor, and you can tell the deacons and the Mission Board that, too. It's a good enough reason that anybody could understand, and it's better to have them blame me. But, Mark," she had said, "I would hate it if you didn't know really that I'm not afraid to have the baby here, if you're with me."

Put that way . . . so their going *was* mostly for his sake; and the word "blame" . . . If that was her chief reason for going, then they had better stay, he had said. He winced now, hearing himself. And he remembered how he had gone on, insisting that just because he wasn't satisfied with his progress so far didn't mean that in time, when he had learned the tongue and was adept at sign language . . . He hadn't looked at Harriet when he said it; he had kept his eyes on his worktable, imagining himself sitting there working. He had even reminded her that he had been able to communicate with Two Knives, and often smoked a pipe with him. Two Knives had given him that eagle feather. "Until this experience with Mrs. Phillips . . ." he had said. His whole ordeal in the Wilderness seemed caught between those two experiences with that woman, both the confirmation of his mission and the negation of it. What did that mean?

But he hadn't finished his sentence about Mrs. Phillips, and Harriet had said, "What, Mark?"

"I believed I could persuade her to talk for me in the services. She could make all the difference."

"But now?" Harriet persisted.

It had been hard to say it; he had never quite admitted it to himself. "Now I don't think I can. I don't know why, but I can't seem to get to her." It was a relief to tell Harriet he had been dreading the winter. "It would be just as you said, I'm afraid." As he thought of leaving, his desire to go became so strong he had crowded it down by talking of the danger of the trip for Harriet. For if something should go wrong, if the trip should be too hard—and she knew anything could happen—she might blame him. That word again. She might not say it, but she might think that if he hadn't been so discouraged—given up is what it amounted to—she would have stayed and had her baby safely, whatever the discomforts, he had said.

Her eyes had held his in a long look again. "Do you really think I am like that, Mark? Don't let's ever think one thing and say something else to each other," she had said. He remembered, too, how they had clung together that night in such oneness of understanding and love that he was absolved, for a little time, of his sense of failure.

Mark was stiff from sitting in the cold, and he got up to hunt for paper he could burn in the study grate. On impulse he opened a drawer of sermons, running his finger over them to read their titles, remembering certain ones quite distinctly. He came on "The Hidden Life" and flipped up the page to read the text. From Corinthians: "For what man knoweth the things of a man, save the spirit of man which is in him?"

No one, not even Harriet, knew the things he had felt, and thought, and tried to do in the Wilderness. It wasn't a bad sermon, but he had hardly understood the full meaning of the word "hidden" when he wrote it. He crumpled the neatly written pages, stuffed them under the single stick that had been left in the grate, and lit them. They flamed up and thrust grabbing fingers at the wood, but fell back again. Still, there was a momentary flash of heat. He went back to his drawer and pulled out another: "April 2nd." The Sunday before he left. He looked curiously to see what the man he then was had preached on.

"Untrodden Paths." Joshua 3:4. "For ye have not passed this way heretofore." That was an understatement! And he had certainly been thinking entirely of himself rather than the congregation. How wrapped up in himself he had been! He tore the pages across, adding them to the fire, and went back to his desk.

It was easier to amuse himself with his old sermons than to force his mind back over leaving the Wilderness: how he had put off going to the Major all that next day, but known he would go. The Major's lack of surprise had given him a flat feeling. Harriet's condition struck him as a quite logical reason—just as she had said it would. He was even a little grateful to give it to the Major.

"A white woman, naturally," the Major had said. The Indian women often dropped back and had their children on the trail; quite amazing. But their grief when they lost a child was more frightful than any white woman's, he believed; Mrs. Phillips was still living in a tipi by herself. Mark began to tell him how he had tried . . . but the Major interrupted him in that brusque way of his saying she had to take it in her own way. A woman like Eenisskim didn't lean on anyone else.

It would always hurt him to remember how little the Major seemed to mind his giving up the mission. Clearly, he felt Mark had been a failure in the Wilderness. Many men were, Mark supposed, not just missionaries. But the Major had been a success; he was as good as any mountain man, could outride, bareback, most of the young braves, and outshoot them, of course. The chiefs listened when he called a council. All of that somehow lined the Major's tone of voice, and the way he made it easy for them to leave. They'd be going that week, the Major had said, while the weather was still good. October first was late; danger of the river freezing before they got down, and snow and blizzards. Mustn't expect an easy trip; part of the way in an open Mackinaw boat. But they'd make it, one way or another. They were taking the two children with them to his sister in Illinois; going to put them in proper schools. Since the younger boy's death, Mrs. Phillips was willing; and he felt it was time for them to be educated like white children. He had been silent for a long minute before he said, quietly, that he was retiring from the fur trade in the spring. Several years ago he had bought quite a piece of country in Illinois, and had a house built. He'd had men working on it, laying out the grounds. It was waiting for them to furnish.

The Major had seemed to forget Mark's presence, and as he stood waiting for him to go on, Mark had wondered how Mrs. Phillips would manage in civilization. Perhaps she would talk English then; she would have to.

Mark went back over to stand in front of the fire. One end of the stick had caught, but the fire was only smouldering. If he had been there at the Fort alone, as he had planned, that first winter, at least, it wouldn't have occurred to him to leave. That thought gave him some small satisfaction. But then, of course, he would have had no legitimate excuse for leaving.

He thought of their departure. He had been as glad to leave the Fort as he had been eager to arrive there. The salute from the cannon as they left belched in his ears with wry derision. He could never forget Aapaaki running along the shore as they pushed off, or the handful of Indians who laughed and pointed at her. Even Mrs. Phillips laughed. Harriet kept her face turned away toward the other shore, he remembered.

When the Black Robe left, Pierre had told him, the Indians, a hundred or more, followed him for three miles to get a last glimpse, and he had to stop and give them his blessing again. "He loved 'em like they were his children," Pierre had told him. When Marcus Ryegate left, he was followed by a single woman, an adulterous outcast with a cut nose. He had been relieved when she stood still; then he saw she was crying, and he had to wave to her.

He and Harriet hadn't talked much about their going, once the Major agreed to it if they thought they could stand the trip. That day when they snagged for the third time in the river, capsizing one boat, so most of their stuff was soaked, Mark had whispered to Harriet that it might be better if they cast Jonah out of the boat. She had known what he meant, but she only smiled and put her hand on his under the buffalo robe.

Mark leaned his head against the mantel. God, he called in his mind. God in Heaven, here am I, back in the place from which I started. Thou knowest that I have failed miserably, that I wanted to leave. But Thou hast brought us safely home after all that long journey, so Thou must want me for something.

He was so tired he stumbled on his way back upstairs, although the morning light was sifting through the stiff lace curtains.

Beneath the layers of sleep Harriet was aware of the sound of swishing water she had wakened to so many mornings, water turning the sidewheel of the Missouri River boat; but there was no movement under her, no sound of timbers straining or of engine chugging, no loud voices. The swishing stopped abruptly, then began again in fast chopping sounds. She sat up in bed and looked around the room, at Mark sleeping soundly beside her.

Crossing to the window, she saw a maid sweeping the white steps of Miss Dinwiddie's house, a woman whose name was Maggie, whom she had known as a child. With a rush of gladness, she realized she was home.

❖ ❖ ❖

But to stay only four months and then give up and come home! That's hardly what you expect of missionaries.

And when you think how hard we worked to raise money to help him build a church for the heathen!

She was there only two months, and we gave her that gold watch with "God bless you and keep you" engraved on the cover! I wept when we gave it to her, thinking she'd likely as not be scalped and some Indian squaw would be wearing it.

She seemed so brave going out there all alone after him.

A woman will follow a man anywheres if she's crazy enough about him. Don't you remember how she used to sit in church and never take her eyes off him all the time he preached?

His marrying her always seemed odd to me. She was so quiet and always had her nose in a book, and she's not what you could call a beauty, by any means.

And he's so handsome! Of course, Judge Tomlinson left her awfully well fixed.

You know Reverend Ryegate would never stoop to marrying for money, or even think about it!

I'm not saying he would. I suppose he was sorry for her, left all alone. But I don't believe Reverend Ryegate would ever have given up his mission if it hadn't been for her. He isn't the kind that gives up.

But, of course, her going to have a child . . .

A missionary's wife has to expect that!

I guess they went through everything making that long trip back so late in the year. It's God's miracle they're alive.

Miracle or not, I still say I think it's mighty queer, their coming back so soon.

◇ ◇ ◇

Chapter Two

IT was fortunate that Calvary Church was still sampling ministers. The Pulpit Committee had meant to take its time. So far, no agreement had been reached. Now Reverend Ryegate could resume his pastorate. Obviously, God had ordained it all.

After the farewell reception when he left, and the constant mention of him in their prayers, and the gifts of money to be spent on building a church for the heathen, a certain awkwardness might have been occasioned by his sudden return; but if so, it was overshadowed by the satisfaction the Church felt at having him back. It wasn't easy to find so gifted a young man as the Reverend Ryegate. He had been called to the pastorate of Calvary Church upon his graduation from the seminary three years ago, at the age of twenty-five. His father had been a clergyman before him. As Mr. Quackenbush said, he was born into the ministry, just like Henry Ward Beecher. His professors at the seminary had predicted a brilliant future for him and had spoken of his remarkable insight into the Scriptures. Although one professor had mentioned a tendency toward too ingenious interpretation and a propensity for reading too symbolically, they were unanimous in praising his natural eloquence.

From Reverend Ryegate's first Sunday at Calvary, the pews had creaked with the weight of the full congregation, which flocked to hear him; two Methodists and a Presbyterian had been seen among them. Deacon Terwilliger said he wouldn't be in the least surprised to have the young man become one of the great preachers of his time. When, moreover, Reverend Ryegate, only a year later, wooed and married Harriet Tomlinson, the twenty-nine-year-old spinster daughter of the Senior Deacon, deceased, their approval fell upon his head like the sweet-scented oil that anointed the head of David.

The enthusiasm of the congregation was not dimmed when the new Mrs. Ryegate preferred to go on living in her own handsome brick house, built by Samuel Tomlinson in 1763, and the income from the rental of the clapboard manse tinkled prettily into the coffers of the Church. The situation was ideal all round.

So it had been disconcerting to the deacons and trustees to have this sudden call to the Wilderness sound so loudly in their young pastor's ears. But his eloquence was no less effective in describing the urgency he felt than in describing the sins of wrongdoers. "The words in Isaiah and the description of John the Baptist preaching in the wilderness burst upon me from the page like the prophecy at the feast of King Belshazzar," he had said. The unfortunate association with the circumstances of Belshazzar's illumination eluded Mark for a moment in his reach for a dramatic comparison, and went unnoticed by the congregation, which was, in fact, awed. The Board of Deacons had voted to grant him a leave, with the proviso that he return when his three-year contract with the Mission Board expired.

Deacon Biddle, however, had cleared his throat and spoken his mind. "I may tell you, Reverend Ryegate, that there has been criticism among the congregation of your leaving your young wife only a year after your marriage."

"I have, of course, Mrs. Ryegate's full agreement and blessing," Mark answered. "She is a woman of rare understanding," he added. "Next year, if I can make proper provision for her, Mrs. Ryegate would like to join me. In fact, the Mission Board really prefers a married couple in the field, but I feel I must first go alone to a place of such danger."

Deacon Biddle had stared at the young man with disapproval amounting to horror. "I would consider taking a white woman to that Wilderness little short of a criminal act, one that would make her father, Whitford Tomlinson, turn over in his grave. I meant, Reverend Ryegate, criticism of your feeling free to answer your call in the first place, now that you are married. Let me tell you, one's decisions are altered after he takes on the responsibility of marriage."

Mark had waited with respect before answering. "It is not a matter of feeling free, but, rather, feeling required to do what I believe is the divine bidding."

So the young man had answered his call, gone forth to the Wilderness and returned, even though it took a little more than forty days. "Got it out of his system," Deacon Biddle put it to Deacon Slocum. And Calvary Baptist had its minister back. Moreover, he returned the gift of money; he hadn't got far enough with the church to need it, he said. The Indians of the upper waters of the Missouri, it appeared, kept moving, so no one location for a church could really serve.

It had been easier than Mark had thought to write the Mission Board; phrases came quickly to mind. "This first trip was, of necessity, one of exploration of the situation rather than of intensive missionary work that could be reckoned in the number of souls saved or in having the church built."

He found it a relief to be so frank with them about the slight progress made. He had worked on the report all the way home, in his mind—at Fort Union, where the question of their staying all winter had arisen and been decided against, and on both the Mackinaw boat and the steamboat. He had been able to copy and mail it from St. Louis.

Irritatingly, though, the phrases he had written kept recurring to him after the report was mailed: "Because of the nomadic nature of the Indian life, the building of a chapel was abandoned; although at some later time . . . Any school will have to be a boarding school; there are no real Indian villages as we had thought of them.

"Preaching and teaching are greatly hampered by the necessity of using an interpreter. A missionary needs to spend his first months learning the tongue. I can only hope that some progress was made in awakening the minds of those Indians who did attend the services." He had thought for some moments, and then added: "Several were baptized in the river before I left, despite the already chilly weather."

He saw Aapaaki as he raised her dripping from the water, her mutilated face more terrible exposed flat to the sun and sky. Had she understood when he told her how Christ treated the woman taken in adultery? Did Pierre tell the story straight? He couldn't tell by watching her expression, but she must have understood, for she came to be baptized. After the baptism he could never rid himself of her.

Of their decision to return, he wrote: "We did not reach this conclusion easily, but after considering the subject in all its aspects, and realizing that my opportunity for work among the tribes during the winter months would be limited, as well as in consideration of Mrs. Ryegate's precarious condition, we yielded to the apparent indications of Providence."

The Mission Board received the communication from Reverend Ryegate calmly enough. Something fruitful had been accomplished; the groundwork had been laid. The twelve-page communication from Reverend Ryegate had given a firsthand report of conditions not before known, and was printed, bound, and duly circulated among all the churches of the denomination. Other Protestant denominations requested copies. For the time being the Mission Board was glad to redouble its efforts in the Orient and let the Wilderness area wait until such time as it seemed advisable to send forth a missionary again. It hardly seemed likely that that time would be as soon as next spring.

But the Board was disturbed about getting back certain supplies that Reverend Ryegate had taken with him: flour, corn meal, molasses, various foodstuffs, cotton flannel, calico, Bibles, spelling and grammar books, and the like, the value of which came just under the sum of one hundred and fifty dollars. If the supplies could not be returned, the Board wished reimbursement. It was disappointing and surprising that Reverend Ryegate had left without making an exact inventory.

Reverend Ryegate wrote back suggesting that the kindness and expense to which Major Phillips and his wife had gone in aiding, boarding, and transporting him and his wife were so great he felt that these supplies should be considered a gift. The Board, however, felt differently, and would write Major Phillips. How fortunate it was, Mark thought, that Harriet had made a gift of the melodeon to the Fort.

There might well have been embarrassment on Harriet's part as the professed cause of her husband's precipitate return from the Wilderness, but she expressed none. Yet she may not have been sorry that she looked so gaunt, or that her eyes seemed to have grown darker under their delicately arched brows. Even the occasional nausea may not have been unwelcome. She lay on the haircloth sofa with the heavy clusters of grapes carved in the polished walnut frame, sitting up against a pillow, when the ladies of the congregation came to call.

Isabelle Cavendish dropped her voice discreetly to say, "But you must have *thought* of the possibility of your having a child when you went."

Harriet lifted her head ever so slightly, her eyes going beyond Isabelle to the wallpaper forest on the opposite side of the parlor. "When one goes to the mission field, Isabelle, one's mind is not on the body."

Isabelle fingered the steel beads on her reticule without answering. Harriet was surprised at the way her answer had come so smoothly to her lips; yet wasn't it true, after all? It was entirely accurate that she had not worried about the pos-

sibility of having a child—although she had not become pregnant in the first year of her married life, she had, indeed, taken
material to make infant apparel should she have need—but
her mind had not been on the mission field, it had been purely
and simply on being with Mark.

Harriet Tomlinson had never been interested in any young
man until Marcus Ryegate called to see her father the week
he began his pastorate. When she opened the door herself,
he had said, smiling, "You must be Miss Tomlinson." "Yes,"
she had said, and it was as though he had just told her who she
was and she had never known herself as a person before.
She had gone slowly up the stairs, listening to the sound of his
voice as he talked with her father. His voice was a Vermont
voice, which was different from a Woollett voice. She waited
from Sunday to Sunday to hear him. When he said from the
pulpit, "Dearly beloved, I say unto you . . ." she heard no
more of the sermon, but her heart pounded and her hands
were cold in their gloves. The wooing had begun.

When he went away for his month's vacation that summer,
the congregation suspected that he might bring back a bride.
But he returned alone. He had gone to refresh his spirit and
do some climbing and fishing in the Green Mountains, he said.
But a minister needed a wife; a Church needed a minister's
wife also, and one of the Deacons told him so. He had laughed,
it was reported, and said he felt rather sorry for ministers'
wives. The women of the Church had been uncertain about
the remark, but Harriet had thought it clever of him; it showed
how sympathetic he would be with a wife.

And then she began to think of herself as the person he
should marry; would, in truth, marry. Once she had thought
of herself as Mrs. Marcus Ryegate, the certitude that she
would be grew in her mind, in the same way that later, once
she had thought of the possibility of joining Mark in the Wilderness, she made immediate preparations for going. She did
nothing to woo him or attract attention to herself, but her

clear eyes brightened when she looked at him. After the service, it was the custom for most of the congregation to compliment him on his sermon or, at least, comment as they shook his hand. Harriet merely shook his hand and met his eyes. She could feel him wondering what she thought, but she disliked people complimenting a minister on his performance, as they might an actor or public lecturer. His eyes moved away from her to the next person, and she went on.

Except for these momentary flickers of concentration on his part, Reverend Ryegate had not really seen her until that day after her father's funeral, when he came to call. Again she opened the door, this time in mourning, and led him into the parlor where the inside blinds were decorously closed. Harriet went at once and folded them back so the sun streamed into the room.

"My father always liked enough light so he could see a person, he used to say."

"I like it, too," he agreed, and noticed the delicate color of her skin, and the way the sun polished her light hair to amber. Her hands were white against the black of her dress.

"We shall miss your father," he began, "and the Church suffers a great loss, but that can hardly be measured against your own loss."

"I shall miss him," she said simply, but in a tone of voice that seemed to close the subject; and although he had thought as he walked toward Deacon Tomlinson's house of what he would say to Miss Tomlinson that he hadn't already said yesterday at the funeral, Reverend Ryegate changed abruptly and asked, "What will you do now?"

Because it had become a fact to her, she said promptly, "I suppose one day I shall marry."

"Then you are engaged," he said, sounding relieved, almost, at not having to worry about her.

"No," she said, and a small silence fell between them, growing until it seemed to her that her thoughts must be audible. He had expected her to go on. Since she didn't, he added, "And until that time, I hope you won't be here alone in this large house."

"Oh, yes, except that Hannah will go on working for me. I shall be occupied in reading and trying to enlarge my understanding." She feared it made her sound like a bluestocking, like Margaret Fuller, but it *was* her plan.

He looked at her with a little surprise and new interest. "What will you read?"

She tried to think of the most impressive author she knew, and settled on Gibbon, but she heard herself saying instead, "I think Lord Byron." She watched the way his smile began far back in his eyes and twitched his lips before he laughed aloud. Harriet laughed with him.

"She walks in beauty, like the night/Of cloudless climes and starry skies;/And all that's best of dark and bright/Meet in her aspect and her eyes . . ." he quoted, and then broke off, for he seemed to be saying these words to her; he noted with relief that her eyes were blue. "Yes, I am sure Byron would be 'enlarging' for the young female mind!" he told her.

"I'm twenty-nine," Harriet said, because it seemed a fact that he should know and one that modified the adjective "young"; she already knew that he was three years younger.

Six months later they were quietly married. And the next year, when her husband felt himself called to the Wilderness field, it was inevitable that she would follow him.

Chapter Three

IF there was embarrassment on Mark's part over the abandonment of his mission in the Wilderness, it was not apparent in his voice as he preached to his congregation that first Sunday after his return. His hair had been carefully cut and his beard shorn by his former barber, who had urged him to keep it. "You've got a good jaw line, Reverend, but a beard would be more impressive for one in your calling, and it's the fashion." Mark thought of the smooth faces of the young Blackfoot braves, and was clean shaven. His face was paler where the beard had been.

"You look less like a prophet," Harriet had teased, and regretted saying it.

"Or more like a false prophet?" Mark said, but there was no time to pursue the subject.

The washed feeling of his skin and the single whiff of cologne on his handkerchief were pleasant to Mark after the constant smell of his own sweat. The starched shirt and high collar felt strange; his black satin cravat had caught on his rough fingers as he tied it. His broadcloth Prince Albert fitted him more snugly, yet he looked leaner.

It had always been his habit to write his sermons out, often hardly blotting a line; to read them aloud in the sanctum of his study until that moment of saturation at which he no longer needed to refer to the script. When he went into the pulpit, he left his manuscript on his desk, able to give forth the sermon almost exactly as written. The congregation of Calvary boasted of his remarkable memory. This week he wrote no sermon.

Now, as though she had never been away, Harriet sat in her pew, dressed in her fine blue merino, which still smelled faintly of moth balls but was saved by the fresh scent of lemon verbena. The small hushed sounds of the congregation settling itself were pleasant in her ears. At the service in the Fort, bedlam often broke out in the yard within the stockade or in the Indian tipis and clashed with the melodeon and Mark's voice.

She looked up at the stained-glass window where the angel with red wings blew a long gold trumpet, at the pointed arches of the ceiling and the gilded pipes of the organ, as at marvels seen long ago, perhaps on her trip to Europe. She was conscious of the eyes of the congregation often turning her way, and concentrated her own gaze on Mark, sitting in the pulpit. He was glad to be back, she had felt that morning. A minister needed a church. In the Fort, at the end of the big rough room where a bearskin and a buffalo hide hung on the wall, he had always looked out of place in his dark ministerial clothes. She rested her hand on the velvet cushion of the pew, caressing it slightly.

Mark stood to read the Scripture; his hand, deftly turning the thin pages of the Bible on the lectern in front of him, was touched by the light through the red wings of the angel in the window.

"I shall read only a few sentences from a letter from Paul to the Corinthians," Mark said. " 'Except ye utter by the tongue words easy to be understood, how shall it be known what is spoken? for ye shall speak into the air. There are, it may be, so many kinds of voices in the world, and none of them is without signification. Therefore if I know not the meaning of the voice, I shall be unto him that speaketh a barbarian, and he that speaketh shall be a barbarian unto me.' "

Mark closed his eyes and bowed his head so abruptly that the congregation was taken unaware, and the organist hardly had time to adjust the music for the hymn that followed the prayer.

"God, keep us from being barbarians one to the other, we pray."

Not only was the prayer disconcertingly brief, but Mark omitted the amen. Feeling the lack, Deacon Slocum supplied it in a sonorous voice.

When Mark rose to preach the sermon, Harriet was no longer the pastor's wife, but that young woman, Harriet Tomlinson, who had sat in this pew responding with all of her being to his voice, his eyes, his least gesture.

"I am grateful," Mark began, "to be safely back with you to bring you a new vision from my experience in the Wilderness, a vision which I hope will quicken the life of this Church."

Harriet's hands clasped nervously in her lap. He wasn't going to tell them about his eagle, was he? They wouldn't understand it. He couldn't make it real to them, although it had been very real to her; he had described every detail to her when she lay in his arms on the fur robe, and her being with him was a miracle in itself, as Mark had said.

"I spoke to a people," Mark continued, "who could not understand what I was saying except through an interpreter, and sometimes could not understand then because the interpreter garbled my message. We were barbarians to each other."

She relaxed in relief, and one hand rested again on the velvet cushion.

"I tell you that it is a great joy, an inexpressible freedom to know that I can speak directly to you and that you will hear and understand. The terrible curse of the tower of Babel rests upon the races of man, but here we speak the same tongue. When we speak, we know the meaning of the words we use. I have come back to speak to you more honestly, more simply, and, I pray, more eloquently than before. But it is not enough for me to speak to you; you will speak to me and to each other out of your hearts. We have too often been people who speak *about* each other, *about* God, rather than *to*."

Harriet began to hear only the pattern of his words—the three adverbs in a row, the rise and fall of his voice at the climax, which he had given up with Pierre translating. He had moved back into his old way of preaching as he had into his Prince Albert coat. But she had never before been so aware of a pattern in his preaching.

"In that Fort where Mrs. Ryegate and I dwelt"—Mark's voice changed, became more conversational—"the wife of the factor of the Fort was a beautiful Indian woman. Intelligence shone in her dark eyes; she graced the head of her husband's table with dignity and courtesy, and offered hospitality, even though the meat was wild duck or buffalo tongue, to distinguished guests from civilization. She once entertained a prince at her table. This woman understood every word of English that was spoken, as well as French; but she did not, or would not, perhaps was too shy to try to, speak in English. My friends, you cannot talk with a person if there is no answer, if she will not speak to you."

Silence held the congregation so tightly in its grasp there was only the sound of a pew creaking and someone's smothered cough. Reverend Ryegate was said to have a gift for illustration.

"Here, we have the tongue, as they say in the Wilderness. But even if we have the same tongue, does it always follow that we speak to God, to our neighbor, even to the one closest to us? How often when we yearn to utter our need, or our love, or our guilt are we dumb, or do we speak one thing while we think another!"

Mark had said if something went wrong on the trip she might not say it was his fault, but she might think it. And she had said, "Don't let's ever think one thing and say something else." Mark had remembered that and put it into his sermon.

"Let us begin now to talk together as never before—clearly, intimately, of the things that matter. Let us talk to God, for God knows our tongue.

"That is the vision, both simple and profound, that I bring back to you from my experience in the Wilderness."

The short sermon was at an end. With dramatic swiftness, Mark bowed his head and prayed: "Oh, God, on that day of Pentecost, when they were all with one accord in one place, suddenly there came a sound from Heaven as of a rushing mighty wind and they were all filled with the Holy Ghost and began to speak with other tongues as the Spirit gave them utterance. We ask not only that we speak with the tongue thou gavest us, but may the Spirit give us utterance. Amen."

In the hush that followed, the roar of the great stove at the rear of the church became loud, but fortunately—or unfortunately—before it was confused with the wind of Pentecost, it was drowned in the silken sound as everyone rose for the hymn. Harriet braced herself to meet the congregation.

◇ ◇ ◇

It seemed good to have the Reverend back in the pulpit instead of some candidate, but didn't that strike you as a poor excuse for a sermon?

There wasn't too much of it. I'd barely got myself comfortable in the pew, and my mind around to listening, when it was all over. The Methodists will wonder if we had a sermon at all, we got out so early.

It didn't have but one point to it, and precious little Scripture. Maybe out there he's got rusty writing sermons.

And I can't say that the one point he did make impressed me as a vision of any great magnitude. I don't know as I ever had any trouble saying what I had a mind to say to anybody.

But I would have liked to see the Reverend trying to talk to that Indian woman who wouldn't say a word to him. That must have got his goat!

It did just occur to me that he was pretty taken with her to put her into his sermon.

That thought went through my mind, too. If she was that

good-looking and intelligent, she wouldn't need to do much talking!

But what I don't understand is why he didn't tell Harriet that she'd gone out there on her own, after he'd left her safe at home with Christian people she'd grown up with, and now she'd have to stick it out, instead of letting her drag him home.

Oh, I can understand why he didn't. Not that she isn't a fine woman, but in that condition she could have carried on and had hysterics and just made his life miserable.

Well, we've got him back; now the Church can settle down again.

◇ ◇ ◇

Chapter Four

THERE was a round of dinners to welcome them back. As Mrs. Quackenbush said to her husband, "We want to ask them before she begins to show." Mr. Quackenbush started to ask, and then grasped his wife's meaning. For the delicate sex, women had a curious way of bringing up indelicate subjects.

At each dinner the Reverend Ryegate was asked to offer grace, and in each grace he offered a variation of his gratitude to the Lord: for bringing them home safely, for the opportunity of being once more in this home; for being surrounded again by old friends bound to them by the bonds of faith and friendship; for saving them from the perils of the elements and the pestilence of the dread disease that laid waste the Indian village they passed; for making it possible to serve once again the Church to which all those present belonged. Deacon Terwilliger, a lively, dapper little man, added as Mark ended his grace, "And so quickly!" The moment hung between proper gravity and mirth; Deacon Terwilliger looked up, beaming, as the bowed heads lifted. The balance was maintained.

Hostess after hostess said, following the grace, with her mind on the roast or the sauce or the new maid, "Now we want to hear all about your experiences. My, we've worried about you, and remembered you in our prayers."

"Someday, you really must make that trip to the Upper Missouri, Mr. Goddard," Mark said. "Just to see a buffalo hunt alone. It's a tremendous spectacle to watch those fearless young Indians riding bareback, close enough to that stupendous herd to shoot their arrows. The most perfect control . . ."

"Thank you, not while they have such perfect control in taking scalps, too," Deacon Goddard replied.

"It must have been terrifying in the dark forest!" A small, birdlike woman seated across the table from Harriet sucked in her breath as she spoke.

"No," Harriet said. "We really weren't very near any forest. That was the way I thought the Wilderness would be, but it wasn't like that. There was no forest around us, and there was too much light, if anything. The Fort was so dark, and then you came out into such bright light you couldn't see for a moment." On Mrs. Quackenbush's best damask cloth, beyond the Haviland china gravy boat, she saw her own shadow stretched on the hard earth under the hot sun and the sky that went on and on. "But it was sometimes terrifying," she finished, coming back from a long way off, and realized she had lost her listener.

"What did the Indian women think of you, Harriet?" Sydney Hall asked. "They were fortunate in the first female specimen of the white race they were privileged to see, I must say!" He bowed a little toward her. Sydney Hall was the Church's most gallant and eligible bachelor, though everyone had given up hope of his ever marrying.

"I don't know what they thought, but they laughed at me," Harriet told him.

"Laughed!" It was a new idea. "I can hardly believe that. I thought they might have been inclined to worship you. Is that really so, Pastor?"

Mark nodded. "I'm afraid they laughed at me, too. Civilized man cuts a foolish figure in the Wilderness. The mountain men, fur traders who know the country, of course, and the Major . . ." But the talk at the other end of the table was on the bankruptcy of a former trustee of the Church, and attention drifted that way.

"Simmons withdrew his membership from the Church, naturally. All things considered, it was more comfortable for everyone. . . . Some question of irregularity."

"But why should he withdraw from the Church?" Mark asked. "I'm sorry to hear that. I shall go and see him this week."

After dinner at the Terwilligers' or the Goddards' or the Quackenbushes', as the case might be, the women gathered at one end of the parlor. Just as the squaws chattered together in one tipi, disdained by the braves, Harriet thought. The men drifted to the other end, in confirmed Woollett fashion.

At the Terwilligers', with the women sitting together, Laura Davies asked the question she had told the Women's Circle she was going to ask. ("Certainly I am; we have a right to know," she had said.)

"Harriet, do you still have your gold watch the Circle gave you?"

"Yes, indeed. I brought it safely home." She had meant to wear it tonight. She wondered if she ought to offer to give it back. "It was a great comfort to me."

"Well, I guess the Lord did bless and keep you, just as we had it engraved," Laura said.

Harriet thought of the times she had looked at its face; how she had waked in those nights Mark was gone with Mrs. Phillips, and wondered if he was safe; or in that dreadful open boat, or during the days they waited at the lower fort. The watch had come to be a sign of the civilization toward which she propelled her mind and body by sheer will some of those days on the way, holding on to it with both hands, the chain twisted in her fingers almost like a rosary when she was afraid the ice in the river would pile up and stop them again. And when at St. Joseph they walked on the big river steamboat, and she could open the cover and check the time with the clock in the salon, she had felt she was back in a manageable world.

At the other end of the long parlor, Deacon Slocum held his fine Turkish cigar in his hand and asked, "Reverend, would that Major at the Fort hang on to his Indian woman, or would he cast her off and take another?"

"Oh, theirs was a marriage of the utmost devotion," Mark assured him. "I am certain that the Major felt himself bound to her as closely as by a marriage sanctified in the Church instead of by Indian custom—the exchange, I understood, of nine horses."

"Horses, eh!" Syd Hall chuckled. "That's not inappropriate, you know!" Chet Quackenbush stared at him. No, he didn't know, but then he had little use for Hall, in spite of his owning the largest paper in Woollett.

"Why didn't you marry 'em while you were there, Reverend?" Deacon Slocum asked, scowling. "I should think that would be part of converting the wife and stiffening the moral fibre of the Major."

"I had supposed that the Catholic priest had performed the ceremony. Mrs. Phillips had been converted. In fact, she wore a cross around her neck. It was only toward the end of my stay that I learned they had been content with the Indian marriage." He felt the impossibility of making the situation comprehensible. "If I had been there longer . . . You can hardly imagine the reticence and dignity of the Major and his wife."

"Did the Major speak Indian or did they just manage without much conversation?" Sydney Hall asked, enjoying his question.

Deacon Quackenbush ignored the remark. "I wanted to ask you, Reverend, were there many on their way to the gold fields on that boat you took up river? Course it's a little far north for gold."

"How many more dinners do you suppose we'll have to go to where we're asked questions about the Wilderness?" Harriet asked as they came back home. "And I'm sure it's bad for the baby for me to eat such rich food."

"You could use the baby as an excuse for declining," Mark said, and then, meeting her eyes with the same thought in them, changed the subject so quickly Harriet noticed. "You know, they think they're interested in hearing about the Wilderness, but it's too remote. And yet they've asked me to give three lectures, open to the public. I've jotted down some subjects; come in the study and see what you think of them."

Harriet curled up on the couch, pulling the afghan over her, while Mark stirred the fire into a blaze. Lying in the shadowed corner and watching Mark at his desk was like being in their room at the Fort, only there was no smell of cured skins, and no sounds of all the other lives going on within the walls of the Fort, and no wind as there had been so incessantly those last days.

"I've got two titles that will do, I think. Maybe you can suggest a third." Mark spread out a paper on his desk. "I thought the first could be called 'The Lure of the Wilderness'—take up the appeal to the artist and the hunter and the historian who have come out there, even from Europe. I was thinking, too, of that artist you told me about meeting on your boat."

"And the missionary?"

"Yes, of course, I mean to end with the missionary, both Black Robes and Protestant."

" 'Lure' seems an odd word to use for missionaries, though," Harriet said thoughtfully. "Something like a decoy."

"Well, it's metaphoric in origin, but I'd be using it in the sense of whatever draws people out there." Mark was a little impatient. "It's a good word for a title. The very idea of the unknown lures you."

Harriet considered, trying the sound of it in her head. "But it sounds as though you were lured against your will. How does that fit with your feeling of being called of God to go into the Wilderness? It's just the word I'm wondering about."

"Words!" Mark grumbled in irritation. "I'll give you its full meaning." He pushed back his chair and went over to the ponderous dictionary that stood on a storklike table supported by one carved leg. The sound of the thin pages turning in his fingers was familiar, and her eyes touched gently the planes of his face as he bent over the dictionary. This was where he belonged, back in a study, surrounded by books.

"Here it is: 'an apparatus used by falconers to recall their hawks, being a bunch of feathers attached to a cord; a representation of this consisting of two bird's wings with the points downward . . .' "

He broke off, looking at Harriet with a wry, half humorous expression on his face.

"It doesn't say eagle wings," she said.

"Or duck's either! But it comes close."

If he hadn't said it . . . but he had! They could say anything to each other. She could even make just a little fun of his vision.

"It goes on to say . . ." Mark was reading. "You might as well hear the rest: 'something which allures, entices, or *tempts.*' " He stopped. "Then it gets worse: 'a means of alluring animals to be captured.' " Mark slapped the cover of the dictionary closed and went back to the desk. His lower lip came up above his upper one, making a pouch at each corner of his mouth. He rubbed his hand over his mouth and chin. His eyes were stormy.

"Was going off to the Wilderness just a lure to me, Harriet? Tonight at dinner, I thought I'd rather be back at the Fort eating stewed deer meat than listening to some of that chatter. Did I just fool myself into thinking I had a call in order to escape all this?"

"Suppose it *was* a lure for you?"

"A lure of the devil, you mean?"

"Or of God," she said calmly. "That poet, Donne, would use it that way. I read the poem—you had it marked—about o'erthrow me that I may stand, you know? And imprison me so I'll be free. 'Nor ever chaste' "—she felt the color burn up in her face, but she went on speaking to Mark's eyes, which had

quickened out of their dullness, and her voice was hushed—
" 'except you ravish me.' "

He hadn't seemed to hear the last phrase. "Catch me in Thy
lure that I may be recalled to Thee, kind of thing, you mean.
You mean I'd flown too high in my ambition and conceit and
had to be pulled back," he went on slowly.

The next moment he was on his feet, flailing the air with his
arm. "Oh, I was a great preacher when I went into the Wilderness, a second John the Baptist, crying out in my eloquence!
I was going to build a church in the Wilderness, and convert
all the savages. I was going to speak with the tongues of men
and of angels, so that even if the savages couldn't understand
what I was saying, they would feel the fire of my words and
hear the angelic swell of my voice; see the holy light in my
countenance. I didn't worry about not having the tongue, not
I! I was a young man with a vision, Mark Ryegate, lifted up
on the wing of an eagle. Even when the eagle turned out to
be a dead duck, I went on believing it was a vision." His self-
disgust caught like phlegm in his throat and had the sound of
a laugh. She couldn't see his face because he had come to stand
in front of the fireplace, but his vehemence and the sarcastic
tone of his voice frightened her.

"Preaching in Woollett, Massachusetts, was too limited a
field for one of my talents, my insight and eloquence. No wonder I felt 'called' to cry out in the Wilderness! For myself."

He whirled around, facing Harriet, and drew himself up in
a stance of pompous dignity. "Ladies and gentlemen"—his
voice aped the tone of the lecturer—"the great unknown and
mysterious Wilderness holds out irresistible lures for men of
varied callings and from all walks of life, from the humblest to
the most elevated. The hunter is drawn by the vision of myri-
ads of buffalo, deer, elk, and antelope fleeing across the vast
plains; the artist longs to picture the countenance of primitive man, never before portrayed; the historian is lured by the
thought of standing upon earth where man's fate is still to be

determined; but these lures are as nothing, nothing I say, to that particular, bright-feathered lure the Wilderness dangles before the would-be, self-appointed minister of God!"

His voice rose and sank in exaggerated eloquence. On the ceiling the shadow of his gestures reached across the room. Harriet watched, her face pale, staring at him with horror.

"Mark, stop it! I can't stand it."

"And before I go further," Mark continued, bowing to her elaborately, "let me pay my debt of gratitude to Mrs. Ryegate, the wife of my bosom, who not only opened my blinded eyes to the true significance of my call to the Wilderness but delivered me—as the children of Israel were led by Moses out of Egypt, out of the Wilderness."

"Mark!" She was crying. In a silken rush of skirts she was across the room, her arms clutching at him. "What have I done? I didn't mean . . . We were only talking about a word, playing with it. I thought we could say anything to each other. I didn't mean to take away your vision; maybe it really was one, or it wouldn't stay with you so. And *you* said that about the duck feathers, Mark. . . ." Her words spilled out on top of each other.

"You were perfectly right, Harriet. You only made me see what I wouldn't face. Just now I saw myself in all my conceit and absurdity. Funny I didn't realize how well I was describing myself when I told them at dinner that civilized man cuts a foolish figure in the Wilderness." His voice was his own now, the bitter edge gone out of it, but its flatness chilled her. She buried her face against his shoulder, unable to stop crying.

"Harriet, you haven't done anything. I got carried away, as I used to do in the seminary. I'd try preaching some of the great sermons we had to read. Once I learned one of John Donne's sentences that was a page long. The fellows used to get me to declaim it, and I'd actually imagine myself in the pulpit at St. Paul's in London. I'd get drunk on the sound of the words and rhythms and my own voice saying them."

He lifted her face so he could see her. "You've just never

seen an exhibition before. Now you know the kind of person you've married. Somebody who has to be heard, who has to feel his own eloquence and power—the power of God through him, he calls it, of course. Maybe John the Baptist was thrilled with his own preaching."

"How do you know that it isn't the power of God?" she asked.

He didn't answer, standing there with his arm around her but not thinking about her, not even listening to her. She moved away from him back to the couch, not able to look at him, looking instead at the fire.

"Mark, I should never have gone to the Wilderness to be with you. That was something you should have done alone; you would have stayed until you worked it out—the difficulties, I mean. Until you had learned the language and could talk directly to them. Now you feel guilty for coming back, and you doubt yourself." She waited for him to say he had needed her there.

But he said, "Maybe you shouldn't have."

She stared down at her hands, clasped in her lap, as though they didn't belong to her. She felt numb. He could hurt her and not care, not even think about it, which was worse.

"I heard you say at dinner tonight that there was too much light in the Wilderness, Harriet. Maybe you were right; too much exposure to the light. It showed too clearly what a failure I was, and how we plotted together to come home."

"Mark! Why do you say a thing like that? I saw how it was, and I know how hard you worked. You did all you possibly could do. You hurt me when you think I don't understand. We didn't plot; we decided what was best."

But he wasn't listening to her. He had drawn into himself where she couldn't reach him. "The wife of my bosom," he had said in that sarcastic tone of voice, as though he meant she was a viper in his bosom. She might as well leave him and go upstairs, but she didn't have the strength. What had happened to them? All this had started over a word; but it wasn't just a word. These thoughts must have been in his mind all the way home. She felt the silence harden around them. There was nothing more she could say to him.

"Harriet!"

She looked up because of the sudden change in his voice. From whatever place he had been, he was back.

"Harriet, forgive me. I'm a blithering, self-dramatizing fool."

He was on the floor with his head burrowed into her lap.

Confused, hardly trusting the swift change, she laid her hands on his head.

"Harriet." The way he said her name made it more than any endearment. "Mark," she murmured close to his ear. They were both afraid of any word but their own names.

"Do you still love me, Harriet? Even when you see me so clearly?"

"You know I love you. Only don't ever go so far away from me again, or talk like that. Your voice was so cold and bitter."

"I'm so sick of myself, Harriet. The only way I could stand it was to take a good look at the ridiculous figure I cut."

"When you do that, you don't see or think of anyone else."

"I see you, Harriet. I know I hurt you. But even that's a way of hurting myself. Oh, I'm a great minister, preaching the love of God!" He got up and paced across the room to his desk. She wondered if he had forgotten her again, he stood there so long. Then he came back to her. "Harriet, let me love you, here by the fire. It won't hurt you, will it? Now, Harriet. I'm so tired of words."

She felt separated from him, uncertain. How could he change so fast? "No, it won't hurt me," she said, but the small consenting words sounded niggardly, cold, as Mark's had been. She wanted to be taken to him, to feel sure again.

"Yes, love me, Mark. Love me hard." She felt his fingers on the buttons of her bodice and reached up and ripped them open. By the firelight she caught sight of her own beskirted shadow on the study wall, as it had been on the clay bank of the river that day with Mrs. Phillips. Loosing the yards of skirts that mushroomed from her waist, she stepped free of them.

"Like the Fort," she murmured as they lay together by the fire, only there had been no firelight and they had lain on a buffalo robe instead of a crocheted afghan.

"Shall I carry you upstairs, Harriet?" Mark said out of the warm stillness.

"Not yet." She didn't want to move out of this peace, but the next moment she said, "Mark, you really, really love me? My body isn't just a lure!"

"Yes, your body is an irresistible lure, and I really, really love you, relentless wench." Mark's quiet laughter was easy and her own answered it.

Chapter Five

HARRIET stood still in front of the window of Newcomb and Walsh, staring at the placard propped against a bolt of new brocade.

THREE LECTURES

BY

THE REVEREND MARCUS RYEGATE
RECENTLY RETURNED MISSIONARY

TO THE

INDIANS OF THE AMERICAN NORTHWEST

February 6th
THE CALL TO THE WILDERNESS

March 20th
THE JOURNEY INTO STRANGENESS

April 4th
THE INDIAN, OUR FOE AND OUR BROTHER

CALVARY BAPTIST CHURCH
8:00 P.M.

She hardly took the words in at first, her eyes catching on "call" and "strangeness," so she went back and read them again.

Why hadn't Mark told her what he had decided on? He had worked steadily in his study, whenever he wasn't making

calls or talking to members of the Church, who seemed to come
to him more than they had before; or going to meetings, or
marrying or burying people. She had expected any day to hear
the study door open with a bang, the way he always threw it
back, and have him come upstairs with a paper in his hand
to read his titles to her. Since that night they hadn't talked
about the lectures, or the Wilderness, but she had gone back
in her mind over every word they had said. Not all at once,
though; a phrase would lift itself suddenly out of other, totally irrelevant thoughts. One day she was regulating her
bureau drawers when she found herself shaping the word "lure"
soundlessly, her tongue curling against the roof of her mouth.
The secret sound was fuller than the sound of a word like
"lyre," and held more music in it.

"You'll want some satin ribbon to match the rosebuds for
binding, won't you, Harriet?" The saleswoman had known her
mother and took great interest in Harriet's buying material
for baby things.

"Oh, yes, thank you, and a spool of pink silk."

Harriet was repeating the titles on the placard in her head
as she sat on the swivel stool in front of the counter. "Call"
would do very well. To the hunter, the artist, the historian,
and yes, of course, to the missionary. He had solved the prob-
lem so simply, after all. "Journey into Strangeness"—that was
beautiful. Sheerest poetry, and true. Going up the river around
bend after bend, through the painted cliffs. . . . But not so
much the strangeness of the journey beyond farms and woods
and everything one had known, as the strangeness at the end
of the journey, living so closely with Mark in that dark little
room, always being aware of Mrs. Phillips. . . .

"Oh, thank you. I guess I was woolgathering," Harriet said
with a smile in answer to the saleswoman's repeated remark.

Mrs. Carey nodded. "It affects some women that way.
Better go home and lie down."

But all the way up Mercantile Street, and High to Elm,
Harriet was back there, going in through the stockade gates,

past the store window where some Indian was trading his skins
for beads or calico or whiskey, into the house they shared with
the Phillipses, on into their own room. She had had to accus-
tom her eyes to the shadowy interior as she came in, and she
could still smell the rat droppings under the planks, and the
smoked moccasins, and even the faint odor of the buffalo hide
on their bed.

As she opened the white panelled front door, Mark called.
The study door swung open with a bang. "You're back.
I thought you'd been gone a long time, and I didn't want to
leave until you were home. Are you all right?"

"Of course." She never got over her delight at his coming
like this to greet her when she returned from an ordinary ex-
pedition. "But Mark, I saw the poster! In Newcomb and
Walsh's window."

"I brought one home from the printer's to show you; that
was one of the reasons I was waiting for you. They certainly
got them around in short order. I wanted to surprise you. What
did you think of the titles?" She could see that he was pleased
with them. " 'Call' works, don't you think? It has none of your
objection to the other." But he made it a question.

She never answered quickly; maybe she thought slowly, or
thought of too many things at once.

"Yes." But she wouldn't avoid saying the word. " 'Lure' had
a magic, but it wasn't accurate. 'Call' fits your purpose better."

"What do you think of the second one?"

He was through with that word, but anyway, she had said it.
"Oh, the second one is inspired, Mark. I walked in strangeness all the way home."

"In beauty, you mean. 'She walks in beauty, like the night.'
Those were the first lines of poetry I ever quoted to you, do
you remember?"

"And then you were embarrassed and stopped!" she teased.
Now he was in high spirits, and he was pleased because she
had said his second title was inspired. "Just reading the title

took me back. Do you sometimes wonder, Mark, if we were ever really there?"

His long, slightly irregular face sobered. "No, I think it's always with me, and writing these lectures I've been there so completely I can hardly believe we are home." They stood in the sun of the front hall, silent a moment. "I have the first one about ready. When I come to the second and third ones— I wonder if there wouldn't be things you had seen and written in your Journal that would add or help me to remember. The trip upriver, especially. You said once that it was so important to have that long journey to separate you from here."

"I'll have to reread it first. I was so young and . . . naïve then. Almost too concerned with myself and my reactions to see what was around me."

"That was so many years ago, of course!" he said. "And you have seen me slightly concerned with myself, as you put it so tactfully." He was laughing down at her.

She was silent, holding her parcel and her handbag, watching his thoughts dispel the laughter. Then he smiled down at her.

"Good-bye, Harriet. Rest a bit, won't you."

She watched his tall, thin figure going down the walk, his head back, his arms swinging, moving with his easy steps, just as she had watched him at the Fort.

What would Mark make of her Journal? She felt now that she had hardly known him then, even though they had lived here together almost a year. They had loved each other timidly then—decorously. No, neither word was right. They had never loved . . . Even that word had to carry too heavy a burden, but there was no other, and it had to change and absorb a hundred meanings into it. Well, then, they had never loved with such need and abandon.

And she had never dreamed of a woman like Mrs. Phillips, who was gracious and merry one time, and could look deep into your eyes, but also be disgusting and savage; who wouldn't try to speak to you, who laughed at you. A woman who could shatter Mark's faith in himself. Did Mark still think about her so much?

She hadn't kept her Journal on the way back. She wished she had written about Mark on that trip, so he could read it. He had been as fearless as the Major, and kept up Mr. Ferrière's spirits in the Mackinaw boat. Once he had quoted the lines from *Don Juan* about people in an open boat living on the love of life and bearing more than they ever thought they could. And the Major had clapped him on the back and said, "That's right, Reverend!" The Major had got over being patronizing to Mark on the trip down. Mrs. Phillips had looked at Mark as though she understood exactly what he said, and poor Mr. Ferrière said they were bearing more than he ever thought he could, all right. But she had known she lived upon the love of Mark.

She could have written in her Journal; Mark had worked on his report to the Mission Board. But she hadn't. Some of the time she had been too frightened or too cold, sometimes too nauseated. Her mind had been too tired to try to put thoughts and feelings into words. Mark must be going to leave out the trip back. His title was "Journey *into* Strangeness," but where did the strangeness end? She took off her wraps and carried her purchases into the sewing room, rather than try to answer her own question.

Chapter Six

K EEP a journal, dear," Mrs. Bascom had said, giving her the green morocco leather book with the year on the front and a strap that fitted into a cut in the leather like the strap of a glove. Harriet remembered holding it in her hands, liking the soft smooth feel of the leather, turning the gold-edged pages that made a picture of Venice when they were pressed together. She had wondered what the pages with the pale-blue lines would contain. Pressed all together, did what she had written hold the "Journey into Strangeness," she wondered now. She sat in the rocking chair by the window in her bedroom and opened the book curiously, almost fearfully. The green cover was stained with candle wax, and the book was warped, crammed as it had been into one of Mark's boots on the trip home.

JOURNAL
of
Harriet Tomlinson Ryegate

I have been standing still in this stateroom with my trunks and portmanteau beside me, wondering how I ever really managed to get here. The minute I made up my mind to come I felt as positive and forceful as Papa. I sat at my desk and simply wrote the Fur Company in St. Louis, just as Mark had done, and said I was going to join my husband in the Mission Field at their trading post on

the Upper Missouri, and asked for information about the
next boat. To have Mr. Ferrière, the head of the Fur Company, planning a trip to that very destination made my
trip seem ordained in Heaven, or else fated! If I could
reach St. Louis by the fifth of June he would consider it a
privilege to escort me. *Escort* me to the *Wilderness!* The
polite word and the wild one hardly seem to go together.
What do I care that the Mission Board protests my
going alone; could not take the responsibility or feel justi-
fied in paying my expenses, since I did not accompany my
husband, which they had expected me to do. I would have,
of course, but Mark wouldn't hear of it. He thought it too
hard and hazardous, but he does not really know my
strength. I took great pleasure in paying my own way.

This is really not unlike sailing for Europe with Papa
when I was eighteen. Captain Latrobe brought me to this
cabin and made a bow and said the boat was honored. No
white woman has gone to the head of the river before,
although Major Phillips' Indian wife had made the trip
several times. He spoke very highly of her. I wonder what
Mark thinks of her. I was surprised to hear she had ever
been out of the Wilderness and am anxious to see her.

It was strange, though, to go off alone with no one to
wave good-bye. I stood on the deck and looked down on
the crowded wharf and didn't know a soul. The people below waved and women cried. Whole families are going to
take up new land. They have chickens and furniture and
tools; there are even cows on the boat. And there are
men going to the gold field. While I was standing on the
deck black cinders came down from the engine pipes or
somewhere and made my white gloves black. I wonder
now that I got myself ready so fast and reached St. Louis
on time. I have never before planned a trip by myself. I
do not do it badly, I think.

Sitting at the Captain's table is quite pleasant. A fiddler plays during dinner and a Negro waiter serves us.

Besides the Captain and Mr. Ferrière, there is a Southerner who calls me Madame Ryegate and made such an elaborate bow when he met me that I was embarrassed —whether for him or me, I'm not sure. His pleated shirt was dingy, I couldn't help noticing. And a German, named Herr Steiner, gave me a brief little nod, but I felt him studying me later through his thick glasses, as though I were a queer creature to be travelling alone. I suppose I am, but I do not care.

Herr Steiner hadn't said a word until we were drinking our coffee at the end of the meal. Then he nodded over at the carved frame of the big mirror behind us and said to the Captain that he had no idea that mermaids frequented riverways. I hadn't even seen the mermaids in the carving until then.

Captain Latrobe said he might discover there were sprites and mermaids and even demons in the river before we reached our destination. Everyone laughed, and when I caught sight of us all in the mirror I seemed as much a stranger to myself, sitting there laughing with five men, as any of them. The Captain asked me to join in the dance after dinner. I declined. I wish Mark knew I was on the way. He will be thinking of me safe at home.

June 8th.

I have just come back to my room from the deck. Herr Steiner turns out to be an artist. He gave me a sketch he had made of a fur trapper on the lower deck. I had seen the very man when I got on, and wondered at him. He seemed all hair and fur and leather, with his face as dark as his leather shirt. I told Herr Steiner that it was a very good likeness. He said he is really interested in painting savages. I couldn't help asking him if he had come all the way from Germany to do that. He said, "You mean I might find savages without leaving home or do you mean they are not worth painting?" I hardly knew what to an-

swer, but without waiting to hear what I thought he asked
what took me to the Wilderness. When I told him I was
going to join my husband who was a Missionary, he said,
"Your husband wants their souls, I want their portraits.
The savages should be honored, or frightened." He says
the oddest things.

June 25th.

I wish we were on the sea instead of this endless river. It
has turned shallow in places and the crew have to pull
the boat by ropes from the shore. They look like slaves,
all tied to a rope, half-naked, cursing, straining till you
can see the muscles in their bodies bulge. Just now we went
between high clay banks, higher than my window, that
made my room so dark I felt I was being buried alive. I
rushed out on the deck to escape.

July 10th.

A shocking and dreadful thing happened today. I am
recording it here to get it out of my mind. I came down to
my room to bathe before dinner, and had peeled my
clothes off to my waist and was revelling in the warm
water the steward had brought me, and my own fragrant
soap and irisroot powder, when a queer feeling and then
the sound of someone breathing close to me made me look
over at the window. Although I had not fastened the shutters because of the heat, I had drawn the curtains tight
and tied them, but a great dirty hand pulled them apart
and an eye was staring in at me. Maybe it was only an
instant, but I had time to look right into the large brown
center of it and see a red line on the white part, even
the eyelashes when the eye blinked. Then the whole great
swarthy face appeared. I couldn't scream or even move
away to get something to cover myself with. I could
feel the man's eyes burning into my skin, and then the
horrible creature grinned at me and pulled the curtains

so far apart the ties that hold them broke. He was all hairy-chested and breathing so hard he was panting. I stood there paralyzed, staring back at him, before I had enough sense to turn my back and reach over to the bunk for my towel. When I turned around his mouth opened in a great wet-lipped kind of grin before he disappeared.

I sat down on the bed because my legs were too weak to hold me and I was trembling so. I have never felt so powerless before in my life. Partly, I think, because not a word was said. He looked like the beast in the picture of Beauty and the Beast that I used to stare at as a child. I never expected to see a human being look so like him. The man was one of the cordellers who pull the boat along. I thought of reporting him to the Captain, but have decided not to do so. How could I explain why I did not scream or cry out? I don't know why I didn't. I shall keep the shutters fastened after this no matter how hot it is.

Harriet laid her hand over the page as though to cover it. Of course, it was nothing to be ashamed of, and yet she was ashamed of the way she had stared back at the man as though hypnotized by his eye. She wondered if she wanted Mark to read this entry. How incredible the incident seemed, here in the safety of her own bedroom.

July 11th.

This is a trying stretch. We are hardly moving. The mud is so thick they have to stop the boat and clean out the boilers. And twice today the boat was stopped because of an ugly snag sticking up from the river bottom. We will not get there before Fall at this rate.

Just before dinner we went around a bend on our own steam, as though we were making up for lost time, when the breeze brought us the most suffocating smell; I thought I was going to faint or be ill and reached in my bag for my smelling salts. It was a dead buffalo, a great bloated mon-

ster floating in the water. I only glanced at it, then someone on the deck below shot the head off and it went up in
the air and came down with a horrid splash and the water
was red all around it. "One of the Captain's demons, no
doubt," Mr. Steiner said. I couldn't help but agree with
him, but then he said, "The river is rather like the human
mind, don't you think, Mrs. Ryegate; you never know
what horrors it can bring up."

"Not all minds," I told him. He smiled and gave that odd
shrug of his, and said, "Maybe. I have an idea that all
minds are pretty well equipped with horrors, but I won't
ask you what yours are." I dislike the man very much.
Mark's mind isn't. Nor do I believe mine is, so speak for
yourself, Mr. Steiner!

July 15th.

We are stuck again on a sand bar. The boat gave a
jerk; then the engine spluttered and stopped. I miss the
fast sound of the water against the side. It is so close to
dark they won't try to dislodge the boat tonight. There is
a good deal of drunkenness, and it is very noisy. The
Southerner is a "cardsharper." I think it strange that the
Captain lets him sit at our table, but I suppose he has
paid for a first-class passage. I have kept to my own room
most of the day. I almost wish I were home again.

July 20th.

I haven't written for some days, but there has been nothing
to recount. One day follows another. The days are marked
off by fights on the lower deck, and the wild game we see.
We are beginning to see more buffalo, not to mention
beaver, deer, and antelope. We had buffalo steak tonight, and it was exceedingly stringy. I am tired of catfish,
too, and thick, sticky corn pudding.

Today, I went to say good-bye to the young woman on

the lower deck whom I have talked with several times. (All the rest of the families are leaving the boat tomorrow.) She was nursing her baby right out on the deck with people all around, men and women. I suppose the Indian women will, too, so I must get used to the sight, but I do not like it. I wonder why a man thinks a woman's breast is so beautiful. Mark once quoted to me the Song of Solomon that likens his beloved's breasts to twin roes. I wonder if I shall have a child while I am in the Wilderness.

I danced tonight and found it not difficult. When I went to Europe with Papa I watched the dancing in the salon, and I admit I have tried a few steps in front of the mirror at home. But how can my dancing hurt anyone when I am in the middle of the Wilderness? I wouldn't do it if I thought Mark would really mind.

I wore my purple silk, the only dress-up dress I brought with me, for I don't expect there will be much occasion to dress up at the Fort, and I didn't have time to ask Mark what I should bring. Mr. Ferrière complimented me. Mr. Steiner, who really dances very well, said, "Ah, the journey is releasing you," staring at me through his thick glasses.

July 21st.

I watched the families leave the boat. I wonder how they will manage in that empty-looking land. What will it be like when I get off? But Mark will be there. I have come down to my cabin to read over for the hundredth time my one letter from him, that he mailed from St. Louis. "I am unutterably lonely for you. This separation is my greatest hardship. At times, the thought of the joy of being together again comes between me and my call."

It seems to me that he must *feel* I am on my way to him. Mark writes things in letters that he doesn't say when we are together. Of course, there is no need, but after this separation, he will, and I shall tell him over and over again how I love him.

July 24th.

This morning the country is completely changed. It hardly looks real. There is no green anywhere, but the land is broken into wild pinnacles and cliffs of rock, colored as though they were painted. This is our hottest day. Mr. Steiner has given up painting. Mr. Ferrière is asleep with a handkerchief spread over his face. Last night there was no dancing. The heat sticks to us all like the mud of the river; even the engines seem to gasp.

The sun, glinting off those painted rocks, is too bright. I took my parasol on deck and one of those insolent-looking black-and-white magpies lighted on it. Mr. Ferrière's clerk caught it and cut its tongue so it could talk. What a horrible thing to do! He has to teach it first; now it only makes a rasping sound, worse than its cry.

"A man would go crazy if he got lost in here," the Southerner said at dinner. I think you couldn't get lost so long as you kept close to the river. The river is the way out of this country, but it is so shallow in places you wonder if it could dry up.

How could I ever have thought this was like sailing to Europe? We were on the ocean and we knew where we were going. All the way, we read about the places and wonders we would see. This trip seems to take us farther and farther into emptiness. There are no people, only savages way off somewhere. I wonder if I should have waited to hear from Mark first, before I came. But then it would have been too late to make the trip.

When we got to the wood-station today to take on fuel there were no piles of wood. The man who went over found the woodchopper killed and scalped by Indians. What if I should find Mark dead when I get there?

Mr. Ferrière seemed distressed that I knew about the

killing. "You mustn't let this frighten you, Madame Ryegate," he said. "You will be very well cared for by Major
Phillips and his wife." Then he told me that Mrs. Phillips had been a guest in their home. I must have looked
surprised, for he said she goes down to St. Louis to buy her
fine clothes and her jewelry. He laughed and said she is
very fond of jewelry; she thinks diamonds are nothing
but frozen drops of water, but rubies and emeralds really
take her eye. I do wonder what she can be like. If she is
so bright and so elegant, I will enjoy teaching her to speak
English. It will be good to talk to a woman again, even an
Indian one. When I thought Mr. Ferrière had forgotten
about her, he said suddenly, "Oh, she is a fascinating
woman, Madame Phillips!"

July 24th.

We are past the nightmare of colored rocks and the river
is deep and fast again, but today we were stopped by hundreds of buffalo. The whole river was blocked by the bawl-
ing beasts. The pilot kept blowing his whistle to frighten
them, and they would plunge and heave and then pay no
attention. A buffalo near the boat lifted its head as it
lunged on the back of the beast in front. It had small
eyes, under all that matted hair, that seemed to stare
at me. The men on the deck began to tell horrible stories
about stampedes and finding an Indian trampled under
their hooves. "Flattened out like a dried buffler chip,"
one of them said, and I foolishly asked what he meant.
Johnny Jessup, the clerk, grinned, actually grinned, and
asked if I knew what cow manure is. "Well," he said, "a
buffler chip is what the buffalo drops." I tried not to show
how I felt at such coarseness, and shall be more careful
about asking questions.

July 30th.

Six days since we stopped at Fort Union. I was encouraged

to see how big it is; a regular little village inside the stockade, and the house of the head of the Fort has wallpaper and painted woodwork. We were royally entertained and much was made of me because I was a white woman. Mr. Steiner and the Southerner and the clerk are staying there. Only Mr. Ferrière and I are left on the cabin deck. The boat is very empty. We should be at the place where a small boat will pick us up to go the rest of the way in two more days.

This evening, the sky turned crimson and pale green, and afterward a lemon-yellow light lay over the earth, giving even the mud bank a color of its own. The boat was moving slowly through a narrow channel between a low island and the shore, and we came on two does standing drinking. They lifted their heads and stared at us, then leapt off into the brush without seeming to touch ground at all. They were so lovely I thought better of the twin roes in the Song of Solomon. There is a delicious scent of wild mint all along the bank. Just as the light faded, a heron started up out of the shadows of the island and flew ahead of the boat. It flew so close I could see its long legs and hear its wings.

July 30th.

This will be my last entry on this boat. I write it with joy. Mr. Ferrière ordered champagne for dinner and proposed a toast to the Captain. This is the quickest trip he has ever made and his last one to the Upper Missouri this year because the river will drop too low. About November, he said, maybe even October, the river will freeze. But I won't think of that now. I lifted my glass and tasted the champagne. Of course, drinking is a sin in the eyes of our Church, but it seemed impolite not to taste it at least.

We have seen Indians in several places along the shore, mostly squaws. I waved my parasol at a woman with a baby on her back. She laughed and said something to the other women, and then they were all laughing. They aren't frightening at all. A group of Indians galloped by on horses, pulling up just at the edge of the cliff. The Captain said these are all friendly enough, but I saw his eyes move away from me and catch Mr. Ferrière's. A chill went over me. It is hard to understand why Mark felt he had to come way out here to preach to these people. The congregation was inclined to criticize him for leaving me. I don't, and I reverence his feeling called of the Lord. Mark is not like other men. And I understand his not wanting me to risk the possible dangers. And yet I can't help but wonder if he has found me lacking in some way, or our marriage. But he couldn't have and written as he did to me. This separation between us came too soon, before we really knew each other. And yet, when I look around in my mind at the married people in Woollett, I wonder if they know each other any better. Then marriage is a sad thing. I hope Mark will be glad I have followed him.

Harriet sat for several moments without reading, her eyes nesting in the tangle of bare branches out the window. She remembered so sharply her sudden misgivings just before she arrived, and how she had told herself she would know the minute she saw Mark's face whether he was glad she had come.

She turned the page of her Journal, and there it was, proof positive.

THE WILDERNESS.
A week later.

I am so thankful that I came. I am happier than I have ever been in all my life. Mark says it is a miracle to him every day to wake and find me here. I think he never really knew before how much he loved me.

"Harriet?" Hannah stood in the doorway. "Do you want I should make a floating island for dessert tonight or a caramel custard pie? The Reverend seems partial to pies, but it's better for you in your condition to eat a little light."

"Oh, yes, Hannah, do let's have the floating island." She began to laugh, it seemed so idiotic. They had lived on a kind of island out there, made of their delight in each other and having nothing to do with one dark little room.

Hannah looked at Harriet, wondering if she was hysterical; but as a child she had always been a flighty one. She should know; she had brought her up since she was a baby. Hannah thought more of the Reverend since he'd had enough sense to bring Harriet back home from those heathen places when she was in a family way. It had surprised her that Harriet had been willing to be brought.

Harriet's eyes flew back to the sentence: "Mark says it is a miracle to him every day to wake and find me here." If he read that now, he would remember agreeing so coldly with her when she said she shouldn't have gone to the Wilderness. Then he would feel guilty, and she didn't want him having any guilt about her. He felt guilty about coming back, as it was; guilty that he wanted to come. If you have done a thing, then you have done it. She didn't like his going over and over it, almost as a way of pitying himself.

She turned the page quickly and went on reading, finding her Journal more absorbing than any of the novels she had read in her father's library. But the Journal began to seem like a novel about someone else, a novel she had read ahead in, so she knew what was coming.

Mark's mind, preoccupied with spiritual things and all the members of the Church, had less room to think about his love. I always knew. We are much closer than we were at home. He tells me all that has happened to him, things he could never have written in a letter without so much explanation. Like the vision he had the first week he was here; very strange and confusing. Mrs. Phillips was playing a prank, of course, entirely unaware that she was the means of a vision, yet it is important to Mark, and he says it makes him sure of his call to the Wilderness. I did not know before that he had any doubts about it.

And it is Heaven to be here with him! I do not care that we live in this dark, cramped room with only one window, high up, nor that I can hear rats running on the roof at night. (Pierre, the clerk, says they are not like Eastern rats, but have bushy tails. That does not make them less horrible to me.) The rank smell of raw hides seeps out from the storeroom, and there is an odd odor from the buffalo robe we have on our bed, too, in spite of the fact that it has been tanned, but I shall doubtless get used to all these things in time. I have used up half of my bottle of toilet water already; I even put a few drops on the wall above Mark's desk.

His desk is really just a rough table, and over it, strung on a leather thong, are lists of Blackfoot words he is learning. I cannot pronounce them, but I often look at them, trying to learn them, too. I shall put down a few, some of which I think I know.

eyes	iwiosoec
nose	ohsusis
mouth	mah oi
fire	steeta
I	nistoa
we	ne stoa pinnan

Mark has drawn a bracket around three words to show, I suppose, how related they are in idea.

Great Spirit	Cristicoom
Evil Spirit	Cristicoom sah
Sun	Cristeque ahtose

Of course, I know "Ah" for "yes," and "Sah" for "no." But the language really does seem hopeless to me. Mark must have a hundred words written there, and he works on them the first thing every morning, or at least he did until I came. He has to get the clerk, Pierre, to translate his sermons, but he hopes to procure Mrs. Phillips' services. He has asked her, but she just smiled and shook her head; he thinks her unwillingness is due to shyness. Mark is wonderfully browned, and when he wears a buckskin shirt and pants, like the other men here, he looks more like a hunter than a clergyman.

Mrs. Phillips is all that Mr. Ferrière said she was. She is shorter than I, and more slender; flatter, that is. Mark says she is twenty-eight, so we are only two years apart. She has three children, the oldest thirteen. She must have been only fourteen when she was married! She is beautiful, with regular features and dark shining eyes. At dinner she always wears a civilized dress, of excellent material and style, a gold cross around her neck and gold earrings, but her hair hangs in two thick black braids, and her feet are in moccasins, so she moves almost soundlessly, except for the soft rustle of her skirt. Although she speaks only in the Indian tongue her eyes show that she understands nearly everything that is said in English, and she is as quick to laugh at any joke in English as anyone at the table. Mark feels she would make such a sensitive interpreter for him if she would only do it. I shall try to persuade her when I know her better, and I shall teach her to speak English so we can talk together. Her children speak a kind of mixture, though Mary, the oldest, prefers to speak English, which is a help to me, but it is often a funny kind of English, with most of the articles left out. The older boy, Raymond, is twelve, and the little boy, Robert, is four. Mark says the Indian women do not seem to have large families.

The Major is a commanding figure who treats me with great courtesy. When I stepped out of the small boat in which we had to make the last three days' journey, he bowed and said he saluted me as the first white woman who has ever come so far up this river, or been in this Fort!

He said I must not mind the Indians and workers staring at me, or even himself, because I was a pleasure to see. I do wonder how he could marry an Indian woman, although she is beautiful—in an Indian way. One thing I do not like about him: I feel there is a slightly patronizing tone in his voice when he speaks to Mark.

Perhaps that kind of a man, a military person and a man of action, feels that way unconsciously toward a man who devotes his life to the service of God. I hope Mark is not aware of it. "We're going to make a fine horseman out of your husband, Mrs. Ryegate; and perhaps even a buffalo hunter!" he said to me a little *too* heartily, as though that would be an improvement! But maybe I am just imagining this.

There is more formality at meals than one would expect. The men, who are called *engagés*, the ones who work here, eat at another table before we do, but at our table Mrs. Phillips sits at the foot and the Major at the head, the children and the clerk and the storekeeper and, of course, Mr. Ferrière and Mark and I along the sides. Mark asks grace at meals. We had broiled beaver tail last night for dinner, and I could see Mrs. Phillips watching to see if I would eat it. I managed to eat all that was on my plate by not thinking what I was eating.

August 8th.

Today we rode out to watch a buffalo hunt. I heard all the galloping outside the Fort, and Mary came running to tell me, but I had no idea that Mark and I would go until he came in more excited than Mary, I believe. He said I must see the Major and Mrs. Phillips riding right up with the hunters, and hear the thunder of the buffalo herd. I hurried into my riding habit, thankful that I have always ridden. They had a kind of side saddle here, made from one of the squaw saddles, but Mr. Ferrière says he will send me a fine saddle from St. Louis. I will have it by next spring.

We were just mounted when Mrs. Phillips came by riding bareback and at a wild gallop. She wore a white beaded and fringed Indian dress and her long black hair flying loose. The Major had a white fringed outfit to match and rode like the wind. I thought privately that they were rather like performers in a circus, but they were handsome and certainly fearless. I haven't seen any war parties since I came; Mark has and says they are terrifying. I got a little idea of how they would look from the young Indians riding out to the hunt. They rode bareback, almost naked; one matched the color of his horse so exactly Mark called him a centaur. I thought Mark looked quite like a Byronic hero on horseback, in his leather clothes Mrs. Phillips had made for him.

There are no roads, no walls or fences or even trees, just endless grassy earth. One can ride anywhere under the sun. I was a little uneasy at first on my odd saddle and strange horse, but after I got used to them I felt an airy sort of freedom and excitement; though I am too timid to gallop very long.

We found our vantage point on a rise of ground just in time to make out the faint cloud of dust moving toward us. I know Mark wanted to ride nearer. He kept pointing out how close in the Indians ride, and the Phillipses (Pierre speaks of them as the Major and his lady) were right up in the front of the hunters, but I kept remembering Johnny Jessup's story on the boat.

Mark said the Indians live for the moment of danger and that civilized man lives for safety, or, at least, not many seek out danger. (But isn't that just what Mark has done by coming out here? And I, too.) The Indians, he said, aren't worried about death or a life hereafter, which makes preaching to them different too. I asked him if he meant because they can't be frightened by the thought of Hell; that I had never heard him do that in his sermons.

And he said with that slight smile of his, that he didn't have to, because the fear was in the minds of Christians already. I shall have to think about that.

Then the herd came nearer and the sound was enough to deafen you; it was like thunder and seemed to shake the earth. The dust was so thick I couldn't really see very much and had a regular sneezing fit.

When the hunters had killed enough buffalo, or, at any rate, when they stopped and the herd were almost out of sight, with only a few Indians still pursuing them, Mark suggested we ride closer. I kept my distaste to myself and rode along. Just as we came up where the Phillipses were standing by a great dusty mountain of fur we saw the most disgusting sight I have ever seen. Mrs. Phillips was holding the brains of the hardly dead buffalo in her hands, eating them! She looked up at us, and her eyes seemed to laugh at us over her bloody hands.

The Major told us that buffalo brains are a great delicacy to her people—which didn't make it any less disgusting! I do not understand how he can tolerate his wife's Indian ways. Mark turned his horse and rode away, and I saw him get off and lie flat on the ground behind a low bush. I knew the sight had made him ill. I don't know why I wasn't sick, too. Mrs. Phillips must have seen him ride away and known, and the Major, and Mr. Ferrière, who was there, too, but no one looked in Mark's direction.

Then Mrs. Phillips wiped her hands on the grass, but her mouth was smeared with blood and there was a horrid stain on her white elkskin dress. She tossed her hair back out of the way, got up on her horse, and she and the Major rode off at a furious gallop.

I waited for Mark, and Mr. Ferrière waited with me. He said that we forgot that Mrs. Phillips, great lady though she was, still belonged to a savage race. I didn't say anything. Mark came back looking very pale. I know it bothered him to see Mrs. Phillips do such a thing, partly because she was the means of his vision. We haven't mentioned Mrs. Phillips or the buffalo hunt since.

August 10th.

The attendance at the service today was very small, smaller even than the one the day after I arrived. It is discouraging for Mark. Those who were there seemed more interested in the melodeon when I started to play the hymn than in what Mark was saying. (Of course, no one was able to play it until I came, or at least to play hymns.) Mark can only speak a few sentences; then he has to wait for Pierre to translate for him. Mrs. Phillips always comes to the service, so maybe she is thinking about how she would interpret Mark's words. The Major has only attended twice, although he wrote the Mission Board that he would be glad to have the Christianizing influence of a Protestant Missionary here, Mark said, and the Major has ordered some of the *engagés* to make dobies for the chapel and build the frame.

A hideous-looking Indian woman with a terribly scarred face is always present. She was unfaithful to her husband and her nose was cut off in punishment! Now she is an outcast, and everyone calls her Kaxkaani, which Mark discovered means "cut-nose"! She isn't thought worthy of keeping her own name. But Mark finally found out that her real name is Aapaaki and makes a point of calling her by it. She must be very pleased, because she follows him everywhere she can, with a grin on her face. I don't see how he can stand her; I can't bear to look at her.

August 12th.

Today was so hot I made up my mind I would wade in the river in front of the Fort where the Indian children are always playing. Mark was away working on the chapel, and I couldn't bear to stay another minute in that dark, close little room of ours. I looked for Mrs. Phillips, but she is usually down at the tipis when she is not riding with the Major. I took off my stays and petticoats and wore just a cotton dress over my underwear, but it was quite thick and gathered full in the skirt. When I came out of the gates Mary saw me and came along, but she laughed and shook her head when I asked her to go in the river with me.

The water felt deliciously cool, rising up my legs through my skirts. The next thing I knew half a dozen squaws stood on the bank giggling and pointing at me. I am getting used to them and their everlasting giggling, and I just waved back.

Then Mrs. Phillips appeared farther up the bank, where the water is deeper. I envied her her elkskin dress. She dove in and swam out under water the way she must have done when she captured the duck for Mark. Her little boy, Robert, came sliding down the bank, too. All the small children run naked here. I smile to myself when I remember how insistent the Mission Board was that Mark take material and patterns for underwear and clothes for the Indian children. The head of the Mission Board wrote Mark that clothing them was one means of civilizing them.

Mrs. Phillips came down-river closer to me, where it is shallow, and took Robert up on her back. She swam out with him and then went under the water, toppling him off. All the children swim like frogs. I held out my hands and he splashed over to me so I could catch him up in my arms, all slippery wet. Then I put him down in the water and he paddled back to his Mother. I shall learn to swim while I am here. It seems easy. Mrs. Phillips gestured toward the deeper part of the river and kept repeating some Indian words.

"Mother say get wet all over," Mary called. Mrs. Phillips held out her hand and led me where the water came up to my shoulders. I had no fear, she is so at home in the water, and she held my hand in a strong grip. The river moved so slowly, the sky and a scraggly tree on the bank were mirrored in it. I could see my own face and Mrs. Phillips' close beside mine. For just an instant I put my face down in the water. When I lifted it the water in my eyes blurred the sky and the Indian squaws giggling on the bank, and ran down my face from my hair. I thought how Mark wanted to baptize a great crowd of converts in the river before the weather turns cold. So far he has converted only one chief and Aapaaki, but he thinks the Indians will understand if they see the baptismal ceremony what "putting off the old man" and "being born again" mean. I believe they would. I felt reborn myself.

I want to write this all down because Mrs. Phillips and I came closer together than we ever had before, but without saying one word to each other.

The squaws were calling out and chattering to her, but their gabble blended with the gurgling sound of the water around the curve of the bank below me, so I wasn't listening when Mary called to me. Then the English words caught my ear.

"Mother hold you up," she was saying.

I looked over at Mrs. Phillips, who held out her arms on top of the water and made a motion of leaning back. I didn't really want to, but I didn't want her to think I was afraid, either, so I went closer to her and leaned back until I was lying on her arms and the water came over my whole body, up to my neck. At first, I held my head up out of the water, but it was awkward, and as she walked, floating me on her arms, I dropped my head back, and felt as though I were Ophelia, drifting with the current. When I looked up at the sky it was unmarked by a single cloud and seemed to curve down at each side like a great empty blue bowl. The water came over my ears and closed off all sound, and I lost any sense of myself. I don't know whether I lay there on her arms only a moment or several moments; then my eyes came back to the smiling face above me, warmed to a copper color in the sunlight, and her eyes were on mine in a long silent look. It was very strange.

I was almost dizzy as I stood on my own feet on the sandy river bottom. When we came out of the water together the squaws were yelling and clapping their hands and laughing up above us. Mrs. Phillips pointed to our shadows traced against the grassless clay bank, her body slim and almost straight in her skin dress, mine bunched out and sagging with my wet clothes. I had to laugh, too. And the little boy's shadow ran along the bank ahead of us.

Water kept running from my hair, so I took out the pins and shook it down. Mrs. Phillips stood still looking at it and touched it with her fingers. My hair is not so heavy as hers, and it is fine, not coarse and strong, but it comes down to my waist. Of course, the squaws pointed and chattered; I didn't mind, I don't suppose any of them had ever seen light hair before, at least not on a woman. When we went back through the stockade the Indians who were there stared and laughed, too. Mrs. Phillips spoke to them, sharply, I thought, but I felt too light and cool for anything to bother me. And I felt less lonely because Mrs. Phillips was with me.

I met Pierre as I was going to our room and he stood still and looked at me. "Madame," he said, "your hair is the color of them willows that grow along the riverbank. In the spring before they got any leaves on 'em the bark get like gold." I think he fancies himself a French gallant, but I don't see any of it in his treatment of his Indian wife!

August 15th.

Mark worked all day making bricks (not really bricks, for they are made out of mud and called dobies) for the Church. It isn't his work, but the men were needed to cut and haul wood, and the Indians are not interested, which disappoints Mark. Only Aapaaki is always there and willing to work. I rode over, and Mary with me. "When I am grown up I am going to live like a white woman," Mary told me. "My skin is so light nobody will know that I am part Indian, will they?" I said her mother was a beautiful woman, but I wonder how it will be for Mary as she grows up.

Harriet heard the door knocker echo through the house, and Hannah appeared to say that Mrs. Sansom and her daughter had come to call and should she serve the caraway cookies with tea? For an amused second Harriet thought of the squaws who came of an afternoon to visit Mrs. Phillips, and of the chatter and laughter that came out of her rooms. One thing she knew—the bugles and bangles on Mrs. Sansom's dress would be laid on as heavily as the elkteeth and porcupine quills on the squaws' best attire.

She had wanted to read the Journal straight through, but she marked her place and went downstairs. It was not easy to come back from the Wilderness in that short descent to the parlor, and she stopped a minute on the landing before going the rest of the way.

"Oh, my poor dear, how relieved and happy you must be to be home! You look better already than you did that first Sunday." Mrs. Sansom clasped her to her wide bosom in a close embrace, planting a heavily scented kiss on her cheek, while her daughter waited her turn.

"I'm dying to hear what it was really like, Harriet," Elizabeth said. "Begin with travelling on the boat all by yourself. No, go back to the very beginning, with the train and the canalboat. Weren't you scared to death! And were you accosted?"

When they had left, Harriet took two more caraway cookies from the plate, poured herself a cup of lukewarm tea, and went back upstairs.

<> <> <>

You can see that the whole experience has been a terrible shock to her system. She doesn't act quite natural to me. I felt it the moment I kissed her. She kinda drew away.

But she did say they weren't attacked or anything, and that the Indian children were as cute as could be.

She admitted that they run around naked, if you can call that cute! I could tell from her eyes that she was keeping a good deal back.

She has pretty eyes; I noticed them.

Of course, Harriet Tomlinson was never what you could call an affectionate, talkative girl; and her mother dying when she was born, and brought up mostly by Judge Tomlinson and the housekeeper made her kinda cold and distant, I always thought.

But she must have loved Reverend Ryegate awfully to go out there by herself so she could be with him.

You notice they didn't stay long after she got there!

But . . .

And I doubt if she ever makes a real good minister's wife! Not one who puts her shoulder to the wheel. When I said we expected her to be head of the Mission Society after the baby was born, she said right off that she "really couldn't"! And why shouldn't she be, I'd like to know? She set herself up as a missionary, didn't she? It would have been much better if Reverend Ryegate had married someone from away, who'd be more worried about pleasing the women of the Church. Harriet is too independent, and you just can't get at her.

❖ ❖ ❖

August 18th.

Almost overnight the weather has turned cold and rainy. The wind blows without stopping. It makes me shudder to think how it will be in winter, when we are closed in the Fort. Food sometimes runs low in winter, Pierre says. The place will smell even more of skins and bodies and wet clothes, I'm sure. Today, nobody kept the fire going, and people were constantly opening and banging the big door and letting in a cold draught. There was another fight in the passageway in front of the store window, and yelling and cursing.

I tried to clean our room, but it will never be really clean. The pegs are hung so deep with clothes they keep falling off, and I packed all I could back in the trunk. I bundled up in my Paisley shawl all day. In winter I shall live in my fur cape. When I went out to the kitchen to make some tea for Mark, because he was so chilled, the cook, who is French Canadian, reached up and touched my hair. "Long time since I seen a yaller-headed woman," he said. He was so dirty I shudder to think he prepares our food.

In spite of the bad weather, the Major and Mrs. Phillips, who doesn't seem to feel the cold at all, and Mr. Ferrière left for an Indian Camp. The Major speaks of these expeditions the way someone from Woollett would talk of going on a business trip to Boston. They left on horseback with two wagons covered with canvas following them.

You can feel their absence at once. Everyone from the cook to Pierre takes life more easily; things seem lax, and the Fort does not seem so secure with them gone. The Major is greatly respected by the Indians. He is not really an Army officer after all, just given that title because he is head of the Fort or, Mark says, for his qualities of a commander. Then, of course, the fact that Mrs. Phillips is the daughter of a Chief of one of the most savage tribes and yet is so civilized gives me a sense of safety. The Indians would listen to her, and understand her. I believe I am growing as conscious as Mark is of how much depends on making one's self understood, and the horrid difficulty of not being able to talk to people of another race.

Last night at dinner the cook put Mark in the Major's place at the table and me in Mrs. Phillips' place, with Robert and Mary on either side of me. Raymond sat by Mark, and then Pierre (who has taken over the storekeeper's duties today because the storekeeper is drunk). I felt as though I was trying to be Mrs. Phillips, but Mark went on being himself.

At the end of the entry she had written in very small handwriting: "I must make note that I missed my time (Aug. 15). It would be surprising if I became pregnant here when I didn't all last year. Perhaps I am late only because of the change in climate."

August 19th. Still Raining.

Mark came back from a visit at Two Knives' tipi greatly encouraged. He said they managed to understand each other remarkably with gestures and a few words. They smoked a pipe together and talked of the Great Spirit whom Mark told him we call God. Mark said the man had a look of deep inner wisdom in his face. Their faces grow on you, he said. Two Knives knows a few words of English and he tried to tell Mark about the Medicine Lodge and the torture he went through as a young man. He even showed him his scars. And he showed Mark his medicine bundle, which is something very sacred because it has to do with some vision he'd had. Mark couldn't get it all, but he tried to tell him about his own vision of the eagle. Two Knives must have understood, because he gave Mark an eagle feather. Mark has it over his worktable.

She hesitated as she turned the page. Perhaps she should tear out these next pages, but that would loosen the others. She would never write out such intimate feelings again, but anyway, she had given up keeping a journal now that they were back home.

August 20th.

Our high window faces due east, and this morning the sun shone right in on our faces and woke me. We had over-slept, and I started to get out of bed quickly, but Mark said not to go yet, and hid my face against his shoulder to keep the sun out of my eyes, quoting poetry to me about the sun having no right to wake up lovers. I delighted in his calling us lovers and his being in such a light and play-ful mood, but I am never quite prepared for it. I thought he had made up the poem, but he said it was by John Donne, who was a minister, too, long ago, and his favorite poet. When Mark was in the Seminary his class was di-rected to read some of Donne's sermons, and then Mark discovered that Donne had written poetry as well. Mark leaped out of bed and produced the little volume with black leather corners and a mottled cover, and read all the rest of the poem to me, though we should have been up and dressed. When Mark finished the lovely, crazy poem, he tossed the little book at me and said I'd find it at least as "enlarging" as Byron. We had to hurry out then to breakfast, which was horrible, as usual; no, worse than usual. The cook doesn't bother as much when the Major isn't here. I have tea rather than drink the muddy coffee. I am thankful I brought five pounds with me; I should have brought ten. But, afterward, I positively fled from Mary and came back to our room and curled up on the bed to "enlarge my understanding"; that has become a special joke between us. This is the stanza Mark quoted to me:

> Busie old foole, unruly Sunne,
> Why dost thou thus,
> Through windowes, and through curtaines call on us?
> Must to thy motions lovers' seasons run?

But it goes on and spins the cleverest fancy.

Some of the poems in the volume are very strange and

hard to understand, and some are quite shockingly flippant. There is one about the flea uniting two lovers by biting them both and mixing their blood, but I did have to smile. The religious poems are like none I have ever read. Most religious poems are rather like hymns, I think, with the same ideas and rhymes over and over, and quite funereal, but not these, which are more like arguments between two lovers, or outright ravings.

One sonnet, beginning "Batter my heart, three person'd God," leaped out from the page because Mark had drawn a heavy line along the margin, and two lines by these words:

> Yet dearely'I love you,'and would be loved faine,
> But am betroth'd unto your enemie:

Why would he mark those lines unless he had felt the same way? From the date on the flyleaf I saw that Mark had bought the book his last year at the Seminary. I wonder if he was not sure then about his call to the Ministry, or even about his faith. Was doubt the enemy to whom he was betrothed? It was not worldliness, that I know.

The lines of the poem grow frantic:

> Divorce mee,'untie, or breake that knot againe,
> Take mee to you, imprison mee, for I
> Except you'enthrall mee, never shall be free;
> Nor ever chast, except you ravish mee.

It is difficult to remember that the poet is really talking to God. I, myself, could say those last three lines to Mark. I could change them to: Until you enthralled me, never was I free, Nor ever chaste, until you ravished me, that night when I arrived. Just writing these words I never say, and hardly thought till now, excites me. I whispered the lines over my way, and then I had to lay my cold hands on my face to cool it. I feel guilty at using them for myself when they were intended for God, yet they *are* true for me. I wonder if I am not a religious person.

Later.

I slipped the little book back between the others on the shelf, almost as though it burned my mind, and went out through the big room, which was empty, for a wonder, because everyone is busy after the bad weather. I hurried through the gate across the grassy land back of the Fort, farther than I have gone before. I had to be alone to think out the meaning of those words for me. I hadn't really understood before how all my being depends on Mark's loving me. It is true! Until Mark—enthralled—me I would never have been bold enough, or free enough, to set out on the long journey by myself to be with him. But I cannot write down all my thoughts, even here.

I walked until the Fort looked as small as it had seemed the day I came. The tipis shrank, too, and the figures moving around them. The barking of the dogs around the tipis and all the confused noise from the Fort blurred into one running, faraway sound.

I wanted to go up to the rocky ridge, above the Fort, that rises straight out of the plain to cut into the blue sky; someplace high enough to match my own exultant mood.

The ridge was farther away than I had thought, but, as I climbed, my eyes went in and out of the fissures and touched the bare rock, and I hid my joy in the secret places, and let the hardness of the rock be proof of its enduring. A magpie flew across the sky, swooping down a little to see what I was, calling out in his harsh, rusty voice, which made me think of the bird on the boat with its tongue split. But a lark sang, too.

Then something terrible happened. The country was so bare and empty and endless from up there that I began to be drawn out of my own thoughts until I was only two eyes looking. Even after the last three days of rain I saw that the ground was already dry again. The grass was pale and made a whipping sound as my skirts brushed it. Grasshoppers sprang out of the grass by the handfuls, hitting my skirt but hopping off again.

I was out of breath and had to stop. But as I stood there, alone under the bright sun, there was too much light. All I had been saying to myself, even the words of the poem, began to fade under the light and lose its meaning, until the words were nothing-words, and I was nothing in all that space.

I started on again toward the rocks; then I remembered that the Major said there were rattlesnake nests in the rocks, and that the rattlers came down to the river when it was hot. I clutched my skirts up above my knees and listened. I could hear only the grasshoppers and the far-away sounds from the Fort, but I felt uneasy and my head ached, so I turned back. I walked faster and faster until I was running. At the gate I met Aapaaki, who grinned at me as usual. The sight of her makes me shudder more than the thought of rattlesnakes.

She wouldn't mind Mark's reading the first part; they had never been so lighthearted together as they were that morning; and Mark would understand her changing the words of the poem and taking them to herself, although the way she had written about her feelings made her seem much younger than she was now. But she wouldn't want him to read the rest. She had been so disturbed when she came in that she had sat down and tried to describe the way she had been drawn out of herself into nothingness, just to find herself again. Her fear sounded silly now as she read, but it had been real. That was why she had said the other night that there was too much light, and then Mark had repeated it and turned her words on himself. "Too much exposure to the light," he had said.

A proper wife of a missionary should have been frightened by an Indian suddenly appearing, something to tell Elizabeth Sansom about, instead of being frightened by a feeling she couldn't explain sensibly. Of course, Aapaaki was an Indian, but she hardly thought of her as one, or as a woman, either; she was more like an apparition.

She couldn't read any more for a while, although there were only a few more entries and she could easily finish them before dinner. Perhaps Mark would forget he had asked to read her Journal. He hadn't asked to *read* it; he had said he wondered if there were things in it that would help him to remember. If she said some of it was too personal, he would say, of course, he understood, but he would wonder what she had written. She would read him parts, skipping others. "Oh, here's something that might be of use," she could hear herself saying.

Chapter Seven

So many attended the first lecture that the audience had to adjourn from the "church parlor" to the auditorium upstairs. Harriet slipped into a back pew, under the shadow of the balcony, feeling that Mark might catch sight at some disconcerting moment of what he had once called her listening face. She had almost said she didn't feel well enough to come. Sitting across from Mark tonight at dinner, feeling his nervousness and eagerness combined, she shrank from hearing him; but here she was. She was annoyed when Sydney Hall sat down beside her.

"You know," he said, "I must confess that I have never felt any call to the Wilderness. If anything, I have a deep urge to go back to Europe. You remember I had a *Wanderjahr* before I came back to the paper, and I've never got over it. Savages and buffalo meat don't particularly appeal to me."

Harriet smiled. Sydney had a relaxed and humorous way of talking that was rather a relief tonight. "I can't see you there, either," she told him, and wondered if he remembered the time she had called him a desiccated raisin because he had called her a bluestocking, back in their teens.

"Of course," Sydney said, "I never had any illusion that I was called to succeed John the Baptist, either."

Now he was going too far. Before she could answer, he said, "I don't believe John the Baptist had a wife to bring him back home after he'd had a taste of it. Mark was fortunate!"

He was baiting her, just as he used to do, but at that moment Mark came out of the door at the back of the pulpit, attended by Deacon Slocum, who would introduce him. A hush fell at once over the lively conversational hum that marked a lecture audience from a church one.

"Or unfortunate," Harriet leaned over to murmur to Sydney.

She writhed at Deacon Slocum's florid welcome to those of other faiths, and at the prolonged eulogy of Calvary Baptist's talented and courageous pastor, summoned back by providential circumstances to his post here. In spite of herself, her eyes met Sydney's, and she was aware of his amusement at her discomfort. He touched her gloved hand in a light gesture of sympathy.

After Deacon Slocum's rotundity of physical figure, which matched his literary phrase, Mark seemed thin as he stood up. The dark eyes in his tanned face seemed to search out each person present, finding them all, even Harriet, in the second of silence he allowed—to separate himself from Deacon Slocum, perhaps, or wait for their full attention. He spoke, as always, without notes, in a voice so quiet and conversational it was a relief after the rhetoric before it. He omitted any acknowledgment of Deacon Slocum's praise or any expression of joy at being back, but began with a direct question.

"Hasn't civilized man always been haunted by the call of the Wilderness?"

"No," a voice beside Harriet whispered, shaping the "O" so roundly she felt it without turning her head.

"Are there many here who can deny that they have heard that call, faint and far away, or taunting, or loud, and difficult not to heed? For some, it comes as a call to freedom from the surface living Thoreau warns us of, the falsity of standards Emerson would have us beware: enslaving routines, the shibboleths of money and prestige. For others, it is a summons to vastness and mystery, and the fearful liberty to discover one's self. . . ."

How could she have feared there might be any hint of that

pomposity of manner and oratory he had poured down on her the other night, or that exaggerated posturing and those theatrical gestures? Then, he had set out to laugh at himself and, as he said, hurt himself by hurting her. She would never get that phrase out of her memory.

He had said, too, in that bitter, sarcastic voice, that he was a person who had to be heard, had to feel his own power. To-night, she set herself to see whether that was true. She had never watched an audience before, or thought about the other people listening beside her. Many of the faces were strange to her. Were they all drawn by the haunting word "Wilderness"? She had found herself saying it soundlessly in her head at odd moments, hearing it when she was talking to callers over tea, or at those dinners to which they were still being invited. There was a sound of wind in it, and the whipping hiss of prairie grass and blown snow. The "wild" of the first syllable became mysterious in the last prolonged "s" sound, because you couldn't cut it off at once by any feat of lips or teeth—or mind. Yet, like Sydney, she would never have heard it if Mark hadn't set it sounding in her ear. She would rather have gone to Europe. But people *were* listening to Mark, really listening. When he began, he had seemed tense, a little uncertain, even though his voice was quiet; now she could see he felt their attention and was marvellously at ease. Oh, yes, he was being heard. But she was hardly hearing what he was saying.

He was talking about the hunter; she didn't know how he had got there. ". . . instinct of the hunt and the chase in every man, and who shall say there is not a vestige of it in every woman . . . for a different prey?" Light, self-conscious, and slightly coy laughter rippled over the audience and gave way to hearty roars as Mark described the Oxford-educated baronet who took forty servants to the Wilderness, including his personal valet, as well as a rubber bathtub and brass bed, which were set up each night on the prairie under a green-striped linen tent; whose lust for killing game by the thousands so shocked the Indians that they protested to the factor

of the Fort, who, in turn, appealed to the government to cur-
tail the baronet's activities. Mark was being entertaining
now.

"I have never shot a gun in my life," Sydney Hall leaned
over to murmur. "The idea is utterly abhorrent to me."

And Mark made them one with him in his expectation of
meeting only the roughest conditions and finding himself instead in a fort five hundred miles from his destination, talking
over a white tablecloth with a botanist from Boston, a cele-
brated historian from London, and an artist from Germany. . . .

She and Mark could have stayed at that fort all winter, and
gone back up to Fort Phillips in the spring. They could have
lived in much more comfort there. Mrs. Phillips would have
come back before the baby was born. Now the baby, conceived
in the Wilderness, would be born in civilization. . . .

"The young man, impatient with the long process of his education, for whom the great events of history all seem beyond
his reach, who wants to measure himself against the fear and
danger that lie beyond civilization so that he may know . . ."

Was that young man Mark, himself?

"He wants, perhaps, to give himself to the most rigorous
discipline—riding hard all day in the saddle, living on pemmican and wild meat, coming up with fur traders and Indians
—and, above all, the rigors of that wild country."

That was the way Mark had lived before she came, very
much alone at the Fort, trying to harden himself physically,
perhaps goaded by that attitude of the Major toward the
hardihood of a missionary. Mark had told her how he plunged
into the river every morning, rode a greater distance each day,
and went out to an Indian camp with only an Indian interpreter, not sure how he would be received. And, of course, he
had worked early and late at learning the language. Had she
spoiled all that for him? She had altered his way of life. The
morning they had lain in bed in the sun while he read that
poem to her came back now in a different context. Perhaps even

his separation from her, which he wrote was his greatest hardship, had been part of the hardship he meant to experience. She had never thought . . . She felt as though she were listening to a page from a journal Mark had kept that had been too personal, too secret for him to let her read by herself.

"Mark always struck me as one to whom the ascetic life would appeal," Sydney murmured.

"He will know for the first time, perhaps, what it would be like to escape the Puritan strictures that our society imposes, and live in a society where there is no struggle between the life of the flesh and the life of the spirit. But do not get the impression that within the pattern of their lives, abhorrent though it may seem, the Indians do not possess . . ."

Mark's ideas about the Indians were going to anger some of his listeners, Harriet thought. He would make statements that they would take too literally, that startled even her. "If we knew their language and could really talk with them and understand their way of thinking . . ." he had said to her.

"Their young men put themselves, in the Medicine Dance, to the test of the most extreme self-torture in an effort to affirm their manhood. They are no more involved with war than Europeans and Americans. The cruelty of the white man over the ages, his greed . . . They are part of the human race to which we all belong. . . ."

When Mark talked of the Indians, would he omit such habits as Mrs. Phillips' eating fresh-killed buffalo brains, in spite of her knowledge of civilized practices? He had forgotten, when he looked at her asleep on the boat and said how beautiful her face was, how sick the sight of her had made him.

"What manner of call moves a man to work at pulling a boat by a rope that turns his hands, finally, into iron claws and grooves his shoulder; wading up to his armpits, slipping in mud, struggling mile after mile against the implacable will of a river that fights him, knocks him down, trip after trip, for a wage he will lose in one night's debauch, if he survives?

Can he get nothing safer to do? Is he too ignorant to know better? Or does even this man feel some strange lure of the Wilderness?"

Mark had said the word! Had he put it in for her? Mark might have understood the episode in her Journal about the cordeller, after all. She hadn't thought Mark was going to get all these people into his lecture, describing the Wilderness through the appeal it had for so many kinds. She had been listening to Mark after all, instead of watching the audience. Some of them were listening eagerly; she could feel their avid appetite for every last, lurid detail. She felt it sometimes in her callers who came to tea. "And did all the Indians practice polygamy?" Miss Printz had asked with a kind of shiver. But she noticed Sydney Hall recrossing his legs as though he was growing bored.

"And then there is the man for whom the call must come quite differently. . . ." She had been waiting to hear what Mark would say about the missionary. He would come last, Mark had said.

". . . not from the Wilderness, but from God, as a vision of what he might be able to do there. Like many others, he goes with a dream in his heart, but not to find wealth or freedom or knowledge for himself, but, rather, to take an inestimable gift to the dwellers in the Wilderness. . . ."

Mark had resorted to trite, noble phrases and oratorical effects to avoid saying what he had felt. She sat back, laying one glove over the other in her disappointment.

". . . which is not to say, paradoxically, that he will not also find something for himself, if only his own spiritual limitations as he comes to know loneliness and frustration and fear, even as the other human beings who venture into the Wilderness."

She might have known he would undercut those first grand statements with the truth, risking his own merciless view of himself, which listeners like Sydney Hall would be quick to perceive. She sat up proudly.

"A European artist on the boat going up the river observed that he was going to the Wilderness because he wanted the portraits of the savages, whereas the missionary was going because he wanted their souls. The savages, he remarked, should be either complimented or frightened."

There was a slight, uncertain murmur of laughter. Mark had used the remark of Steiner's she had told him about. His mouth had twisted, she remembered, and he had said her artist was obviously pleased with his own cleverness, but he had gone on thinking about it.

"He was quite mistaken about the missionary," Mark went on. "Not the missionary, but God, wants their souls. God makes use of the faulty, uncomprehending, clumsy human material, even as Christ used it for his disciples, but He must first perform a miracle with that material, changing repugnance and fear toward the savages to love, before those too ordinary human beings can become worthy of the calling of missionary."

Harriet thought about the word "love." Could anyone love Aapaaki? And those wretched hags scraping buffalo skins on the ground in front of their tipis; she had seen one thrust a puppy into a kettle of boiling water, making sport of it. Mark had been angry at them when they laughed in the service; he had been frightened sometimes. His not being able to feel love for them gnawed at him. "Loved," he had said that night in his sleep, and then, "God so loved." The night he came back from Mrs. Phillips.

The quietness of Mark's voice interrupted her thoughts.

"Only two hundred years ago this very city was just such a Wilderness, to which other generations of men were called, for different reasons. Now civilization has conquered that Wilderness, how completely I leave you to consider in your own minds. But this I can assure you: We are never far from the Wilderness, be it that mysterious vastness I have attempted to describe, two thousand miles and more from here, or the wilderness within ourselves."

The audience sat still. His conclusion was hardly startling, in either the words or the idea, yet Mark did have the power of awakening a response in his listeners. She felt it in herself, and even Sydney was attentive. Was it by the vibration of his voice, then, and the intensity of his gaze, which seemed to look into each person's eyes? And he felt he held them; she could tell by the way he didn't move for a moment after he had stopped speaking. Perversely, she resisted that hold and began fastening her cape.

Sydney Hall leaned toward her. "You're breaking the spell," he whispered, raising his eyebrows. But applause broke out before she could answer.

Applause that, as Abigail Dalton said to her husband on the way home, seemed out of place in a house of worship. "Did you notice there wasn't a word of religion in it, Mr. Dalton? And he had a good chance with so many people there who didn't belong to our Church."

"Oh, yes, he talked about what God has to do to turn out a missionary. But I didn't just gather whether the Lord had finished the job on Reverend Ryegate or given it up," Mr. Dalton observed.

"Well?" Mark asked when they were home.

"Oh, Mark, I could hardly hear you some of the time, because I was remembering and seeing, and seeing us—even missing it at the same time. And I never expected to."

"I'm satisfied then."

"You know, Mark, you're wrong. It isn't that you're a person who has to feel his own power over an audience. It's that you have to make somebody else see what you saw and feel what you felt. And you did it! People who would never dream of going to the Wilderness—even Sydney Hall—began to see."

"You're hardly a judge, my darling. You had seen it for yourself, remember."

"But I didn't see all you saw, or as you saw it."

From the Woollett *Republican:*

A RARE TREAT FOR WOOLLETT RESIDENTS

The first of three lectures on his Wilderness experience by the Reverend Marcus Ryegate was pronounced a distinguished performance by the large and discriminating audience who attended. With eloquence and rare powers of observation and interpretation the clergyman evoked for his hearers the mystery and appeal of the colossal territory at the head of the Missouri River, describing its untouched resources and particular attraction for the hunter, scientist, artist, and missionary alike. By the time he was through, an entire cavalcade of humanity on their way to the Wilderness had been portrayed.

The lecture was not only informative but often humorous, and philosophical as well. If any criticism can be found, it is in the impersonal nature of the Reverend Ryegate's account; only brief instances of his personal experience were given. This first lecture cannot fail to whet the appetite of his audience for the viands to be served at the two subsequent lectures.

From the *New England Reporter:*

RETURNED MISSIONARY
GIVES FIRST OF THREE LECTURES

Over three hundred persons felt the fascination of danger and mystery of the Northwest Wilderness as they listened spellbound to the Reverend Marcus Ryegate last evening at the Calvary Baptist Church discourse on the reasons that draw Europeans as well as Easterners to the Wilderness country. From the man with the dream of making money in furs to the man with the dream of winning souls, he covered a wide range of human motives. It is to be feared that he may have set the Call of the Wilderness resounding so loudly in his listeners' ears that it will drown out the sound of Indian war whoops and the howl of wolves also present in the wilds. The Reverend and Mrs. Ryegate were unable to stay in the territory until it became a frozen waste, cut off from the rest of the world, nor did they experience an Indian attack, which may account for his enthusiastic view of the country and his appreciation of the virtues of the Indians! The fate of those Missionaries beyond the Rocky Mountains offers a different view. In his next lecture, entitled "Journey into Strangeness," the Reverend Ryegate will doubtless deal with the nature of the Wilderness and its inhabitants from a different, perhaps a more realistic, angle.

From the Woollett *Bugle:*

FIRST-HAND REPORT FROM THE INDIAN COUNTRY
By a Non-Indian Fighter!

According to the glowing description of the appeal of the Wilderness for all sorts and conditions of men, the Upper Missouri country will soon be well populated unless the numbers are kept down by the zealous efforts of the present inhabitants, namely, the Indians. Some disappointment may have been felt on the part of the male listeners that the Reverend avoided all mention of two prime attractions: its *relative* closeness to the gold fields and the "beauty" and availability of Indian squaws. Come now, Parson, tell us more!

Chapter Eight

T HE next morning, Harriet read the few remaining entries
in her Journal.

September 16th.

About midmorning the salute from the cannon went off
to greet the Phillipses like a Monarch and his Queen returning to their kingdom; but, of course, they are a kind
of royalty out here. Pierre says there will be a ball tonight
and the Major will give a dram of whiskey around. I asked
Mark if he would dance. He looked surprised at my question, and said that he had never danced, and as for dancing here, that he felt he suffered enough by comparison
with the Black Robes in the eyes of the Indians without
dancing. So I shall not either, though the Black Robes
didn't have wives to compare me with! I don't believe I
shall tell Mark about dancing on the boat. Oh, yes, I will,
at some later time, but I do not want him to feel I am a
poor excuse for a Minister's wife.

The moment the Phillipses and Mr. Ferrière came in,
the atmosphere of the Fort seemed to change. Mrs. Phillips wore her Indian dress, with her black braids tied with
red cloth. The Major told how far they had ridden and
that Mrs. Phillips had killed a young antelope which we
would have for dinner. He sounded like a husband in
Woollett boasting of his wife's cake!

"And how was it for you?" Mr. Ferrière asked me. I

assured him that we had managed very well, but I was happy to see Mrs. Phillips back. He told me he was afraid the Phillipses would be gone for some months, for they were going East with him to Illinois, where the Major has had a home built for his retirement from the Indian country. I was so shocked that I wanted to cry out that they couldn't do that, go off and leave us alone here all winter; but I managed to ask only who would be in charge. He said Pierre, and that Mark's presence would help in controlling the men at the Fort and any drunken Indians! "The activity dies down pretty well in winter, until the skins come in," he said. I had the feeling that he was going to say more and then thought better of it. I am very much disturbed.

Over a hundred Indians have been here at the Fort this afternoon to talk with the Major. Some of them were men of importance in their tribe. The Major introduced Mark to them at the end, and Mark talked to them through the Major, who, he said, made a fine interpreter. It was a relief to Mark, I think, to have a chance to speak to so many. But they seemed frightening when they stared at me. I disappeared at once.

Mrs. Phillips was visited by many of the squaws, and I never heard such a chattering and giggling. Indian women laugh much more than white women, and differently. I stayed in my room most of the afternoon, but when I started out into the enclosure I saw Mrs. Phillips taking little mincing steps in front of a group of them, obviously showing them how I walk, holding up an imaginary skirt with one hand and a parasol with the other. She was nodding her head and talking quite fast, and the Indian women sitting on the ground laughed so hard that one fell over backwards. Then Mrs. Phillips held out her arms and moved slowly in front of them, showing them how she floated me in the river. There was no mistaking what she was doing. I was furious, and hurried back into our room and slammed the door. Mrs. Phillips must be laughing at me all the time behind those shining black eyes, even that time when she held me and I felt that our eyes met in understanding. I have decided that I will tell her at dinner that she is a *very* clever actress. She will know then that I saw her. But how can she change so? She is a different person when she is with the Major or Mr. Ferrière or Mark and me; very much a lady, and as dignified as you please.

I waited in my room after I was dressed for dinner in my purple, with Mama's amethyst brooch and drops, until I saw Mrs. Phillips go out of their apartment. She wore her red silk dress, which must have been made for her in St. Louis, with her gold earrings and gold cross, and was polite dignity itself! The Major was wearing the blue coat and high white stock he wears on special occasions. There will be none of these occasions in the long winter if the Major and Mrs. Phillips are away. I don't like her laughing at me, but I am coming to listen for the sound of her laughing. At least there is always life where she is, and a feeling of security with them both. I feel they can control any danger.

After Midnight.

How ironic my last sentence seems now. But to go back and try to set down the sad events of this night in order: the table was set with more formality than usual, and only the adults were there. Mark began the grace, but he only got as far as "God bless" when the heavy door banged open and Mary came running in saying something to her Mother. Mrs. Phillips jumped to her feet, shrieking some Indian word in such a terrible voice it went right through me. Then she ran out the door. The Major called her by her first name, Eenisskim, and rushed out after her, and the rest of us sat stunned while Mary told us she couldn't find Robert anywhere. He was by the river, she said.

"Maybe he drown. Little Crow see him near deep current, tell him get away." Mary was crying between her words.

I have just come in. Torches are burning along the river where the deep water swirls at the point of the island. It seemed as though everyone in the Fort and the tipis is there. A white face jumps out in the flare of light, and then an Indian face. I could hear the Major's voice above the mixture of Indian and English and even French, and the sound of the men and canoes splashing in the water. The men are dragging the river with a crude kind of frame. As I stood watching, Mary brought me her Mother's red silk dress all in a heap. She said her Mother had torn it off and dived into the river to find Robert's body. Now the poor woman is sitting wrapped in a blanket, waiting. I was glad Mark was there beside her. I feel for her.

It was almost dawn when Mark came back to the room. They found the little boy's body. Mark said he had never seen anyone so overwhelmed with grief as Mrs. Phillips was. She sat there, swaying back and forth, moaning. When he tried to speak to her, she didn't seem to hear him, or notice when he said a prayer. The Major couldn't get her to go back to the Fort, so he finally left her there. She was still sitting on the bank when Mark came in, but other Indian women were with her, wailing.

I thought Mark had fallen asleep when he said that word Mrs. Phillips called out at dinner meant "owl." The Major told him an owl woke her the night before and frightened her so she wakened him, saying it was a sign of death. The old superstitions have such a hold on her, Mark said, it was hard to reach her.

Mark held a funeral service this afternoon here in the Fort. I played softly on the melodeon. All the men and many of the Indians who had come to trade crowded into the room; I could hardly breathe in the foul air. Mr. Fer-rière stood beside the melodeon but on my other side a half-naked Indian was so close I could see his chest rise and fall with his breathing and the sweat glisten through the streaks of paint on his face. Mr. Ferrière whispered to me that he was Mrs. Phillips' brother. I found myself staring at the human scalp locks sewed into the seams of his buckskin pants.

Never, I thought, did a human voice hold more tender-ness and compassion than Mark's. In his prayer he asked the Lord to "bear up this Thy child unto Thyself, gently as on eagle's wings." I felt Pierre must be trying harder than usual to translate Mark's words exactly. "Warm him in Thy bosom and give him everlasting life," Mark said. I wondered if Mrs. Phillips would remember holding the bird over Mark, but, of course, she didn't know anything about his vision.

When I turned around from the melodeon, I very nearly screamed. Mrs. Phillips had chopped off her long black hair and streaked it with mud or ashes, and painted her face with black, white, and green stripes, so her eyes seemed to look out between bars. She had cut gashes in the skin of her arms and smeared them with blood; I saw a trickle of blood still running down her forearm. She wore an old elkskin dress, all streaked with ashes, and she had left off the cross she wears so much. The Major stood beside her, his face stern and closed. Mary had streaked her hair, too, but not chopped it off or painted her face. She stood next to her Father and Raymond, not lifting her eyes from the floor.

Two Indians, relatives of Mrs. Phillips' I learned, car-ried the little coffin, made that morning in the carpenter's shop. Mrs. Phillips walked behind it, then the Major, then the children.

We all went in a procession up to the burial ground; there must have been forty or more from the fort and the tipis. On the way the Indian women, the very ones Mrs. Phillips had sent into gales of laughter yesterday afternoon, kept up that unearthly sound, half wail, half moan. They, too, had their faces painted. Aapaaki walked a little way behind them, her face more horrible than any, with her mouth open in a wail.

The burial ground has only wooden markers, and not more than a dozen, although there are more mounds than that. Except for a few clumps of sage, there wasn't a bush or a flower. The fenced-off space seemed unutterably desolate out there in all that emptiness of sky and grass. I thought how it would be completely lost this winter under the snow. I would come by there and remember this day when the big cottonwood tree along the river was just beginning to turn yellow and the cold wind was blowing the leaves wrong side out. I wished there had been hot sun, but the sky was covered with clouds.

Even after the burial the women kept up their wailing. The sound presses down on your nerves until it would be a relief to cry out yourself. Mark and I came back to our room, but he was worried about Mrs. Phillips and went to see if he could talk with her. The Major told him she had gone off by herself to mourn up on the flat table land they call a butte. After all, he said, she was an Indian woman and had to take her grief in her own way. The Major is taking Robert's death in his way, I felt. He came to dinner and did not mention his wife's absence or the tragedy. None of us made much attempt at conversation.

Mark has just left to find Mrs. Phillips. He couldn't bear the thought of her off on the mountain alone. The Major tried to discourage him and said it was a long way and that he could do her no good when he did find her; but Mark said that if it was worth while for him to come way out here to bring the message of Christianity, it was worth while for him to try to take that comfort to Mrs. Phillips.

The Major sent an Indian guide with him, and Mark has taken a bedroll and some food and his New Testament inside his leather shirt. I noticed that he put his eagle feather inside the Testament. I went outside the stockade to watch them go; it scares me to think of Mark off out there in the dark, but he was so set on it, I kept my fears to myself. He wouldn't even carry a gun, but, of course, the guide was with him.

When I came back in, the Major was still there. "Your husband is a stubborn man, Mrs. Ryegate," he said, "and a brave one, but he doesn't understand Eenisskim." We stood there a moment, and for the first time, I thought of the Major as old. His eyes looked tired above heavy pouches and lines cut deep into the leathery tanned skin of his face. His calling his wife Eenisskim made her seem more Indian.

What had she written along the margin? Then she remembered. "I am sure now that 'I am with child.' I like the Biblical phrase. How strange it is to be sure of this just as Mrs. Phillips has lost a child."

September 18th.

Mark has been gone two nights. The Indian guide returned the next day and said they had found Mrs. Phillips on the butte; that the Short-coat, as the Indians call Mark, was staying with her. Pierre told me this.

Tonight at dinner, I had no intention of doing so, but I heard myself asking the Major if he thought they could have met with any accident. From some hostile Indians, I said. I hadn't mentioned their names but of course he knew whom I meant. He shook his head and said Mrs. Phillips could take care of herself—and Reverend Ryegate, he added. He said that if they didn't come tomorrow he would send someone to take more food. Mr. Ferrière gave his dry little cough and said it was turning so cold there

might be snow in the mountains. I think he is shocked at
Mark's staying out there with Mrs. Phillips, and Pierre
looks at me and moves his eyes away again quickly, but
I understand how Mark feels and that he had to go to her.
He would be no Missionary if he didn't go. What I don't
understand is why the Major doesn't feel *he* must go to
her. I dread another night with Mark away.

September 19th.

The day has been endless. Most of the Indians have gone,
leaving such a litter where their tipis were that I cannot
look at the place. Crows keep cawing overhead and swooping down to pick in the refuse. Nor can I bear to look at
the river, glittering in the cold sunlight. I keep remembering little Robert running on the shore and laughing after
he had toppled off his Mother's back in the water. Mrs.
Phillips must be thinking of that day, too. Maybe the
pain of all those gashes she gave herself distracts her
mind from the worse pain of losing him.

Raymond, who is seldom inside the Fort, came to my
room while Mary was with me having her reading lesson.
He is a handsome, dark-eyed boy, but very shy. He just
shook his head when I tried to have him sit down with us,
but he went on leaning against the door. He wants to be
an Indian brave, Mary told me scornfully. Perhaps in the
winter he— But he won't be here. The Phillipses are taking the children with them, Pierre says. I can't bear to
think of being shut up here in winter. The wolves must
howl every night.

I overheard Pierre telling Mr. Ferrière about a mad
wolf attacking some hunters in their tent. One of the hunters was a young man from New York. He went mad from
the wolf bite and tore off all his clothes and ran screaming
into the dark. "Never found any trace of him but his
clothes," Pierre said. When Pierre finishes a story, he just

stops, but I heard Mr. Ferrière swear under his breath in French.

After dinner tonight, perhaps because he regretted his remark about the snow, Mr. Ferrière took pains to tell me we were bound to have a fine stretch of Indian summer after this little cold spell. "Most glorious time of the whole year out here," he assured me; he only hoped it would last for their trip down-river. I thought again of the Phillipses gone and being left here in this lonely outpost. All the time the baby will be growing inside me. I wonder if that will help the desolateness or make it worse.

Mark is back! I am so thankful.

He opened the door while I was sitting here writing and came in as though he couldn't take one more step. I've never seen him look so awful. "I failed utterly," was all he said, and he dragged himself over to the bed. I tried to pull out the buffalo robe so he could lie on the blanket, but he seemed to be asleep already. I got off his moccasins and the Indian leggings he wore, but I let him sleep as he was and covered him with my Paisley. Once he coughed so hard he half sat up, but he lay back again without really waking.

The Major just came to the door and handed me a bottle of whiskey. He said to see if I couldn't get Mark to take some; that he looked in bad shape. I wanted to ask about Mrs. Phillips, but I didn't.

When Mark's coughing woke him just now I told him the Major had brought him some whiskey. I didn't think he would touch it, but he sat on the edge of the bed and drank from the bottle, saying that ought to warm him up and keep him from coughing his head off. It was good to have him say something. When he started to go out to relieve himself I wouldn't let him. I didn't even go out of the room. I am becoming primitive myself. I wonder how we will be by the end of the winter, living in this place. But we will be together, anyway.

It is cold in the room, so he only took off his leather shirt and put on a woolen one and got under the blankets and robe, seeming almost desperate to get warm. I wanted to ask what happened and why they stayed so long, but he went right back to sleep. The smell of the whiskey mixes with the everlasting smell of hides so our room smells like the store.

I am sitting at Mark's desk with the one candle making a dim light in the room. Mark breathes so heavily and is talking in his sleep. He keeps repeating words from the Bible, all run together. I can see how it must have been with Mark saying these words to Mrs. Phillips. Just now he said "the resurrection and the life" and "beauty for ashes" and then fell to coughing. "Comfort ye, comfort ye, my people," he said in a whisper. I wondered if Mrs. Phillips would understand.

His face is hot now and he has thrown off the buffalo robe. I wiped his face with water from the pitcher, but it is too cold, and I felt him shiver, so I stopped. While I was sponging his face, he said as clearly as though he knew what he was saying, "loved . . . loved, I tell you. God so loved," but he couldn't get any further with it. His fever makes him delirious.

It is only eight o'clock, but I can't sit here and listen, so I'm going to crawl into bed beside him without even undressing, and try to sleep.

She had come to the last of the entries in the Journal. It seemed a queer place to break off. Nothing about the day she told Mark of the baby coming, and no mention of their deciding to leave. In the beginning she had written down everything she felt and thought; now she had no desire to put her thoughts into words. You remembered well enough what you wanted to remember, and what you didn't, too. Everything was there in your mind. You didn't get rid of it by writing it down, or understand anything better. The words weren't always the right ones. All the Journal really showed was a younger person whom she found a little boring now.

If anything, she was more interested in the picture of Mrs. Phillips. She hadn't realized how much there was about her. Yet she hadn't written about the evening Mrs. Phillips appeared for dinner two days before they left. She had grown so used to not having her there that when she heard the soft pad of moccasined feet she had been startled.

Mrs. Phillips came in with the Major and took her place at the table without looking at any of them. The paint was off her face but seemed to have taken with it all expression. Her short, uneven hair was greased down so it made a rough cap around her head, almost spoiling the beauty of her face completely, making it round and stolid. She wore her black dress, but neither earrings nor cross. No one spoke to her during the meal, not even the Major or the children, so it was as though she sat by herself, walled off by the talk of the others among themselves. Mark's eyes were often on her, Harriet remembered, and he, too, was silent at the meal.

Harriet wondered now how she had dared hurry after her when they all got up from the table. She had had to call her name, and when Mrs. Phillips stood still, the words tumbled out of her mouth, saying how sorry she was. Only for a flicker did Mrs. Phillips' eyes meet hers, but they had a blind stare. She had spoken quickly, trying to get past that blank look. "Mrs. Phillips, I'll always think of Robert running ahead of us on the shore that day, of his shadow dancing on the ba—" She had stopped, horrified at her own words, but Mrs. Phillips' eyes had brightened.

"Ah," she said. Then she moved away on her moccasined feet, leaving Harriet standing there. But she must not have minded; and they had spoken together.

She had told Mark about it when they were back in their room.

"That's more than she said to me the whole time," he said. She thought he would go on then and tell her how it had been, but his eyes went back to his book and he was silent.

They had talked very little about their going, once it was decided; Mark was occupied with his own thoughts, packing away the things he would leave behind, she with hers. Nor had they loved. That was the beginning of the journey into strangeness.

Two days later they started for the lower fort in one of the two flat-bottomed boats making the first part of the trip. The boats looked too small, and the cabins on them, open in the front, were better for bales of skins than passengers. She listened to the slap and swish of the water against them. The river *moved*, flowing between the banks, around snags, and lapping against islands. She was never going to see it frozen solid as she had seen it in her mind.

Aapaaki ran along the shore a little way; but although Harriet didn't look at her again, or back at the Fort, she could at this minute clearly see both Aapaaki and the Fort, and the fenced-in burial ground, and the rock ledges against the sky above the Fort. Instead, she had kept her eyes on the other shore, where patches of red, from rose hips and the bush with the Indian name, were just beginning to show in the early morning light. She watched the sun skim off the milky mist from the river and slowly warm the mudbanks into color, pale pink and mauve and, finally, deep gold. She had looked over at Mark. His face was set, almost sad, and he was looking back at the Fort, but he was relieved to be going, too.

Chapter Nine

THE Major lay on the buffalo robe thrown over the bed of willow branches Nisskim had made. He smoked his pipe, watching the spring dark come down. Mild for early April, and no wind, but snow up there on the rimrock, and the mountains would be still covered. They were snug in the shelter of the cottonwoods against the bank of the river if a wind did come up. A curlew called. Pretty; more mellow this time of year. He remembered when a call like that used to raise the hair on the back of his neck, he was so sure it was one Indian signalling to another. He couldn't be fooled now.

A pair of geese let themselves clumsily down on the island in the river. Just the two of them, cut off from the rest of the noisy honkers, like Nisskim and him. He watched her moving around, hunting wood. She'd let the fire get low to broil the deer liver for him, and eaten a piece raw herself. Made him think of poor Ryegate turning green around the gills when he saw Nisskim eating raw buffalo brains! Broiled liver and berry pemmican Nisskim had got from a squaw in a Piegan lodge, and water from the river, cold enough to feel all the way down. Made as good a meal as he knew.

Tomorrow by noon they'd be at the Fort, but he was in no hurry. They'd never been away so long before. Well, this was the way it was going to be from now on. They'd get back every summer, but not for as long as Nisskim thought. She'd stood up pretty good. Once they'd got to the lower fort, she'd put away her mourning for Robert deep in her mind; hadn't spoken of him but once, after they'd left the children at their schools. Raymond ought to do all right, if he didn't break too many rules. He'd take to the cavalry stuff, anyway. The Major wasn't so sure how Mary would do at the Sisters' school, except she wanted to be like a white girl. Nisskim had said they were safe from the river and wouldn't drown like Robert, as though that was the whole reason they'd gone east. A queer thing, the way losing Robert had had a lot to do with her willingness to go. He wished he had a picture of Robert.

He'd let his pipe go out, thinking about Robert, so he sat up and filled it and got it lit, and moved his thoughts to Nisskim. She always liked being in St. Louis. He'd bought her everything she wanted, and Ferrière had seen to it they were gay there. He'd worried about how she'd take to the East for living, but she liked the house, 'specially that long glass they'd bought for the front hall; laughed at it every time she came downstairs. And the Illinois country was enough like the plains . . . No, it wasn't either. Too many damned farms, and no mountains. Maybe that would be harder on him than on her. Anyway, he'd bought enough acres so she'd have plenty of space; wouldn't have to see a single God-damned farm. When they went back down in July, they'd ship some more animals, pair of antelope and a couple of buffalo. He started figuring how many bales of robes would equal the weight of two buffalo. Better have the buffalo brought down earlier, when it wasn't so hot.

Nisskim liked the blooded horses all right. The one he'd bought for her was the best money could buy. He wasn't quite satisfied with his own. When they got to raising horses, they ought to get some beauties.

Stars were coming out now, still pale and cold-looking. He lifted his head to see where Nisskim had got to, and she was close to him, she'd come so quiet. He watched her push the ends of the fresh logs into the fire. One was a beaver log; he could see the beavered-off end. They'd have beaver, too, in the pond on their place. That painter ought to have the painting of this country done by the time they got there, spread across the whole long wall of the parlor. There'd be mountains in that! He'd almost told Nisskim about it, but better to keep it for a surprise. He heard her with the horses now.

He took a deep breath of the air down into his lungs. Fresh, almost cold, and edged with smoke from the fire; river smell in it, too. Almost three weeks they'd taken coming five hundred miles, and not a day too long. Holed in two days because of the snow, to lie snug in the shelter Nisskim had made. They'd raced their horses and shot game, and stopped off with a lodge of Piegans on the way. All the time, the feeling that he was a fool to change this way of life nagged at him, but he'd always meant to get out at the right time, and this was it, before the country was full of settlers coming west, and the Fort was nothing but a trading post for 'em. The fur trade wasn't anything like it used to be. Even Ferrière was thinking of selling out. And he'd made what he set out to make. Wasn't many could say that.

He heard the pad of Nisskim's feet on the grass. "You drink?" she asked, holding the wooden cup of water out to him. He drank it and pulled her down beside him, spreading the robe up over her.

"Not cold." She pushed it off. "Meessionary wife always cold." And then she giggled over the word "missionary." She always said that one word to him in English, turning the "i" into an "ee," sticking out her chin as she said it.

"She was all right on the trip," he said. "That was a rough one."

It was almost too dark to see, but he felt Nisskim's hand come up and her fingers dispose of the hard trip, or Mrs. Ryegate's hardihood, with a gesture that made them nothing. Sometimes he thought Nisskim was jealous of her, but she didn't need to be. Mrs. Ryegate was a shapely enough woman, and a pretty one, with that pale gold hair and light skin. He liked her eyes, but she thought too much; they got a worried look in 'em sometimes. Sometimes she seemed younger than Nisskim, though she was two years older; but she wasn't dumb, or silly, like a lot of white women. He puffed at his pipe, pondering over Mrs. Ryegate. Quite a thing, her hightailing it out here alone to be with her husband!

"I was glad when we got 'em on that steamboat. They were, too," he said aloud. "I don't think they'll ever try going to the Wilderness again."

Nisskim made no answer. She often didn't, yet he had the feeling of carrying on a conversation with her. All the time he'd been lying here thinking, going round and round over his plans and reasons for leaving, he'd been half talking to her. It had been that way so long he was used to it; his serious talks with her often went on in the silence of his own mind, sometimes underneath her chattered accounts of some Indian gossip. But he had the feeling she knew what he thought; all that mattered, anyway.

Jealous or not, Nisskim liked the Ryegates. She laughed at Missus, but that was natural. He laughed a little at her himself. He'd hoped Nisskim'd talk English with her to get herself ready for their move to Illinois, but she wouldn't. She didn't like to feel at a disadvantage with anyone. Maybe she never would talk English, even after they were living back east. If she didn't, she'd get lonesome for squaw talk. Well, then, he'd bring an Indian girl down for her. She'd have Mary on her vacations from school, but Mary and her mother weren't ever going to be much company for each other, he could see that. Mary'd just as soon forget that she could talk Blackfoot. Well, Nisskim could do just what she wanted, and the society of Brighton, Illinois, would have to take her as she was. He'd cut a big enough figure so they'd want to.

He still wondered how Ryegate had fared those nights alone with Nisskim, but he had a good idea. Nisskim must have wailed most the night, calling Robert's name over and over again, and that would be enough to drive a white man, even himself, half crazy. He'd warned the Reverend; there were times when you had to leave Nisskim alone, but he was all-fired to go to her. He looked as though he'd been through something when he came back. Made him think of a Blackfoot brave, slinking back after going out on a fast to get him a vision, and not having had any. Except the Blackfoot would keep his fate to himself, but Ryegate came right to him, holding on to the door, he was so done in; said he hadn't been able to do anything for Nisskim, clearly feeling that it was his failure, and as clearly ashamed of it. Didn't help any to tell him this was the time for Nisskim to mourn; nobody could do it for her, and she couldn't lean on anybody. At that, it was better than the way some white women held their sadness underneath and sucked on it all the rest of their lives; drove their husbands to drink because they couldn't ever laugh again. He'd seen 'em. But he didn't think Ryegate had got over those nights out there yet. He'd seen him studying Nisskim on the boat, not able to make her out, but he noticed he didn't try to talk religion to her. The Black Robes did better out here in the Wilderness, he had to admit. He didn't know just why. Weren't so bothered by themselves, maybe; didn't expect too much of the Indians, and forgave 'em anyway.

The Major tousled the dark head against his arm, ruffling the hair that had grown down to her shoulders, brushing it over her face until she pulled her head away and bunted it hard against his ribs, laughing all the time. He put out an arm and held her still, but she wriggled and fought like a wild one, so he had to move his whole weight over on her to hold her down. Then he put his mouth on hers and felt her arms go around his neck and her legs spring around him, holding him tight in their own embrace.

He didn't go to sleep, even with his body satisfied and Nisskim lying close beside him. He listened to the river, high and loud with the melted snow in it, and heard a splash—beaver prob'ly—below them. Stars were closer, almost sticking to the high branches of the cottonwoods.

"Nisskim, you pick out some good skins for the tipi you're going to pitch out there." He didn't need to tell her he meant back in Illinois; she knew. "When we get tired of the house, we'll sleep in the tipi."

"I sleep there alone," she teased. "I Medicine Lodge Woman."

She could be. She was wise enough, for all her fooling, and chaste. Ferrière had looked at him in a funny French way when he let Ryegate go out there to stay with her those nights. Maybe Ferrière got the idea when he told him Nisskim could take care of herself and Ryegate. Hard for a Frenchman to understand.

He didn't go on with the playing. He was thinking she was going to need that tipi when civilized living got too much for her, or it was too hot in an Illinois summer. He only gave her a little push away from him, but she moved back, close against him. He hoped to God they didn't hear any owls screeching tonight.

Fort Phillips Journal

April Sat. 4

About noon, much to the delight of all in the fort, Major and Ldy. returned. Rec'd them with proper salute. Pressed 104 Packs Robes, which makes us over 1300 Packs to date. Major gave men a feast and in the evening a ball, at which two only of the number made a sorry display of their reason. Light snow.

Part Two

EASTER SUNDAY

Chapter Ten

BUT I mean, you and Mark came back changed. You know that, don't you?" Sydney Hall leaned back in his chair, gently stirring the lump of sugar in his teacup, enjoying the effect of his remark. "Both of you."

He had felt a difference in Mark right away. When Mark first came to Calvary he had seemed not quite real, the handsome, eloquent young preacher; a quality of purity about him, of celibacy, he had thought, too. He had been surprised when Mark married Harriet Tomlinson. Harriet was attractive enough, even rather lovely at times, and she had a mind, or at least wit, but she was a type, the New England type that produced so many strong-minded spinsters; spinsters of their own volition, more often than not, he surmised. Mark had a harder edge about him now; something not less dedicated, but less ascetic. Sydney felt more drawn to him.

Harriet's eyebrows arched a little higher, the twist of her mouth made light of his remark. She stirred her tea without answering, which was disappointing. He hadn't felt the change in Harriet until the night at Mark's lecture, when she hadn't hung on every word Mark said, the way she used to do in church. Pregnancy made some women's faces softer, gave their skin a flushed, rather dewy look, but Harriet looked sallow, so that her eyes seemed a darker blue. He rather liked the effect, preferred it to her usual high color. And then all that hair of hers, caught in a velvet snood at the back of her head instead of on top, made her neck less long and her head, somehow, rather Elizabethan. If she had risen to his remark about being changed, he would have told her she had come back more worldly, but that was a crazy thing to think about somebody back from the Wilderness. Harriet, though, was less interested in hearing what you thought of her than most women were; as if what you thought was of no real importance. She had been that way as a girl growing up, just down the street from him. Only she always had a retort for you in those days. That time in church at some young people's meeting, he had told her she would be a bluestocking if she wasn't careful, with her head always in a book; and she had told him, under the cover of the hymn they were singing, that he would be a desiccated raisin. He couldn't see a raisin yet that he didn't think of it.

"I would say that, by now, half of the people in Woollett feel that they've been to the Wilderness, too, after hearing Mark's lectures," Sydney said.

"But are hardly changed by the experience." Her tone of voice mocked him. He remembered how Harriet had stirred almost impatiently when Mark finished his lecture that first evening.

"Well, let's say few of them would ever dream of leaving Woollett for any place but Boston or the grand tour. And I think, myself, that it's rather difficult to get absorbed in Indians once you've outgrown playing you're big chief what's-his-name, except to shudder at the thought of their massacres. Though I admit Mark was pretty convincing about their having a kind of—well, call it culture. I was going to print that second lecture of his in the *Republican,* until the news of the family of settlers in Iowa being wiped out by some Indians hit the press. After that, I didn't really think Mark's ideas would have much appeal. It seems all the more remarkable that you and Mark survived."

Harriet shrugged. "We were never really in danger."

For the first white woman to go up that river, so far into the

Wilderness, she was certainly cool, but he had a feeling she had things to tell, if she would.

"Too bad you missed the last two lectures. After the last one old Sutton asked him what he thought of the Iowa massacre. He expected Mark to defend the Indians and was all set to go after him, but Mark said, oh, yes, they were quite capable of that, seeing settlers take over their hunting land. Sutton said, 'Well, do you think you missionaries can ever change them?' That was a moment! Mark let it run full sixty seconds before he answered. Then he said, 'If you mean in Christ's image, not under the present circumstances. If you mean in ours . . .' Sutton didn't say anything, but he was as red in the face as the carnelian stone in my signet ring."

"I know. Mark told me about Mr. Sutton," Harriet murmured, setting down her cup without drinking the tea in it.

"I don't suppose you really got to know any of them, uh, well, yourself?"

"I was there less than three months."

"Of course." Sydney would have liked to pursue the subject—he had always wondered about that—but decided against it. That would lead to the subject of her pregnancy, which he avoided, naturally. But Mark had told him it would be good for Harriet to have him drop in, now that she wasn't going out very much.

"I think Mark was wise to change the order of his lectures and end with 'The Journey into Strangeness.' He took us there, all right. Pardon me, Harriet, I'm talking too long and tiring you." He had the feeling that she wasn't really listening to him.

"No, I'm interested. I minded missing Mark's lectures. Go on, please. Let me give you another cup of tea."

The niggardly April light of late afternoon reached across the sombre room to catch her face, pale and almost gaunt. What she needed was a glass of port wine, but, of course, the Church didn't . . . "Thank you, Harriet, no more. I must go;

tell Mark I was sorry not to see him, but that I'm still wandering around in his Wilderness."

When Sydney reached his own house, he left his hat in the hall and went straight to the sideboard to pour himself a glass that caught the same dreary light but buried it in the wine's rich color. As he sat in the high-backed armchair that had been his grandfather's, his legs on an ottoman, his thoughts went back to Mark. He couldn't get some of those phrases of Mark's out of his mind: "All the fears you ever had are subsumed in Fear itself, so palpable it is a live presence hovering just behind you. . . . Divested of the pride of articulateness, you talk and talk to a people who can't understand you, and so you lapse, finally, into silence."

Mark's saying that in the Wilderness you came to know what Lear meant by unaccommodated man had made him drag out his copy of Shakespeare. Man without a thing but himself. Sydney had seen himself as a naked, forked man. Everybody quoted Shakespeare in their lectures, but Mark could make the words into an experience rather than a quotation. Sydney had looked at himself that night, naked, in the long gold-framed mirror in his dressing room, and for the first time in his life thought of himself as a rather weak, grotesque-looking creature. He had sometimes admired his head, his lean body tapering from his shoulders to his hipbones. Not too far from Michelangelo's *David*, he had once thought in the secrecy of his own mind.

In the Wilderness, Mark had said, death was so unimportant that a warrior swaggered with the proofs of the deaths he had committed worn at his belt or stitched into his buckskin trousers. He had some Indian word for those deaths; "coups," maybe? It would be a relief to live in a world where people weren't worried about death or Hell, or the brevity of life. But none of that had impressed him so much as Mark's saying the Indians never worried about any conflict between the flesh and the spirit, except in the endurance contests for the young braves, and then only a few of the braves. They weren't aware of such a conflict—he meant in the way all Puritan New England damn well knew it.

The very idea pulled Sydney out of his chair and sent him to pour himself another glass. On his way back from the dining-room sideboard, he tapped the edge of his wineglass against the bell jar with the stuffed owl beneath it, not so much listening to the ring as carrying out what had become an amusing ritual. As a boy he had been afraid of the owl's fierce stare, but he and the old fellow had a kind of communication between them now. He carried his glass back to his chair.

Yet beyond what Mark had said, really, although he'd shot more than one bolt at them, was some note in his voice; almost a challenge. No, not that, an arrogance, perhaps. Because none of them knew at first hand the world he was talking about. It made Mark seem more remote. An uncomfortable excitement stirred Sydney. He thought of Mark's face as he had stood there for a moment, silent, seeming himself to be lost in that strangeness. He had felt close to Mark. He wanted to say to him—oh, not in so many words, but to let him know, somehow—that he knew that feeling of strangeness. Mark made him feel less lonely.

Harriet sat still, glad Sydney had gone. Hearing Mark through Sydney was disturbing because he made her sense the spell Mark could cast. Well, why wasn't she proud of it? She felt it was Mark's enemy—or was it hers? Was she jealous of it in Mark? That idea had never occurred to her before, but perhaps she was, because it separated them.

Mark had been elated when he came home after the last lecture. "Should I have been there? Was it your best?" she had asked, and Mark, paring an apple, handing her a quarter on the point of his knife, had laughed and said it was, but that he was glad she hadn't been there.

"Why do you say that?" she remembered asking, a little hurt. And his answer had come back to her more than once. "I was at it again," Mark had said. "I got so involved describing the strangeness that I felt myself weaving a circle, only I got myself caught in it."

For a moment, after that, there was only the sound of their teeth biting into the apples. Something ominous in the word "caught." She had almost told him that if he couldn't stop thinking about the Wilderness, he would have to go back there, but instead, she had reminded him that he was finished with his lectures, that sermons were less dangerous. Then he had pulled out of his pocket the letter from the Directors of the Lyceum Bureau asking him to repeat his Wilderness lectures in Boston.

"It could be interesting," he had said, and she had seen how much he would like it. "It might even lead to a call to a church there—I mean, I'd come to the attention, at least . . ." But his voice had trailed off as he met her eyes, and he'd quoted from Milton about a desire for fame being the last infirmity of noble minds. "You would like that wouldn't you?" he had asked.

How instantly they each saw themselves transported there; yes, she supposed she would like it. Mark had smiled and said that was counting chickens, but the next instant his face changed and became sober, and he said that it seemed he was more successful bringing the Wilderness to civilization than spirituality to the Wilderness. He said it wryly, and then, before she could answer him, he had come over and kissed her good night and taken the plates with their parings downstairs. She heard him going into his study. He would have been too stirred up by the lecture to go to bed and would sit there, going back to the Wilderness, perhaps. Or would he think about Boston? Then he would read himself back to quietness. Poetry, perhaps, or the Scriptures. Job, perhaps; he loved the last chapters of Job. She could see him as well as though she were sitting on the couch in the study. Mark had no idea how close the stillness of the house could hold them. It was less necessary for her to talk, but words were always necessary for Mark.

*

"Sitting here in the dark, moping!" Hannah came in from lighting the hanging lamp in the hall. "That isn't good for you, Harriet."

"It's hardly dark yet," Harriet said, almost apologetically.

Hannah held her match on the long rod up to the chandelier, turning the gas key under each globe. Flames sprang out like fans, lighting up the trees and deer etched into the glass. Harriet thought how she would hold the baby up to see the deer. Another six weeks, Dr. Fothergill said. Way after Easter.

She went to the piano, playing chords, a little aimlessly. If she were at the Fort, would Mrs. Phillips be back by now? There must still be snow, but only in patches; most of the river would be running free again, wouldn't it? Along the bank where the sun was warm there would be clumps of those willows, leafless, but their bark would be gold colored.

She dropped her hands in her lap. Why did she think of bright yellow willows against the riverbank? She had never seen them, only dry-leaved in the fall; yet she saw them now as clear as clear.

Chapter Eleven

MARK walked home slowly from the meeting with the deacons. What was this reluctance in him to hold a revival meeting? To bring souls to Christ? Wasn't that what he'd gone into the Wilderness to do? He had writhed inwardly at those veiled allusions to sin in the congregation. Not among those present, not in their pastor, but in all those others: Simmons, who would come to trial next month; and Mrs. Fainall, who had gone off and left her husband. Yet nodding their heads when he told them they all needed a call to a deeper life of the spirit. He himself, most of all.

He had felt himself unequal to his task in the Wilderness; was he now to feel himself even less adequate at home? He drew back from rousing the emotions to such a state that they would be stirred. He had heard Finney once, when he was in the seminary. Finney could count his converts by the hundreds, and Mark had wanted, then, to be able to do the same, but now . . . Going from those stolid, uncomprehending Indian faces to faces that hung upon his words with moist, parted lips and bright eyes; the Amens called out, the organ music in a low tone, and then only the voices singing "Just as I am without one plea," until there was the sound of someone weeping, shuffling steps coming down the aisle.

He wondered if he could do it. Could he manage to preach to them night after night, every night of that week before Easter, speak words that would stir and move? Every night, give the invitation to come to God, to claim Christ as their

Saviour—run the whole gamut, from stern warning of the road to destruction to tender pleading. Reach out a hand to those who came down that aisle of red carpeting. Kneel with them there, feel something himself. . . . But wasn't that what he had gone into the ministry for?

Had something hardened in him, making him shrink from stirring a congregation? Was he afraid of anything emotional? Something within him had frozen, as hard as the ice on the river. There was no least sign of spring in that wilderness where he still dwelt half the time.

But this was the spring of the Christian year. The time when the heart thawed; the hard crusts of selfishness and hate, misunderstanding and sin melted; the waters of love broke through and sent the ice blocks crashing. . . . He stopped himself in disgust. Gibberish! Those weren't really his thoughts. He was making up phrases to use the first night of the revival.

Revival! The word itself repelled him. But he had never questioned it before. Hadn't he been taught that the healthy church, the strong church, was measured by its converts, and the minister by his power to move men to a fresh realization of their sins? Yet when he thought of Christ's ministry, he saw a man speaking quietly, telling a story, attending a wedding and changing the water into wine. Raising his voice only as he drove out the money-changers from the temple. Not John the Baptist's way.

Revival. His mind took hold of the word it had rejected and, plucking off the old meaning, reached into the green heart of it. Not revival with its brown sheaf of stock responses and half hysteria, but revived, renewed. The word seemed to burst into flower and fragrance before him.

There was some verse—Kings, was it? Hosea maybe. It was Hosea who depicted the sins of Israel and ended with the promise of reviving. Mark muttered as he walked, "Revive as the corn. . . ." Something about his shadow . . . Then he had it: "They that dwell under his shadow shall return; they shall

revive as the corn, and grow as the vine: the scent thereof
shall be as the wine of Lebanon."

Revived from the deadness of complacency and unaware-
ness and lovelessness—every one of the members of Calvary
Church.

But what about Mark Ryegate, their pastor? Would he revive as the corn and grow as the vine?

He had returned, even if he had left failure behind him.
But the time out there wasn't all failure. He had come back
a different person; his old mental skin seemed smaller. And it
had been a slight thing, but a satisfaction, to find himself
equal to some of the rigors of that life, to feel he could have
survived physically.

He remembered his apprehension, fear almost, the first time
he had forced himself to plunge into the cold river in the early
morning with the Major and strike out across the current to
the other side. He had thought he might have to turn back, but
he had made it. And he remembered climbing up the bank into
the warmth of the sun, feeling the strength of his body, and
something more; feeling renewed.

Why should that physical sense come back now and make
him feel a renewal of his spirit? He didn't know; it didn't matter, but he felt suddenly that he could do this thing.

◇ ◇ ◇

How many were there; have you any idea?

*Over three hundred and fifty, I figure. I know every pew
was filled and they had to bring up chairs from the cellar.*

A pentecostal meeting!

The Spirit moved tonight!

*I couldn't keep back the tears when I saw Mr. Simmons go-
ing up to shake the Pastor's hand.*

*And did you see Mr. Fainall, as if he had sins on his own
soul, for all he blames his wife!*

I thought the Reverend was inspired last night, but tonight I hardly knew he was speaking; you know what I mean?

Yes, yes, I know.

I'll tell you one thing; this has been a week Calvary Church will never forget! Must have been twenty strangers answered the call.

Thank the Lord for bringing the Reverend back from the mission field. He's got a greater mission here.

◇ ◇ ◇

People still lingered, waiting to speak with Mark, after the sexton had turned out the main lights. A young man under the shadow of the balcony sat with his head bowed in his hands. A couple Mark did not recognize murmured together down in front. He went from one to the other, heard their halting confession of sin or despair, felt their relief—as much from getting it out as from his words, perhaps. "Comfort ye, comfort ye my people, saith your God." That was what he had tried to do for Eenisskim, but she wouldn't listen. Here he could do it. The words came; he had a sense of sureness, that he was being heard and that they were the right words. He felt compassion even for the woman who responded whenever an invitation was given, each time with the same tears and dramatic protestations that she was not saved. "God so loved," he told her gently, as he had told Eenisskim. . . .

And finally they had all gone, their steps shuffling over the carpeted aisles; there were the sounds of the door into the vestibule, then the outer door, opening, letting in the chill of the spring night.

"Good night, Parson. It was a spiritual night!"

"Yes, Hodges. You go ahead. I'll lock up," he told the sexton.

And then he was alone in his church. He sat down in a pew at one side, too exhilarated, too spent to leave for a moment. Sweat had soaked his broadcloth coat under the arms and stood out on his forehead, and his hands were clammy as he rubbed them over his face. Tonight he had got rid of himself; he had been a tongue speaking for the Lord. He had yearned over these people, felt love for them. What he had feared he could not do, he had managed; God through him. Relief lifted his heart. He could have sunk to his knees by the pew himself, as people had done that night. He had an impulse to pray in audible words, but he wouldn't say "I" tonight. He sat still in the pew, not the pulpit. "Peace that passeth understanding," he murmured. Then he went to the study to get his coat before he turned out the lamps along the wall and locked the heavy wooden doors behind him.

Someone was leaning against the iron fence in the shadow. "Mark!"

"Why—Sydney?" He was touched that Sydney had waited for him. He often walked as far as his house with Mark, but not when Mark was held there so long.

"It was a stirring performance. You were great, simply great! I thought I'd wait and see if you weren't satisfied yourself."

The words "performance" and "satisfied" crashed in on his peace. He found it hard to speak. But Sydney went on.

"I wish you could have seen how you held them! Even I felt I'd been lost in that wilderness of sin, you made it so vivid." Sydney's light, only half-deprecating laugh raked across Mark's mood, and Sydney's hand rested on Mark's shoulder. "You can do more with your image of the Wilderness than the fire-and-brimstone boys ever do with their descriptions of hell-fire. That part about the loneliness in all that empty space when the sickness of self-loathing really gets at you—you seem to know. . . ." Sydney broke off. "Stop in for a bit, Mark. You must need to let down."

"No, thank you, Sydney. I—I admit I'm pretty well drained. I think I better get on home." He turned up his collar against the raw air.

"Good night," Sydney said a little abruptly.

Mark walked on slowly. He should have gone in with Sydney. He had felt a kind of urgency in Sydney's voice. Had he wanted to say something that was on his mind, to confide in him, even? With all the times they had talked together, Sydney had never spoken of his own beliefs. Perhaps he had been wrong, Mark thought, not to have talked to him about his faith, but he had respected Sydney's privacy.

Or was it because he hadn't wanted to risk putting Sydney off—for fear of losing him? He was grateful for Sydney. His ideas often whetted his own, and he could talk with him as he couldn't with anyone else here, about politics—or poetry, for that matter—concerns outside of the Church and Woollett. Perhaps tonight was the time to break through the cynicism and reticence he always felt in him. Sydney had seemed unusually keyed up, put his hand on Mark's shoulder with a kind of affection he had never shown before—almost a reaching out.

Mark hesitated, wondering if he should go back. He wished that he had gone in, but by now the right moment would have passed. To go in and say, "I felt you had something you wanted to tell me"—that would be too direct. Sydney would answer with some offhand remark. He had thought of the meeting as a performance—that was all, a "stirring performance." Mark went on again.

Yet what a hunger there was in people, even the most self-sufficient, to talk with someone, to strike a response—so that one's heart burned. "Did not our heart burn within us, while he talked with us by the way?"

The familiar words came into his mind that he had read just yesterday in Luke about those two apostles walking to Emmaus after the crucifixion; having to talk of their terrible disappointment in the man they had thought would be the Messiah. Then the stranger coming up beside them, falling into conversation. When they came to the inn they couldn't bear to have him leave them and begged him to come in. Not until the stranger blessed the bread did they realize who he was.

And afterward they said to each other, "Did not our heart burn within us, while he talked with us by the way?"

That was what he would use for his Easter sermon. He saw it clearly. Why did their hearts burn? What was it about Christ's conversation? What did he say to them?

He hadn't been satisfied with the sermon he had written about the women at the tomb. And this might speak to Sydney after all, better than he could have done if he had stopped in.

The Day before Easter.

I am starting a new Journal. I might just go on in the one I kept in the Wilderness, but that time and this are too separate. It is as though the whole long river divides them. Anyway, I don't believe I want to connect them.

I get bored staying in so much, waiting for the baby to be born. Today I went over to Miss Dinwiddie's for tea, but that is next door. I think pregnant women make too much of a thing of it, or other people do for them. Even Sydney has stopped dropping in to see me—but have I really grown too large to look at? Why shouldn't women go every place, even if they are out of shape? After all, it is the shape of life. I take an odd comfort in the fact that everyone had to be carried the same way in the body of a woman.

The Indians make nothing at all of pregnancy. I remember the pregnant woman I watched that day when the Indians moved camp. She drew a loaded travois behind her like a beast of burden. (Inside and out!) And somewhere on the trail she would stop and have her child. Mrs. Phillips doubtless rode horseback right up to the last hour! I am going to Church tomorrow, but I have not mentioned it to Mark, or, most especially, not to Hannah.

Mark is entirely absorbed these days with the Church and now his preparation for Easter Sunday. He has lost his restlessness, I think, and any sense of guilt at coming back, because he can see how much he is doing here. He feels this week of Revival Meetings has given the Church a great impetus. I don't see much of him, because every morning he works on his sermon for the evening meeting and in the afternoons he makes calls on people who have been converted and are joining the Church. And, of course, his Easter sermon. Yesterday he told me he was going to preach on the incident of the two Marys coming to the garden and finding the stone rolled away. "Think of the miracle of it," Mark said, "to go there to mourn, like Eenisskim up on that butte, and find Christ alive and gone from the tomb." I think he will always remember Eenisskim in her grief, and always suffer because he couldn't comfort her.

But something has changed in Mark. My awe of him that I had when I first met him is coming back. I am not so close to him as I was at the Fort, yet I think I would rather look up to him. I was upset when I felt his discouragement and weakness. No, I'll cross that out; it wasn't weakness.

Tonight was the last of the Revival Meetings. They always make me uncomfortable, and I was not sorry to stay home, but I was anxious to hear how Mark felt this one had gone; whether it was the climax of the whole week. He was very late getting back, so I went on up to bed, but my light was on, and I read until he came.

I could see at once that the meeting had gone well, but he didn't talk about it, except to say that he didn't get in his own way, and I knew what he meant. Sydney Hall walked with him as far as his house and gave Mark a new idea for his Easter sermon. How surprised Sydney would be if he knew it. Mark is now going to preach on the episode of the two disciples on their way to Emmaus. It seems too bad when he has his sermon already written, but he said he wasn't satisfied with it; maybe he could use it for the evening service. I could see he was excited and would stay up half the night writing it. He was part way downstairs when he came back up and told me he had a verse for me he had copied off some time last week and forgotten to give to me. It was from a letter of St. Paul's. And then Mark stood waiting for me to read it. I'll copy it here.

But he that is married careth for the things that are of this world, how he may please his wife.

"I thought that would make you indignant," he teased. And I said that Paul never had a wife, so he didn't know anything about it, and, anyway, he was always hard on women, almost as though he were scared of them.

Mark said I held Paul's not marrying against him. Then he said a lovely thing (which is why I am writing all this down here). He said I often lifted him above the things of this world. I would like it to be true, but I cannot think how that can be. If I ever do, it cannot be by what I say. We seldom talk of religion, and I am often critical of Mark's sermons. But I must always say what I think. I could never bear to have any doubt or uncertainty between us.

How swiftly Mark's mind moves from deepest seriousness to teasing or joking. I love it. I am always surprised by him. Even yet I sometimes wonder if I know him.

Chapter Twelve

THEY were singing the first hymn when Harriet reached the church. The heavy fragrance of flowers drifted out with the alleluia. The voices came at her with such a burst she knew the church must be full. She pushed the door open just a crack, but Mr. Warren's broad back blocked her view.

> The powers of death have done their worst,
> But Christ their legions hath dispersed:
> Let shouts of holy joy outburst,
> Al . . . le . . . lu . . . ia!

"Why Mrs. Ryegate!" Mr. Warren opened wide the door.

"Somewhere in the back, please," she murmured. But she could see that there were no empty places and chairs had been moved in.

"The only place, I'm afraid, is your own pew," Mr. Warren whispered noisily. "I put Mr. and Mrs. Albee there because they were such friends of your mother's, but there's room for you."

The voices burst into the next stanza with redoubled volume:

> The three sad days are quickly sped;
> He rises glorious from the dead:
> All glory to our risen Head!
> Al . . . le . . . lu . . . ia!

One voice held the alleluia beyond the others.

Harriet followed Mr. Warren to her pew, glad of the torrent

of sound almost submerging her, holding her cape closely around her. When the congregation settled themselves in their seats after the last alleluia of the last stanza, Mark saw her. His pleased surprise must have been visible to everyone, she thought, lifting her head ever so slightly.

Mark was reading about the women at the grave, after all. He must have gone back to his first sermon. He seemed crowded by the pots of lilies so close to his feet; the back half of the platform that covered the baptistry had been removed, and the dark-red velvet curtains trimmed with slightly dusty fringe were tied back at each side. Mark had said his sermon must be short because there were so many to be baptized—thirty-one, the most at any one time in the history of Calvary Baptist. They were sitting together in the front pews. The women wore white gowns, the men black, over their underwear. Mark would be tired, lowering and then raising all those people.

Harriet felt herself rising a little ponderously for the next hymn, but buoyed up on the swells of the triumphant music. The sun was too pale to shine far enough through the red wings of the angel to reach Mark's hands as they held his hymnal.

"Give us the words thou wouldst have us speak, O Lord, that they may move and comfort and lift the hearts and minds of those who hear thy servant," Mark prayed.

Then the expectant hush before the sermon, never as intense as her own expectancy. Mark stood silent longer than he usually did, as though the crowded church stirred him too much to speak. In the silence, a sense of intimacy seemed to grow between Mark and every person there, and when he began, in his low, conversational tone, he seemed to be speaking directly to each one; but most of all, Harriet felt, to her.

"I have written a sermon for this Easter Sabbath morning, which lies on my desk in the study. It is based on that incident that you know so well; an incident in the lives of those first Christians as they came to know the overwhelming joy of the

Risen Christ. But very late last night, I decided not to preach
that sermon, not to preach any sermon at all, but to try to
come to a deeper realization of the joy of the resurrection of
Christ by telling you of the abysmal darkness of death without
it, as I witnessed this tragedy in the life of a human being.

"I am going to tell you of the death of a mother's son that
took place not far off and long ago in Jerusalem, but last year
in the Wilderness of our own country."

Why did Mark do this on Easter? People didn't want to
hear about an Indian woman and her son; they were tired of
his talking about the Wilderness. Maybe she was, too.

"In September of last year, about three weeks before we
came away from that far outpost, the little son of the head of
the Fort was drowned in the treacherous river that connects
that Wilderness world with civilization, in that river where I
also held a baptism, so it became to me, in a very real sense, a
river of both physical death and the rebirth of the spirit.

"Just at dusk, as we sat at dinner, word of the boy's dis-
appearance was brought to the mother. She uttered a scream
which I can still hear, a scream such as those Israelite moth-
ers uttered when their first-born were slain. When she heard
her little son had last been seen playing by the river, this
mother ran to the bank, stripped off her dress, and dove again
and again into the water, searching on that muddy, snag-in-
fested river bottom for his body. But not until nearly dawn
was the child found. . . ."

Harriet could see Mrs. Phillips sitting wrapped in a blanket
on the bank. She remembered Mary coming to her with her
mother's red silk dress and the heavy gold cross.

"The next day I conducted a Christian burial service for the
dead boy, but the bereaved mother attended clothed in her
Indian elkskin dress and moccasins, with her hair chopped off
and streaked with ashes as a sign of mourning. She had painted
her face with black and white and green paint so that it became a grotesque mask of death through which her eyes stared
unseeingly.

"She sat stolidly through the service and the burial, but as soon as they were over, she set off alone to keep a pagan vigil of mourning, a desolate vigil without hope. The words of comfort I had spoken at the Christian service had fallen on sorrow-deaf ears. She had suffered the service only because of her husband's wishes; then she repudiated all that it stood for and went back to the darkness of her primitive despair.

"I couldn't let her be alone in her desolation, so I went to her husband and got his permission to follow her."

Harriet was thankful he had said that. People—Mrs. Terwilliger or Mrs. Sansom or Isabelle—might have thought . . .

"He sent a guide with me, for I could never have found my way alone. It was dark before we had gone far, and I rode my horse behind his, unable to see my guide at all. The very darkness and cold and my ignorance of any sense of direction seemed to me symbolic of a world without belief in God.

"We were still a long way off when out of the dark came a desolate wail, rising and falling, interrupted at intervals by the name of her son, Robert, called into the night. I have heard wolves howling across the river from the Fort and shuddered, but not as I shuddered at this human cry that was, at the same time, inhuman, demonic, lost.

"When we reached her, I confess that it took all my courage to go in the dark toward that voice, calling her by name. Even when I finally came to her, there was no recognition of my presence, no interruption in that wail. I took my blanket from the horse and sat down beside her to wait. Surely her breath would give out and she would stop, out of exhaustion. But the wailing went on, sometimes low, sometimes rising, broken only by her calling the name of her son, which was the only English word I have ever heard her utter.

"The Indian guide who had come with me put the bundle of food beside me, and I reached out to touch his arm, to bid him sit down, but he moved away, and the next minute I heard the sharp sound of a rock struck by his horse's hoof and realized he was riding back to the Fort.

"Can you imagine what the night was like? I tried again and again to speak, but this woman at whose table I had sat, in whose home I had been living as a guest, this woman seemed unaware of my existence. The sound of my own voice half frightened me. I grovelled around on the ground for pieces of wood, stumbling over rocks and bushes, and came back to try to get a handful of sticks and some pine needles to burn. It took me a long time in my ineptness; finally, a small flame shot up like a hope of life, but in the sudden flare of light this grieving mother became all the more terrifying. Her eyes, usually bright and quick with understanding, stared blindly. I was not even sure that she saw me. Certainly she did not hear my prayer; and in the end, I prayed for myself, for knowledge and strength to reach her. I tell you frankly that I was afraid, but finally I must have dozed, huddled there in my blanket. When I woke, the fire was only an ember, and I went again to hunt for wood. With the first gray light, I poured water and offered it to her, but she pushed the cup away, so it spilled out on the ground. I ate a piece of dried meat I had brought, but I knew it was no use to offer her any."

The scent of the lilies lying on the silence of the congregation seemed suffocating to Harriet. Mark hardly looked conscious of the faces in front of him, or of the thoughts forming behind those faces. He was back with Mrs. Phillips. Why had he never told her how it had been? She hadn't asked him because he had come back so depressed. He was making Mrs. Phillips so real as a woman they wouldn't understand his meaning. They would be shocked. Harriet kept her eyes on Mark, making her attention a little rapt so that if anyone looked at her, they would think she knew all about Mark's experience.

"Except for brief intervals, I sat with that grotesque creature, who seemed hardly human, holding myself there through the second day, waiting for an opportunity to speak. It became a trial of endurance. Once in the dusk of the second evening her cries mounted to frenzy, and before my eyes, she hacked new cuts in her arms so the fresh blood trickled down over the dried blood. . . ."

Harriet heard someone moving in the congregation, then the sound of the swinging door. Oh Mark, stop! she cried out in her mind. You've forgotten that you are talking to anyone; you're just reliving your own experience. The silence after the interruption seemed more tense.

Sydney Hall moistened his lips, his eyes never leaving Mark's face. This was the strangeness of the strangeness. Mark seemed to be speaking out of a trance, out of some compulsion; his voice was preternaturally quiet.

"I was sickened, revolted even, by this suffering human being as she became more and more demonic. I was frightened—by what?"

Harriet tightened her hands in her lap, praying that he would stop talking of his own reactions and feelings.

"Frightened by this affront to my shocked sensibilities? By fear of what she might do to me? She would do me no harm; she was scarcely aware that I was there. What I was afraid of, to my soul's depths, although I did not know it then, was the sight of despair more complete and hopeless than any I had ever witnessed at any bedside of death. I was seeing a human being driven by her grief over the loss of her child to a subhuman, animal state. I knew—as I thought I had known, but had previously perceived only intellectually—the depths of the desolation in the face of human death if we had no concept of the immortality of the spirit.

"I tried to think how to speak to her of God in her own terms. An elk came near us, so the fire was reflected in its eyes, and I wanted to say in her tongue that there was the presence of the Holy Spirit, or to point to the mystery of the fire and say it contained the Holy Spirit, but her wailing, sunk now to a melancholy moan, rendered me dumb.

Harriet could see it all; for her, there was no congregation, only Mark telling her at last about that time.

"Suddenly, a miracle happened," Mark said in a hushed

voice, his eyes alight in his pale face. "I loved that wretched, dirty, sorrowing human being beside me. My repulsion and horror dropped away. I went to her, and put my arm around her, and called her by her Indian name. I understood, as never before, something of the love with which God must view our blind, suffering, grotesque humanity. I told her that God so loved her that He let his son be tortured and killed that her little son might live. . . ."

The outer doors of the church slammed so loudly that Mark's next words were lost, but Harriet was seeing Mark's face, lit by firelight. She heard him pleading with Mrs. Phillips. When she felt his arm around her, how could she not have heard him?

Sydney Hall sat where he could just catch sight of Harriet's face, looming white within the shelter of her bonnet. Then his eyes came back to Mark. Was he really so naïve that he didn't realize his obsession with that Indian woman? Self-deceived, maybe, rather than naïve. Mark was earnest enough, and honest to the point of embarrassment, but couldn't he see that he was scandalizing the very people he had brought to their knees last night? Once he had been put off by the sense he had of Mark's cold kind of asceticism, but that was only one side of him. Mark had his sensual side, too. And this Indian woman would be far different from poor Harriet.

"I felt that the love God had poured into my heart must reach her, but she was too lost in the depths of her pagan despair." Mark paused. As though pronouncing his own crime, he said, "She didn't hear me. My words, the pressure of my arm around her, my eyes on hers never spoke to her."

Harriet shivered at the accents of sadness and finality in Mark's voice. That was the way he had said "I failed," when he staggered into their room that night at the Fort.

"At length, on the third day, I followed her back to the Fort with a sense of failure and inadequacy I have lived with ever since.

"For many days this bereaved woman lived apart, speaking to no one, not even to her husband and children, until the time

came when she had paid to death and grief what her pagan
custom demanded; then she stoically returned to ordinary living. She removed the bars of paint, but the closed expression
of her face showed her still imprisoned in utter desolation,
shut out from that comfort and joy we celebrate today. Do
you realize what that would be like?" Mark demanded in a
voice so loud that the question seemed to fill the room, echoing
from the arches, and wakened Mrs. Pillsbury out of her sleep.

He leaned on the open Bible before him. "Dearly beloved,
I don't care whether or not you attend all the services of this
church, or even that you are immersed—although these are
the foundations of our denomination—so much as I care that
you understand today what the divine love means to you.

Mark bowed his head, but Harriet couldn't hear the words
of his prayer because Mrs. Albee, who had sat beside her,
reached over and pressed her hand as she and her husband
pushed past her into the aisle.

"Love Divine, all loves excelling. Joy of Heaven, to earth
come down . . ." the choir sang lustily. The word "heresy"
floated to Harriet's ears on its hissing "s" above the "Joy of
Heaven," and she raised her own voice for the next line.

"Fix in us Thy humble dwelling . . ." Mark had disappeared to get ready for the baptismal service.

"End of Faith as its beginning, set our hearts at liberty!"
Some confusion became evident in the first row. On the last
stanza, the converts to be baptized always marched out, singing, to await their turn in the baptistry, but as the sixth and
last stanza dragged out its course, most of the occupants of the
first pew remained in their places. All the eyes in the congregation watched; necks craned; heads leaned toward each other
to whisper. "Ten" drifted in a shocked whisper through the
air.

"Lost in wonder, love and praise. A . . . men."
If the front pew was still well filled, the audience room of
Calvary Church was no longer crowded. The sound of the

swinging doors interfered with the hush that should precede
the baptismal ceremony.

Mark came through the water to the front of the baptistry,
leading Laura Marchant by the hand; and the sound of the
water was as loud as when she was wading out into the river
to take hold of Mrs. Phillips' hand, Harriet thought. She remembered how the water had crept up through her clothes,
deliciously cool and clean against her sweaty body.

When she was baptized here at Calvary Church at the age
of twelve, she had felt the heavy weight of her sins clinging
to her more closely than sweat, and afterward had had a
guilty feeling that she had left them like a scum in the water
for the next person to wade through. But she was disappoint-
ingly the same Harriet Tomlinson, aged twelve. She had expected to feel different.

Walking out in the river where the water ran freshly against
her, under the blue sky and the hot sun, she had felt different
—clean and light and free. She remembered understanding
what reborn meant, as she never had before. The tin tub and
the fringed velvet curtains and the watching people were all
in the way here.

Laura Marchant leaned back stiffly, trying to hold her
head with its corkscrew curls up out of the water, her eyes on
Mark's as Harriet's had been on Mrs. Phillips'. That was the
way she had held her head at first, Harriet thought, and the
cords of her neck had strained; but when she dropped her head
back on Mrs. Phillips' arm, the whole sky arched above her
in that enormous blue curve, and the water covered her ears
and shut out all sound, until she had lost any sense of herself. . . .

"I baptize thee in the name of the Father and the Son and
the Holy Ghost. Amen," Mark pronounced, lowering Laura
until the water covered her face, then lifting her quickly.

For a minute, utter stillness fell over the congregation, in-
voked by the names of the Trinity, mysterious, incomprehen-

sible, awe-inspiring. The music of the organ rose; voices sang softly. Laura Marchant bowed her head so the water could run off, and as she went out her robe was bunched and sagging with water. Harriet remembered herself coming up out of the river, and the squaws laughing on the bank.

Mark came forward again with a man taller and heavier than he, red-faced and apprehensive. Mark's lips moved, and the man closed his eyes and thrust back his head obediently, like someone baring his throat for an execution. But as he came dripping up out of the water, his face shone with relief— or grace.

Two Knives, the Indian chief Mark had baptized, had held his eyes wide open, Harriet remembered, and his body rigid as a board. Mark had been a little unsure about his understanding, whether he wanted to be baptized only as a means of securing additional "good medicine." But, Mark had said, in a way, he supposed, that was why they were all baptized, only the Indian concept of "good medicine" and the Christian's differed. He had said it with that wry half-smile of his that she loved. Mark had hoped that once a chief, even an old chief like Two Knives, had been baptized, others would be; but only Aapaaki was.

And Aapaaki . . . It had been a relief to have her poor face hidden a minute under the water when Mark baptized her, but she had choked and gasped as he had raised her. The squaws crowding along the shore had giggled, but they hadn't dared call out. Harriet remembered wondering how Mark could look at that face, but he had looked right into her eyes and said above the sound of the water, "Our Lord said, 'Woman, thy sins are forgiven thee, sin no more.'"

Had it made any difference in Aapaaki's life? Except that she had followed Mark more closely than ever and brought him gifts that Harriet was glad they had had to leave behind.

When the Indians wondered at the strange ceremony of immersion, since the Black Robe had only dipped his fingers in water and made the sign of the cross on their foreheads, Mark had told them how Christ, Christ who was the son of the great God—it had seemed so complicated to explain—had been baptized that way, going down into the water. Mark had tried to learn the jumble of syllables Pierre had given him for the word "baptize" but he had never been quite sure he was saying them right, or even that they really formed the correct word. Pierre kept saying, "Sure, sure, is right," and shrugged, as though he was tired of talking about it. The Major had said he really didn't know, and when Mark asked Mrs. Phillips she had just nodded and smiled. Some of the Indian boys had dived in at once after they saw Aapaaki, and had come up grinning and calling out the long word. It had been so hard for Mark.

And now that he was back where everyone understood the meaning of baptism, he had—had brought the Wilderness into his sermon, so all those people sitting in the front row wouldn't be baptized. Why hadn't he *known* the congregation would be shocked?

Mark came back to the front of the baptistry alone. Harriet heard the indrawn breath, the rustle, and the squeak of a pew as the audience stirred. Mark's eyes seemed to rest a long moment on those in the front row in their baptismal robes. Then he lifted his hand and pronounced the benediction, and she saw him again, standing in the river under that wide sky.

As though in relief that the service was over, the organ burst instantly into full volume with Mark's last word, covering over the frowning silence in which many of the congregation moved up the aisles, and the murmured comments of others.

Harriet sat still in her pew, waiting for Mark. It always took him longer after a baptism because he had to get out of his hip boots and the gown he wore over them, so he couldn't stand at the door shaking hands. Harriet was thankful. She could sense that some of the congregation were too shocked by his telling about Mrs. Phillips to shake his hand. Those around her either passed in an embarrassed silence or stopped to ask too solicitously how she felt. "My dear, what you have been through!" Mrs. Sansom said, shaking her head sorrowfully over her.

When Mark came out the door at the side of the pulpit, and up the aisle, Harriet went to him, putting her hand on his arm so they could walk out together. She took pains to smile and bow to each one they met, but there were few still lingering. The Adamses and the Browns spoke to her without glancing at Mark.

She was relieved to step outside Calvary Church and draw in a breath of the fresh air, unweighted by the sweetness of the lilies.

"I was so surprised and delighted to see you come in, Harriet," Mark said.

"I planned to come on Easter Sunday," she murmured, bowing to Mr. Hodges, the sexton.

Sydney Hall walked with them all the way to their house. He was trying to show his support of Mark, Harriet felt, but knew that Mark was unaware of it, he was so deep in his own thoughts.

"Mark, would you come over after dinner? I feel it's rather urgent," Sydney said as they paused at the iron gate.

"Of course, Sydney, if it's important. I can only stop a few minutes before Sabbath school, and I have to prepare for the evening service, you know. I want to make some calls on some of those who weren't baptized," he added slowly.

"I should think you might well preach one of those sermons you have already written. The congregation were pretty upset by the lack of a conventional sermon this morning, you gathered."

"So I saw," Mark said.

Sydney lingered, and Harriet went on up the steps of their house. She had to lift the knocker because Mark had the key and, as she waited for Hannah, she remembered that other time, when they had just come home from the Wilderness and Mark had to climb in through the study window.

"It didn't tire me at all," she said to Hannah's question. "The walk did me good. Yes, the Church was crowded. Hannah, those lilies the Terwilligers sent smell too strongly for the parlor. Put them in the pantry, will you please?"

But when Hannah was gone, she lingered in the hall as she slipped out of her cape and took off her bonnet. She felt oddly like that other time, too.

Mark came in as she stood there. "Harriet, how could they misunderstand everything I said? After the revival I wanted to speak so simply, so truthfully—to let that experience with Eenisskim make them aware as it did me. . . ." His face was strained in its urgency. His eyes implored her. "Couldn't *you* see how clearly it showed the difference Easter makes in our lives? Couldn't you?"

"Yes, but I was there. At least, I was at the funeral service," she corrected herself. "You forget how far away Woollett is from the Wilderness."

His eyes were stormy, his mouth set in a stubborn line.

"Why didn't you preach the sermon you had written? What made you tell them about . . . Mrs. Phillips? You never even told me about those nights with her."

Mark pushed both hands back over his head and brought them down in a hard fist. "Because I saw last night in the study what I'd never seen before, Harriet. I always knew that what was wrong with my mission wasn't really all the things I wrote the Board, though they were a part of it, and true enough— the language difficulty and the nomadic life; you know, all those things—but that the real trouble was that I had gone out there to convert the heathen, to make civilized Christians out of them, to move them by my own eloquence that was going to grow out there, but I had no real *love* for them. If I had had, I suppose I couldn't have left."

He turned away from her as he talked, hanging up the hat he wore only on Sundays, and his coat. "It always bothered me that Pierre said the Black Robe loved the Indians like a father, and they felt they were his children, so they followed him by the hundreds when he came to leave. You saw that only Aapaaki followed me very far!"

"And then last night, Harriet, I was thinking of Eenisskim's grief and despair in the face of death, and how I was actually repelled by her even though I went out to help her—almost afraid of her—but then how that second night I found myself yearning over her. And I realized, Harriet, that I had loved, really loved one human soul out there. Don't you see what an enormous relief that was?"

He turned so suddenly to her she was startled by the way his face lighted up.

"Heaven knows, I've talked about God's love enough at the revival—about his love for sinning, stupid, blind humanity—so people believed in it, but last night I think I myself understood for the first time what it is really like, Harriet. I remembered how my disgust and fear left me and I was able to love Eenisskim, in all her paint and filth and misery, and I could put my arm around her. I realized last night that that must be the way humanity looks to God. That I could make the congregation see how God feels toward us, if I told them about her and my being able to love her."

When Harriet was silent, he went on. "Most of the congregation who are so worked up about the slaves, who help them escape, don't feel any love for them as human beings. They're repelled, just as I was by Eenisskim.

"But that was the trouble, Mark. They only saw you with Eenisskim—with your arm around her—and they were shocked. You should have told them how you suffered before over not being able to feel any love for the people you went out to convert," she said, thinking carefully.

Harriet was glad to sit down at the dinner table and go through the ordinary motions, making small sounds with silver and dishes. She understood Mark, and yet . . . She looked across the white cloth and the cruet set into his eyes, which were dark and brooding.

"Why did you realize just last night that you had been able to love her?" she asked abruptly. "You must have known it before. That night when you came back, you kept saying in your fever, 'I loved,' and then without finishing your sentence you'd say, 'God so loved.' You must have known it then."

Mark shook his head. "All I remembered that next day was that I couldn't make her listen to me; she didn't seem to hear me. I felt I'd failed with her, and with the whole mission. Well, I had. You felt that, too, or you wouldn't have made it so easy for us to leave."

"By having a child—for that reason!" She couldn't have said why she laughed. The sound startled Hannah, coming in again with the sweet potatoes. Whatever it was about, she noticed the Reverend didn't laugh—but on the Sabbath, and Easter Sunday at that, she should hope he wouldn't. Harriet was like that.

"Or did God make this happen just to rescue his servant, Mark, lost in the Wilderness?" Harriet asked when Hannah had gone out. "Oh, Mark, I didn't mean that. Only it is hard for me to believe we're so much the center of God's attention. I know 'His eye is on the sparrow' but I never can quite . . ."

"I am self-centered," Mark said. "I have to guard against it. But my relationship to God has always been personal, the most personal one I know. I suppose that's why I'm so drawn to John Donne's sermons and religious poetry. It was for him, too. I believe it should be for every human being, Harriet."

Harriet was frowning. There was something wrong in the tone of Mark's voice. And he meant closer than his relationship to her. She didn't want any relationship to be closer than that. Was that so bad? It made her uncomfortable to be so personal about God; it was like appropriating him. And yet, that day when she had walked up toward the rimrock, and the sun stretched her shadow out on the grass until she was nothing in all that space, she had been frightened. Even now . . . She moved away from the memory.

"What will you do about the Church, Mark?"

"Over their being shocked? I'm going to talk about that at the service tonight. If they want me to resign, that's entirely up to them, but I shall make them understand a few things first. They are not children. We're living in a time when there is so much hate and anarchy and violence, they need to understand the nature of love."

Mark's eyes could burn so the dark brown lightened and the white seemed almost blue. His head lifted. How could anyone not believe in him, she wondered. He never worried about what people said or thought about him. She liked that in him.

Hannah, coming in with the pie, put it down quietly, but Mark pushed back his chair. "I've got to go and see what Sydney has on his mind, and I have a couple of sick calls to make; then I'll be back. I think I'll not go to Sabbath school today."

Harriet didn't eat her pie either. She was gaining too much, she told Hannah, and escaped from the Easter-lily smell. From her window she could see Mark way down the street, hatless, but walking more slowly than usual. She was always standing here in the window, watching him go away from her, as he had gone to the Wilderness.

Now he was out of sight, and she crossed the room to lie down; but she caught sight of herself in the mirror over her dresser—a woman with a sallow face and a swollen body. She stood so still she saw the movement beneath the folds of her dress, which hung straight from her shoulders, and she crossed her arms around herself, over the life that was hers and Mark's.

◇　◇　◇

An insult and a disgrace to Christian people, that's what it was!

Wasn't that terrible when only ten were willing to be baptized!

I don't blame them. Laura Marchant told her mother she didn't feel good having Reverend Ryegate's arm around her, after he'd put it around that Indian woman.

And poor Harriet Tomlinson, sitting there in her father's pew, hearing him tell about the nights he spent loving that woman! It was enough to have an effect on her unborn babe!

Of course, he did say the Indian woman didn't listen to him.

I don't care about that; what I care about is Reverend Ryegate's actually coming out in church and saying he loved that woman.

He meant in Christian love, I guess.

What he was talking about was a whole lot different than any Christian love I ever heard about! And what he meant and what he did are two different things.

Harriet had her hand on his arm when they went out of church together.

Just putting a good front on it, if you ask me! The Tomlinsons were always proud people, but it's a lucky thing for her husband that Whitford Tomlinson isn't alive. He'd have him run out of here so fast he wouldn't know what happened to him.

Look, there's the deacons talking together right now!

❖ ❖ ❖

Chapter Thirteen

SYDNEY swung back the door and, seizing Mark by both hands, drew him inside.

"Mark, are you mad? You can't tell a church full of people that you loved a woman and have them think it has any relation to religion. You poor, simple-minded fool!"

"It seems that I was," Mark said. He resented Sydney's whole manner. "I was speaking out of my heart and soul and the experience I had had, as God led me."

"Well, come in and sit down. Nobody can get at you here, and they'll be calling on you, you can count on that. I saw Quackenbush and Slocum talking together in the back of the church, right after the service."

"I'll be glad to talk with them. I'm not ashamed of anything I said, fool though you think I was."

"That's why I wanted to see you. Good God, man, those self-righteous Puritans are in no mood to listen to anything you say. They'll just ask for your resignation. It might not have been so bad if there hadn't been a baptismal service. That was really a debacle! There they were down in front, the whole flock of them, whispering together during the hymn, and when the time came for them to file out, most of them went on sitting there, stubborn as mules."

Mark sat silent in the big leather chair across from Sydney. On the marble-topped table, in his line of vision, stood a glass bell jar protecting a stuffed owl that clasped its claws around a moss-covered branch made out of velvet and growing from a black velvet mound. "Siipistto," he remembered, was the name for owl in the Indian tongue; the word that Eenisskim shrieked out at dinner. Mark's eyes came back to Sydney.

"If that was the depth of their purpose, it was just as well that they weren't baptized. One of the reasons I'm a little reluctant to conduct revival meetings is that I've seen people too often raised to such a pitch of emotion by the words of the preacher that they declare their desire to follow Christ, and when that wave of feeling ebbs, they revert to their former state."

Sydney clapped his knee in despair. "That's the pity of it. You were magnificent conducting those revival meetings. I told you that even I was stirred out of my usual laconic state. . . . You had the whole Church in the palm of your hand."

"I don't want the Church in the palm of my hand. My intention was to rest it in God's," Mark said stiffly. "And I consider it a failure if you were busy thinking about *how* I conducted it. That's why I wanted to tell about that Indian woman this morning; tell it as it happened, as simply as the writers of the Gospels tell those incidents." But he was startled by Sydney's reaction. He had thought Sydney would understand what he was doing.

Sydney had been filling his pipe; now he pointed it at Mark. "All right, maybe you could have told it, though I can assure you that a congregation wants a sermon, pure and simple, with an illustration or two thrown in to highlight it. And it better be something that happened to someone else; you can't use a word like "love" about yourself and a woman not your wife and not expect consequences."

Mark started to protest, but Sydney went on. "Oh, I know you're one of the pure in heart, old man. I'm not even sure you understand love in all its ramifications, but I do know that most of the world *isn't* pure in heart."

Mark sat back in the chair, sucking in his cheeks, his mouth tightened in a crooked line.

"Be that as it may," Sydney went on, "can I have your per-

mission to go to Quackenbush and Slocum and the rest of them
and explain to them what you were trying to do? You can talk
to them later, but if you meet them now, you'll only get in
deeper. I just might be able to talk them out of their sense of
outrage. And in the meantime, you stay here."

Mark sprang out of the deep chair so quickly Sydney
dropped his pipe. "Thank you, Sydney. I appreciate your kind
intentions, but I'll do my own explaining. I wouldn't want any
such committee calling on Harriet."

"I was thinking of Harriet. Of course, everything depends
on poor Harriet. People are shocked and angered partly on
her account. It can't have been exactly easy for her to sit there
this morning and hear you talk about loving another woman,
you must admit." He watched Mark's face.

But Sydney's saying "poor Harriet" irritated Mark so, that
he was oblivious of the rest of his remarks. He moved toward
the door. Sydney's hand gripped his arm. "You know I'm here,
Mark, if there's anything I can do. You can count on me. I
think I understand you better than you know."

Mark hardly heard him. He walked back up the street in
the thin April sunlight that came through the haze of green
barely showing on the trees and slanted off the short new grass.
It seemed to encase him like the owl in the bell jar, one made
of green glass, shutting out the real world. He felt unable to
make himself heard or understood through that transparent
wall. Last night in his study, seeing so clearly the meaning of
his vigil on the mountain, released in some way from his sense
of failure, he had been in the real world.

How could they not see what he tried to show those people
in front of him this morning? That Eenisskim was the very
symbol of human misery and blindness. . . . As he walked, he
went over each point in his sermon to see where he could have
failed to be clear. That he, defeated and repelled and frightened as he was, could feel such a surge of love toward her was
in the smallest but truest way indicative of that incredible

love of God for humanity. The idea of using that incident to make them aware of the joy of the resurrection, by showing Eenisskim's despair, had come to him like an illumination, and he had realized then his own love toward her. Why didn't they understand him?

He kicked a stick off the brick walk. Did they think the word "love" had no meaning other than carnal? Were they children, that their minds couldn't follow his meaning? And this uproar—none of it was real, nor was the sense of depression he felt. He turned the key in his own door.

Harriet was sitting in the parlor on the sofa, just sitting there.

"I hurried back, Harriet, for fear you'd be bothered by a visitation. Sydney seemed to think—"

"Deacon Slocum and Deacon Goddard were here."

"I'm sorry. I don't like you to have to—"

"They were very kind, Mark, and troubled. . . ."

"And they choose not to understand a word I said."

"Not as you meant it. Deacon Slocum was shocked that you could say you didn't care so much about immersion as—"

"As I do about their understanding the love of God. I don't."

"You see, that's heresy to them, Mark. I tried to explain, and they listened to me, but I'm afraid I—didn't convince them."

He sat down beside her and took her hand in his. She remembered that he had sat here like this the afternoon he had asked her to marry him.

"They felt your telling about putting your arm around Eenisskim served no purpose—that was their expression. That it was shocking. I'm only telling you, Mark, just what they said."

"Yes, I know. Did they never feel the arms of God?"

"No, I think not so . . . so physically," Harriet said. "Did you, Mark?"

"Yes! 'Underneath are the everlasting arms.' We both felt

them when we were coming down those rapids in that shell of a boat. Why do you suppose John Donne uses those images of physical love in his 'Holy Sonnets'? You were moved by them."

She didn't answer. Mark had forgotten how she had taken them for herself and her love for him. Then she remembered that Mark didn't know; her feelings were locked safely in her Journal. She forced herself to go on. "They were concerned about the effect on the converts, and the—" but she must use their exact words, however they angered Mark—"the scandal and talk that will be connected with Calvary Church. I told them there was no scandal," she added quickly.

She had never seen Mark's mouth set in such an ugly line. He stood up. "They had no right to talk like that with you. Why didn't they have the decency to make their utterly false charges to me? I'll go and see Slocum. I may as well tender my resignation while I'm about it. Did they suggest it?"

"Mark, please, don't do anything. They really are upset. I led them on to talk. It seemed . . . better. And I could explain what you were trying to do, what you meant by saying you loved Eenisskim." She hurried on to the end of her sentence, making her voice matter-of-fact, but her eyes followed a green tree on the wallpaper forest.

"It seems I always need interpreters," Mark said. "Thank you, Harriet. I'm sure you calmed them, but I don't like your having to. If you had been still awake last night, I would have told you what I had just realized about Eenisskim and that I was going to use her instead of a regular sermon. You would have understood and urged me to."

"No, I would have known it wouldn't do; anyone would know that, Mark, but you. A church congregation couldn't understand."

The glass of the bell jar seemed to encase him again. In the greenish light of the parlor he said, "But you do, Harriet. You understand what I was trying to do." He didn't make it a question.

"It isn't easy, Mark." She helped herself up from the sofa

by the cluster of grapes carved into the arm. She saw that he was so sure of her faith in him that he was not really concerned about her answer. He wasn't really thinking about her. "I think I'll go up and lie down," she said.

"Of course, dearest. They must have tired you out!" Mark said, his whole attention coming back to her.

"Mark, promise me you won't go to Deacon Slocum or anyone now. They're going to meet with you tonight after the service." She started to leave him, but he looked so grim—so troubled, standing there—that she laid her hands on either side of his face, gazing into his eyes.

"Thank God for you, Harriet."

"And Mark, be careful what you say to them."

"I'll have to say what I feel, Harriet. You wouldn't have me do anything else."

She turned away without answering. She felt hopeless about his meeting with the deacons. And something else lay in her mind, deeper than the trouble with the Church. She waited, wanting to speak of it, but she had asked him once. She still couldn't understand why he hadn't remembered—he said "realized"—until just last night that he had felt such love for Mrs. Phillips, or why he hadn't told her when he came back about everything that had happened, about what he had done. If he had told her then, she would have understood better. As she had told the deacons, what he felt was entirely different from the way a man felt for a woman he loved. They had been startled and uncomfortable at her speaking so frankly. "You're a remarkable woman, Harriet," Deacon Slocum had said, but he had meant she was a simple-minded one. "No," she had told him, "I know my husband."

"Go now, Harriet," Mark said. "Don't worry. I'll make them understand what I meant." He went with her to the stairs.

◇ ◇ ◇

A lot of the old man in her! Faced right up to us.

I didn't like talking to her about her husband that way, and in her condition, but she kinda asked for it.

When she said we were making the greatest mistake and there wasn't a more honest, God-fearing man in the world than Marcus Ryegate, it took the wind right out of your sails!

Many a wife's been mistaken about her husband. Besides, her kind's bound to be loyal.

Not when her husband gets up in the pulpit and tells about loving another woman—a heathen Indian squaw at that—and putting his arm around her! My wife's so mad, I don't know as she'll ever set foot in the church as long as he's there.

Half the congregation feels the way your wife does. We're going to have a split right down the middle. . . .

It's more likely to be the whole Church!

The damage is done as far as the scandal and gossip are concerned. I can see the Methodists as pleased as the devil about it, too!

It's what he said about immersion that bothers me. When you think what Roger Williams went through so Baptists could baptize the way the Bible said it ought to be done, it makes you feel Ryegate should be read out of the denomination.

He did say immersion was the foundation of the denomination, only . . .

Only love *is more important!*

We've got to make up our minds about what we're going to say to him tonight.

Tell him he's not the man we want as pastor of Calvary. We're going to be in hot water, one way or another, as long as he stays. You can never tell what he's going to say next.

I think myself that it was going off to the Wilderness that unsettled him. I put the whole blame on the Wilderness. He's never been the same since.

◇ ◇ ◇

Chapter Fourteen

Easter Sunday Night.

Mark has gone to the evening service. I asked him if he didn't want me to go, but he said no; that I had done enough, acting as interpreter. It's true, as he said, he does need one here almost as much as he did at the Fort. People don't understand him easily. Yet I do. Mark is completely honest, as I told Deacon Slocum. The trouble is that most people aren't, so they cannot believe him.

I wish I had gone. It makes me nervous to sit here at home, wondering how the service is going. He told me the text he wanted to preach from, and it wouldn't do at all. Mark does not always have good judgment. He wanted to preach on "strong meat belongeth to them that are of full age, even those who by reason of use have their senses exercised to discern both good and evil." He wrote it out for me. He would have told them that his sermon this morning seemed to be too strong for them because they couldn't discern good from evil! But he promised he wouldn't. He said he would save it; it was too good not to use.

I wonder how Mark happened to love me? He didn't fall in love (that silly expression people use) because of my beauty, although I prefer my appearance to Elizabeth Sansom's (who is considered attractive). I think our minds met first. We talked about poetry the first time we talked together. I wonder if Mark ever wondered how I happened to love him? People should wonder more about love; I mean the miracle of it—that this man and this woman should be drawn to each other.

Of course, Mark was trying to show the miracle of God's love for man in his sermon. They were stupid not to understand—although even I was a little startled at first.

I saw him so clearly sitting there beside Eenisskim. But his saying "I loved that human being. I went to her and put my arm around her" came out too suddenly.

Harriet dipped her pen in the ink and crossed out the sentences until the words were entirely hidden and the entry ended with "They were stupid not to understand." She put away her Journal in her secretary.

The service must be over by now. Mark would be talking with the deacons. And he wouldn't be careful. She was counting on what she had said to them to alter their feelings, rather than on what Mark would say.

She went downstairs to the study to wait for him, and bent clumsily to build a fire. The house seemed cold.

She thought of Mark hunting in the dark for wood to build a fire, and then sitting with that hideous creature—with her bloody arms and her painted face. No wonder he used her as a symbol for all the ugliness and unlovableness of humanity. He hardly thought of her as a woman.

Mark was very late. Wasn't that a good sign? Perhaps he and the deacons were really talking together.

Over on Mark's desk she saw the Testament that he had had at the Fort. She brought it back to the fire. It was full of markers Mark had stuck in, and she laid it on her knees and let it fall open at each place. There it was—the eagle feather. He had kept it all this time because of his vision.

She wished she had told Mark about her dream. "I had the most outlandish dream, Mark," she could have said, half laughing. "You and Mrs. Phillips were riding up in the sky on a great eagle. And I was standing down below on the ground

trying to run after you, but that hideous Aapaaki held me
there." If she told him her dream, maybe that would rid her
of it. Wasn't that why people told their dreams? She could
still tell it to him.

In a movement so sudden she had to lean against the mantel
for support and the Testament fell to the floor, she dropped
the pale-gray feathered shaft into the fire. An acrid smell
tickled her nose an instant as the feathers burned, leaving the
shaft itself glowing red before the color gave way to black.
Harriet picked up the Testament. The cover was smudged,
but when she wiped it against her skirt she saw the stain was
an old one, in the shape of human toes, as though a muddy
foot had stood on the cover. Hurriedly she put the Testament
back on the desk.

Mark closed the front door too quietly; now he was hanging
up his coat and hat. This winter, because she was always at
home, she was aware of each sound of Mark's returns and de-
partures. No, it wasn't just this winter; she had always been.

"I'm in here, Mark," she called; he would expect to find her
upstairs. But he didn't answer. Then there he was, the outcome
of the service and the meeting quite clear from his expression.
He sat down in the chair across from her, leaning a little forward, his hands one on the other, empty. He was looking at
the fire instead of at her; she had never seen him so angry.

"There were ten at the service tonight, besides the whole
array of deacons. Deacon Wattrus said the church had been
thronged to the doors this morning, and I could see for myself
how I had driven them away by my sermon." There was no
expression in his voice.

"I hope you told him it was thronged because of your sermons, because they go to hear you!" She offered him comfort
and defense, but he refused it.

"Deacon Slocum thought there was no use holding a service.
He suggested we omit it and have the meeting of the deacons.
I told him that as long as I was minister at Calvary I would

hold the service that was announced, whether there was anyone there or not.

"The organist hadn't come, so I started the hymns myself.
Sydney was there. I never realized what a good voice he has."

Harriet listened in silence.

"But it went all right. I preached the sermon about the walk
to Emmaus. It really wasn't an Easter sermon any more. You
should have heard me developing my three points. I didn't
bring in any illustrations, and I quoted Scripture enough even
for Goddard. I thought Quackenbush squirmed a little when
I came to the sentence 'What manner of communications are
these that ye have one to another?' It made its point."

Mark's tone was harsh, almost as though he were justify-
ing himself. She thought of Pierre telling about protecting
himself from two hostile Indians by showing them his watch,
saying, "You use what you got." Mark had used the sermon.

"I think they were a little embarrassed when they came to
the meeting with me. I asked them if they would like me to sit
up in front like a culprit in the dock and Quackenbush glow-
ered at such levity."

"Oh, Mark, you shouldn't have said that!"

"I said it just to relieve the solemnity. Of course, they said
the same things they said to you, but they've lost faith in me—
that's what it comes down to. Because of one sermon! Slocum
got red in the face and thundered at me, 'Reverend Ryegate,
we want a preacher at Calvary Baptist who preaches the Word
of the Almighty God.'

"I told him that, oddly enough, that was what I had been
trying to do, as I was given the vision to see it."

Harriet's eyes moved to the fireplace. On the tiled hearth below the andirons lay the burned spine of the feather, black but
unconsumed.

"So I shall tender my resignation to take effect in six months'
time, more or less. Meanwhile, I will occupy the pulpit when

they don't have a candidate, which will be a little awkward. Still, I wouldn't like to think I'd preached my last sermon there. Oh, yes, Terwilliger said he didn't want to hear the Wilderness referred to for the rest of the time I'm at Calvary. I'll have to watch myself. It's become such a part of me. They've decided in their wisdom that the Wilderness has unsettled me!"

She supposed the Wilderness was part of her, too, only what did that mean? And their child was conceived in the Wilderness. . . .

"They didn't listen this morning," Mark burst out. "And they deliberately misunderstood my remark about immersion. It was a fortunate thing they saw you first, Harriet. Your showing your faith in me impressed them. I think before that they felt I'd betrayed you." His disgust came out in a wordless sound of impatience. "Like so many suspicious old women. Oh, the word 'love' is a dangerous word. You've got to be awfully careful of it if you're preaching Christianity!"

Mark got up restlessly and went over to stand by the desk, looking down at it. Harriet was silent, watching him. Could the deacons be right that the Wilderness had unsettled him? Or was this the way he was and was his need to go to the Wilderness part of some strange restlessness in him?

He came back to her as abruptly as he had left, and sat down facing her squarely.

"But Harriet, I don't regret my telling that incident this morning. I don't regret anything I said. If they had had ears and hearts to hear, it could have been an Easter sermon they would never have forgotten!"

"They probably never will, anyway," Harriet said.

The clang of the knocker on the panel of the front door made them both start.

"Who now?" Mark exclaimed in irritation. "Deacon Slocum has doubtless just remembered something he forgot to say."

As he went to the door, Harriet stooped and picked up the

burned spine of the eagle feather from the hearth, and went past Mark up the stairs. She was at the landing when she heard Sydney Hall's voice.

"Mark, I couldn't not come. I just heard, and I'm outraged. You mustn't leave here."

Would they leave here? She hadn't thought of that until now. But, of course, Mark was through.

Part Three

THE WILDERNESS

Chapter Fifteen

MARK began to see his congregation: the ones who crossed the street to avoid speaking to him, and those who came and confided in him, now that he, too, had confessed to an aberration of accepted behavior. There was one who said, "Reverend, I know most folks were shocked, but I can understand how you came to love that Indian woman. I, myself . . ." Mark was appalled, but it seemed useless to try to set him straight, because the man was already telling in painful detail of his own love affair with an Irish girl. The word "affair" hung in Mark's mind, false and unpleasant, but persistent.

He saw Harriet on that endless day and night of her labor, her face pale and distorted in pain, but uttering no sound. Her stoicism awed him. Once, after a pain in which her hand tightened on his with more strength than he had known she possessed, her lips pulled back over her clenched teeth in a grinning grimace that was almost savage. Then she sent him away, and he waited first downstairs in the study and then in the bedroom across the hall, but still Harriet made no groan or cry. If she had, it might have pierced through his unreal world and penetrated his mood of detachment. When, finally, he heard the infant cry, that, too, seemed unreal. He looked with incredulity at the face of the small, perfect girl child who was his own flesh and blood.

When the baby was several days old, he sat alone in the nursery with her to bring himself to some more intimate feeling. Would she ever know that she had brought her parents out of the Wilderness? Perhaps she would like to boast that she might have been born there. But, his mind automatically added, they could all say that, anyway, all the children of Adam. He tried saying her name aloud, sitting in the rocker beside her. "Marcia." A gentle name—Harriet's mother's. Then the baby woke and began to fret, screwing up her face. It was an odd little face, puckered like that. But when the fretting turned into crying Mark took the baby in his arms for the first time and carried her in to Harriet, who was leaning against the dark polished headboard of the bed.

"I didn't know you were home, Mark," Harriet said, taking her from him.

"You forget, I don't preach this week. Calvary is having a 'promising candidate.'" He said it humorously, but her face sobered. "It seems strange, doesn't it? I'm not going to attend the service tomorrow, either. I'm going over to the Methodist Church, where Wendell Phillips is preaching on the antislavery movement. I've always wanted to hear him."

Harriet's head was bent over the baby at her breast, and small sucking sounds began; then the room was quiet. Harriet looked at Mark, feeling his restlessness.

"If I'm not preaching they really don't want me at Calvary, Harriet. I discovered that last Sunday. My presence seems to embarrass them. Last Sunday's candidate prosed on for an hour and a half without ever saying anything illuminating; I never knew before how hard those pews could get. Afterward, Slocum made a point of assuring me that the candidate was very sound in his orthodoxy and that made up for many other attributes. By all means, I told him, and we both bowed civilly."

Harriet smiled at the picture. She could see Mark agreeing gravely yet making Deacon Slocum uncomfortable by the mockery there would be in his eyes.

"I don't like this marking time, Harriet; sometimes preaching, sometimes not. Oh, I'm getting a chance to do some studying I wanted to do, but as soon as I delve into something a sermon begins to shape up in my mind. And when I've made notes I want to write it all out, and preach it while it's hot."

"But you know you'll use it, if not this week, next."

"The whole thing changes if you let it get cold," he muttered. He stretched out on the bed beside her, watching the baby, but Harriet saw that he wasn't really thinking about Marcia. He had that moody look he had had so often at the Fort when he felt things weren't going well.

But he laughed and sat up. "This afternoon, I felt like one of the young braves lazing around the stockade, waiting for someone to spot a war party or a herd of buffalo. Then I'd spring on my horse and gallop into action!"

How strange it was that their minds had converged back there, Harriet thought, smiling only faintly.

"It's true. I feel just as idle. Only, of course, the young braves weren't cursed with any guilt feelings about being idle!"

The baby was satisfied and Harriet held her up for Mark to see. "Isn't she lovely, Mark!"

"Can't tell yet," he teased; then he asked abruptly, "I wonder what she'll make of her father when she grows up?"

"She'll be proud of him, of course," Harriet said.

Harriet's words kept sounding in his ears as Mark walked out of the house, and he tested them for their ring. "Don't let's ever think one thing and say something else," Harriet had said that time. Why should he question that she meant what she said? Hadn't she defended him to the deacons? Yet there was that little pause, and a hint of insistence, as though she had thought "must" instead of "will."

Harriet hadn't asked what he was going to do, where he was going to go. She assumed, like everyone else, that he was waiting for a call. Well, he was.

As Quackenbush had said, trying with heavy tact to gentle their action, no doubt, some church in a larger city would "snap him up." The inference was that such a church would not be so particular about his orthodoxy—or was it his morals!

He had had difficulty ignoring the remark, and he hadn't repeated it to Harriet. Nor had he told her about the church in Northampton that had asked him to come as a candidate and then written a few days later to say that "under the unfortunate circumstances of which they had just become apprised" they had decided to revoke their invitation. He wouldn't want that particular church anyway, but he had minded. He had never thought of having to *hunt* for a church. There was something to be said for the organization of other denominations, one with a bishop who knew a man's gifts and knew also how a church congregation could misunderstand.

Since he had walked in the direction of the church, he thought of a book he wanted that he had left in the study. Even to himself he did not say *his* study any longer, since the candidates also used it. Finding the key in his pocket, he let himself in. He never had liked the way they kept the church locked except for services. He would insist on keeping his next church open.

In the late afternoon, the windowless vestibule was dark, and even the auditorium as he pushed the door open was heavily shadowed. The figures in the stained-glass windows on the west were dark and featureless. Stillness filled the place, except for a faraway slow sound of water dripping, but that would be in the baptistry under the platform, and harmless. The air smelled close, yet it was familiar and not unpleasant to him. He never minded that lifeless air in the closed church because his thoughts had their own life.

Since he had come down the center aisle instead of going around the side to the study, he went up on the pulpit. There was something about mounting a pulpit and facing the pews that stirred him. Even as a boy in his father's country church in Vermont he had had that feeling. He walked over to the reading desk and leaned his arms on the big Bible. As a boy, he had tried declaiming Patrick Henry's words to empty pews, or praying in the manner of various members of the church, but he neither prayed nor preached today. He stood waiting.

It had been so long since he had felt any sense of nearness to God. Words from one of his own sermons rose in his mind to mock him. "Once you have felt that nearness," he had said, "that mystic union with a power so much greater than yourself or your wildest imagining, you are always seeking it, consciously or unconsciously. Its continued absence is the greatest weariness the human spirit knows." He had had some glimmer then of what he was talking about, but he hadn't known as he did now, either the nearness or the weariness.

Since he had written those words, he had come nearer than ever before in his vision of being borne on eagle's wings. . . . If he could stand here in this pulpit now, at this minute, and feel again that sense of being drawn up, a sense of the Infinite, he would be sure.

He waited, hardly breathing, trying to relive that feeling. Then he stopped trying. It was no use. The vision was only an illusion of his own imagination, and the doubt he had tried to shut his mind against all week was back. Had he mistaken his call to the ministry, as he had his call to the mission field? It was just as well that he had lost his eagle feather; keeping it had been a superstitious, childish thing, but he had hunted all over the floor of the study for it.

Yet he went on standing there in the empty stillness, distracted by the intermittent dripping of water in the baptistry.

The door at the back of the audience room opened, letting in the stooped figure of Hodges, the sexton. Each man stared at the other, too startled to speak. The sexton withdrew, banging the front door after him. Mark went home without bothering to get his book.

◇ ◇ ◇

Yep, just standin' there, like he was prayin'. A sorrowin' an' sin-sick critter as ever I see.

Looked like a ghost. Wouldn't never been able to know who 'twas if he hadn't been so tall an' thin. An' he was standin' kinda hangin' on to the Bible.

Didn't say a blamed word. Just stared, crazy-like. Enough to scare you outa year's growth.

How I happened to go in was I went to fix the drip in the baptistry. The pipe kep' drippin' an' I was goin' to stuff it, 'cause I guess we won't be needin' it for a spell. Jus' like a man's conscience remindin' him of what he done, I thought to myself.

I got out an' left him there. Let the House of the Lord work on the Reverind if it can, I sez to myself.

He didn't look like he knew me, even.

Yep, it's a pity! A good man like that! An' over an Indian squaw.

◇ ◇ ◇

Chapter Sixteen

IT was unfortunate that Calvary Church must go through the business of sampling ministers again. Yet easier in a way. As Deacon Slocum said, "Last time we were trying to find a man who could preach like Reverend Ryegate, almost a second Ryegate, you might say; now we aren't. What we want is someone sound in his orthodoxy, who sticks to the Bible for his subjects." The others agreed emphatically.

"Still," Deacon Goddard commented, "Ryegate can start out with a text from the Bible and turn it so you wonder if the Lord himself knew what it said; like that one about Christ saying 'What manner of communications are these that ye have to another?' The next thing you knew he was making it say *we* were the ones whose conversation wasn't just right!" A small silence enveloped their meeting, while each man thought his own thoughts.

"To return to the business in hand, gentlemen," Deacon Slocum began with great formality, "since we have no promising candidate for next Sabbath, shall we let this antislavery speaker fill the pulpit? I guess he's been preaching all over the state."

"Ryegate suggest him?"

"Well, yes, he did. You see, we thought we had someone coming, so Ryegate agreed to speak in Worcester. He's giving all his extra time to the movement, and he's got in thick with all the top men. Now our candidate can't come."

Deacon Terwilliger gave a short laugh. "Heard Ryegate

spoke up in Manchester, New Hampshire, an' had eggs thrown at him and heckled to beat the band, but he outtalked 'em and had 'em joining up at the end!''

"He could. He could answer anyone's arguments. His mind works like a steel trap. And when he sends his voice out over a crowd and then drops it down so you have to lean forward to hear, he can move a stone. I'd like to have heard him.''

Only Deacon Slocum failed to join in the pride in the exploits of someone who, when all was said and done, still belonged to them. With his fingers moving steadily in their pill-rolling movement he asked, "Is Ryegate going to get out of the ministry and go into the antislavery movement full time?''

"I don't know about that. He seems heart and soul in it. And he preaches for it most Sundays when he's not here, claims the Christian Church has to fight slavery or lose its own soul.''

"Why don't he preach against slavery when he's here?''

"I guess he knows there's no argument here, so he saves his breath,'' Deacon Terwilliger suggested.

"He likes to preach on love here!'' Deacon Goddard commented.

Their discussions on Reverend Ryegate usually ended in uncomfortable silence. Deacon Slocum sometimes wondered if it wouldn't have been better for the Church to have asked for Ryegate's resignation after his Easter sermon and have him gone. The situation wasn't simple. There were people in the congregation who were beginning to change their minds about him. Six of the twenty who had refused on Easter had been baptized by him since.

And now that Harriet's child was born, some of the women had begun to murmur about the pity of the Ryegates' moving away.

"Prettiest little thing you ever saw; has the Tomlinson eyes,'' his wife had told Deacon Slocum. "They've named her for Harriet's mother, Marcia Tomlinson Ryegate. It's just a pity. . . ."

"Yes, it is a pity," he said, "but there are things a Church can't take."

"Oh, I know, I know," Mrs. Slocum agreed. "I meant it's a pity Harriet Tomlinson ever married that man."

The women tried to show their sympathy for Harriet by bringing gifts for the baby, until the drawers of the nursery dresser were full of sacques and bonnets and shawls, and the baby was equipped with two silver cups.

"It's really a christening cup, I suppose," Mrs. Biddle said apologetically, when she brought her gift. "I was born out of the Church, you know—an Episcopalian—but you can call it a milk cup."

There were two silver porringers, a galaxy of silver spoons, a gold locket, a tiny ring with a diamond chip in the center, all brought as gifts for the new baby.

Harriet sat on the porch in the warm June sunlight, looking off down the back garden, and talked with each caller who came to see the new baby. Each one carefully avoided the subject of the Church or its pastor, or if either subject crept inadvertently into the conversation, the visitor took her leave soon after. It was convenient for the callers that Reverend Ryegate was away so much of the time; they had no way of knowing how far away Harriet was also.

Isabelle Cavendish settled down in the rocker for a good chat. "Harriet, do nurse the baby out here. It couldn't be more private," she said, as Harriet took the baby from the elaborately woven bassinet, swathed in point d'esprit. Isabelle looked delicately off toward the lilac bushes and the beech tree at the end of the garden while Harriet unbuttoned the loops of her bodice and held the baby to her breast, feeling the sun warm on her skin.

Everything reminded her of something else these days, Harriet thought under cover of Isabelle's talk; of that night in the study when she had worn this dress and stepped out of it by the fire; of the woman nursing her baby on the deck of the boat going up-river and how she had wondered if she would have a child in the Wilderness. She looked down at the small head against her breast and saw the filigree of shade the syringa bush laid over it like a lace cap.

"Of course, you know you look quite lovely that way, Harriet; like a modern Madonna," Isabelle chattered on, but that was not what she had come to talk about, and she was not inhibited as the older women of the Church were.

"Oh, Harriet, I meant to give you a compliment. Dr. Fothergill's nurse told Mama that you were simply wonderful during your labor; that it took thirty-six hours and the baby came feet first and it was terribly painful but you never uttered a sound. So there! She couldn't say as much for me. I simply shrieked, and I don't care who knows it. If I'm pregnant again, I'm going to scream even louder. I told Peabody that."

"After all, an Indian woman often drops out on the trail to have her baby," Harriet said. "She manages the whole thing by herself, wraps the baby in moss and puts it in a papoose case on her back, and then catches up with the rest."

"Well, really, Harriet, we're not primitive Indian women!"

"No." Harriet's light laugh hung a moment in the air like a hummingbird, suspended by the invisible fanning of her thoughts. During her labor she had imagined herself a primitive Indian woman, walking on a trail that wound up the faraway rimrock toward those mysterious cypress hills, with the sun flattening her body on the ground in a shadow and emptying it of all pain or feeling. Or she was in the dark little room at the Fort, looking up into Mrs. Phillips' eyes and holding onto Mrs. Phillips' hand, holding hard. Once, when the pains were worst, she had thought she heard Mrs. Phillips laughing and had closed her lips tight so not a sound could escape. She had grinned back at her once, even if she couldn't manage a laugh.

Isabelle was pleased with the turn the conversation had taken, so she plunged in quickly. "I still can't understand how Reverend Ryegate ever happened to tell about that awful Indian woman on Easter Sunday. He might have known it would shock people into fits!"

"I wonder if people really listened to what he was saying," Harriet lifted the baby over her shoulder and fastened the bodice of her dress.

"Harriet, this is just between ourselves, of course, and I wouldn't ask you if we hadn't grown up together, and you know I was crazy over Mark Ryegate from the moment he came to Calvary Church—I was furious when you so neatly snared him—but honestly and truly, didn't that Indian woman have something to do with your coming back home so soon? You know, I never believed it was because you were pregnant."

"Isabelle, I believe you've been reading novels! You get the wildest notions." Harriet's laughter trickled through her words like empty squaw laughter. "I would have screamed if I'd had to have the baby out there. Without any conveniences, can you imagine what it would be like?" She held the baby close to her, as a shield. "But there were other reasons, of course. Mark felt that his first trip was really an exploration and—"

Isabelle cut in impatiently. "All right, Harriet. You always were closemouthed. What he was talking about certainly sounded to me like more than any Christian love."

"Can any love be?" Harriet asked, smiling ever so slightly down at the baby as she put her back in the bassinet. "Now that *is* heresy!" She no longer needed a shield. She could manage Isabelle Cavendish.

"Really, Harriet! I don't mind admitting that Peabody was absolutely gone on Cora Ambler, the soprano in the choir last year. That was while you were away. I teased him quite openly about it, and he got over her. And, of course, there was nothing *real* between them. Men just can't help being attracted to some women, and primitive women, especially. I know that."

"Unless it's their souls they are concerned with." Harriet was tired of this and she wished Isabelle would go. She had sounded sanctimonious and irritated Isabelle.

"I suppose the clergy are quite different from other men," Isabelle retorted. "But I have heard that some quite handsome runaway slaves come up through here. In Reverend Ryegate's new work he may find some to try to convert—through Christian love, of course." She stood up. "Harriet dear, you know I didn't mean it, but you really deserved something after that smug remark. I know you're going through a trying time, and I'm disgusted with the deacons for wanting Reverend Ryegate to resign. Don't mind me!" She pressed a quick kiss on Harriet's cheek.

"Of course not," Harriet said, "but keep an eye on Peabody!"

But after Isabelle had gone, Harriet sat still, with the shadow of the syringa falling across her sober face and eyes. Isabelle was a silly little fool and always had been. Nothing she said could bother her. But how sordid; they had sounded like two women condoning the ways of men, as though love were nothing. She was tired of the word.

Mark said if he could have really loved the Indians he never would have left. But was that true? He didn't *love* the Slocums or the Terwilligers or the rest of the congregation here either, really. The word became nothing when you tried to use it toward more than one person. And did he *love* the Negroes he was trying to help? What he cared about was seeing them free, because he loved the idea of freedom. Wasn't that it?

Yet it was a relief to have him stirred up and excited about something, after all those days when he was so restless, working in his study and then flinging out to take long walks. But his work took him away so much, and she was lonely, even with the baby. Thank goodness, he would be back tonight in time for dinner. Perhaps she would tell him what Isabelle had said. It would make him angry first, and then he would put back his head and laugh, perhaps; anyway, they would be very close.

But Mark didn't come in time for dinner, and Harriet went down to eat alone in the room with the blue Staffordshire dishes in the corner cupboard and the hunting paintings on the white panelled spaces on either side of the door. Her father had brought the paintings back from Europe before she was born, and they had grown to be merely part of the wall for Harriet. But tonight, moving her eyes beyond Mark's empty chair, she was caught by the dark-hued oils. In one, a bird hung by a string to a shadowy nail. The head drooped on its breast, but its plumage glowed out of the dusky brown background, a flash of bright green and deep blue, and the soft down around the legs palest gray. The short legs ended in red webbed feet. If you held the duck by the feet, the cold water would drip from the spread wings. . . .

Getting up from the table, she climbed on one of the leather-seated chairs and unhooked the painting from its nail, banging it clumsily against the chair back as she got down. She turned it to the wall, pushing the chair against it. Where the painting had hung, all the years of her life, the unfaded square of brown wallpaper, covered with small gold figures, stood out like a placard covered with print.

"Whatever have you done?" Hannah exclaimed when she came in to bring the dessert.

"I've always hated that painting. I decided to get rid of it. Take it up to the attic tomorrow, will you please, Hannah? Who wants to look at a dead duck!"

Hannah's mouth compressed in disapproval, but she carried the painting as far as the kitchen. Harriet was lonely with the Reverend away so much; that was what ailed her lately, and worry. The stories Hannah had heard about the Reverend and some Indian woman shocked her, but she had told everyone who asked, "He's a God-fearing, loving man in the home, from all I ever see." Still, she did wonder why he went off and got himself mixed up with a passel of troublemakers. Let the South take care of its own troubles.

Harriet avoided the study and went on into the parlor, where the lamps in the chandelier spread a coldly remote light on the horsehair upholstery framed in walnut, the horsehair giving back an impervious sheen, the wood taking the light deep into its grain. She raised one of the long windows, but the early evening hung so still the lace curtains held their stiff folds without moving, and the scent of syringa and honeysuckle pressed in on her. The fragrance was as sickening as that of lilies. It came from flowers growing in fenced and green-hedged gardens, not any wide sweep of sage-dotted prairie rising to a broken rim of rock.

The room was too quiet. Only an occasional buggy driving by on rubber-rimmed wheels made any sound. Harriet sat down at the piano, picking tentatively at the keys. She had hardly touched the piano since she came back. After the little melodeon, the big square piano was too massive.

Hannah had placed the hymnal on the rack as the proper music for the role of parsonage, which the Tomlinson house had assumed, but underneath the hymnal was all her old music, just as she had left it. "Fleecy Cloud" and the "Spinning Song"—never played to her father's complete satisfaction—and "Restlessness." How dramatic she had felt playing "Restlessness," telling herself it matched her own mood because Mark had gone away. Then she had followed him, and the music had stayed here all the time.

She played the first chords, but the music was more difficult than she remembered, and she got in the way of her own light. She had to lean forward, her head out awkwardly toward the music. She made a mistake and played the passage again with her right hand. The tentative notes stopped.

That time she was playing at the Fort, the sound of someone coming up on padding, moccasined feet, too shuffling for Mrs. Phillips . . . Harriet hadn't looked up, only felt someone standing close to her and smelled the wild garlic and grease and dirt. A rough, red-tanned hand slid onto the edge of the melodeon, plump but not large. The breathing and the smell came closer, until Harriet had looked up, frightened, straight into that flat, scarred face. Her eyes had fled back to the keys, and she couldn't manage to speak.

She had been ashamed of her relief when Mary came and drove Aapaaki out with a shrill voice, calling her that ugly word, "kaxkaani," that meant cut-nose. "She knows better than to come in here with us! We don't want anything to do with her," Mary said, with a glance that was too knowing for a fourteen-year-old.

But how could Mary not know everything there was to know, growing up there? How would she get along with properly brought-up young girls in a convent school? "Everything there was to know" was a queer expression, a disgusting expression—it suggested that what men and women could do to each other was all there was to know in life.

She began to wonder about Aapaaki. Had the young braves dragged her out of her lover's tipi, or had they come on her in his arms in some hidden place? Did she cling to her lover, screaming? Or run from them until they overtook her? If Aapaaki had been given by her father to someone she didn't love; if she really loved someone. . . .

Harriet had never thought of Aapaaki as a young girl in love; hardly thought of her as quite human. . . . What had happened to the man Aapaaki loved? Did he just slink off without trying to protect her, or did they drive him out of camp? She wished she knew. She had never really looked at Aapaaki before because it had been so horrible to have her follow Mark—even when they were leaving—and the squaws pointing and calling and giggling at her.

As though Aapaaki were offering herself to Mark, or as though . . .

Drawing her hands back too quickly from the keys, Harriet

struck a discord. She clasped her hands together in the folds of her skirt, staring at the polished wood that gave back dimly the image of her own face.

Why had she had that nightmare of Aapaaki holding her down to the ground while Mark went off with Eenisskim unless there had been some truth in it? There was always some truth in dreams, Hannah said, or a warning.

Why didn't the young braves go up on that butte where Eenisskim sat with Mark's arms around her and drag her out and chop off her nose with one swift flash of a knife? Eenisskim would have screamed then. Her blood would have run down over her mouth and chin, and the sight would have made Mark sick. Maybe Mark had kissed her mouth to stop her wailing, but he hadn't told that.

Or in his love for her, his Christian love, would he see only her great dark eyes and look past the raw holes in her face?

If her face was butchered, Eenisskim would be as ugly as Aapaaki. Mark wouldn't think she was beautiful then! And the squaws would laugh at her instead of at Aapaaki—or the missionary's wife. The Major would drive her out of the Fort. She herself would pass by without looking at her. No, she would stand still and stare at her, and then she would laugh, too.

Harriet clasped both hands around her neck in horror. What was she thinking! Never before in her life had she ever wanted to see someone hurt. That she could even imagine such a thing shook her whole being. It was hideous. Her hands covered her face, rubbing down over her eyes, flattening her nose and clawing at her mouth. She took her wet fingers out of her mouth and threw her arms around herself as though to protect herself from the wrath of Heaven.

Then she sat up straight, staring down at the black and white keys. What was the matter with her? There had been nothing *real* between Mark and Eenisskim. It was natural for Mark to want to comfort the wretched woman in her grief; that was like Mark. He wouldn't have told about her in a sermon if there had been anything to hide. Hadn't he been bewildered when the congregation was shocked? He had had no idea that they wouldn't understand why he was telling them about his love toward her. "But you understand, Harriet," he had said.

She pushed down first a black key, then a white one, the length of the keyboard, listening to the thin sounds climb in the hollow stillness.

She did understand. . . . Eenisskim had bewitched Mark! She had held that duck over his face, fooling him into thinking he had a vision. She had made him feel the closest to God he had ever come. How ridiculous that was, when she was nothing but a primitive Indian squaw; that's what she was, even if she was supposed to be an Indian princess. How could a man like Mark be so fooled?

And when he loved her—whatever kind of love it was—he thought it made up for not loving the whole Indian race. He tried to make a parable out of it. If he hadn't been bewitched, he couldn't have thought such a crazy thing.

Eenisskim was the cause of all his trouble at Calvary. It wasn't the Wilderness that had unsettled him, it was that woman. Her very silence made her seem mysterious to Mark. If he could have heard what she said when she jabbered with the squaws, maybe he wouldn't have found her so mysterious, or cared so much about her talking to him.

But that time in the river, lying on Eenisskim's arms, looking up into her dark eyes . . . Harriet stood quickly, to rid herself of the memory. Oh, she saw how Eenisskim had laid hold of Mark.

What use was it to burn Mark's feather? He would never get Eenisskim out of his mind.

"He was so bewitched he will never again belong completely to me," she whispered in the silent room. "Even though I followed him to the Wilderness and brought him back."

Harriet's hands writhed nervously inside each other. Her mouth trembled so much that she caught her lower lip between

her teeth, biting it without minding the hurt. She would *tell*
Mark he was bewitched; shout it right out at him and bring
him to his senses. Hadn't they promised each other they would
say what they thought? Not say one thing and think something
else, something secret and hidden?

Chapter Seventeen

THE cab bringing Mark home stopped in front of the house. Always before when she heard it she rushed downstairs to open the door. But tonight she sat in her room, fully dressed, with her Journal open on her writing box. She had written only two sentences on the white page: "I loathe myself tonight. I have found that my mind is capable of demons, too; but it is Mark's fault." Then she had had no desire to go on. Perhaps she had now become a person who didn't commit her thoughts to paper. Once she had asked Mark why he didn't keep a journal at the Fort, and he had laughed and said his thoughts lay too deep. He had said it to tease her, but maybe he was right. Maybe he didn't want to see them spelled out on a white page.

She moved deliberately, putting her Journal away in the writing box and turning the key before she put the box in the drawer of her blanket chest. She stopped in front of the mirror and brushed the hair that framed her face so it was smooth and shining, but she barely met her own eyes. Then she put on her amethyst earrings.

All the time she had followed Mark by the sound of the key in the lock, the creak of the hatrack as he hung up his coat, his steps moving through the house. He hadn't come running up to her; had he gone into his study? She heard the pantry door. Perhaps he had had no supper. But even at that thought, she made no haste. Slowly she moved down the chasm of the stairway.

When she pushed open the door into the kitchen, Mark was sitting on the table, his coat off, cutting slices of meat from the joint of mutton she had had for dinner. She had to take hold of the doorframe to keep from running to him because of the habit of gladness at seeing him. Then she remembered, and said only, "You're back."

"Harriet! I thought you must be asleep. Didn't you hear me come in?" Wiping his arm across his mouth, he came over to kiss her so eagerly he was unaware of the tightness of her lips and the stiffness of her body. His face was rough with a day's growth of beard, and his shirt was limp. Excitement seemed to steam from him.

"We had such an uproar at the meeting I couldn't get away in time for the early train. You've never seen anything like it." His face was alight with all he had to tell. He felt himself coming to her with his success in his hands. He had been good. He had moved the crowd and held them. Now he knew that this work was what everything that had gone before had prepared him for. Seeing the Indians free in their primitive lives had given him forever a sense of man as born to be free. He had found his right work.

"You're as excited as an Indian brave just back from a war raid," she said.

"War raid? Not yet, though it's going to come to—oh!" He laughed. "Well, I won't have any more time to lounge around the Fort. This last meeting was close to a war raid. Some of the slavery men grabbed down the lamps around the walls and set fire to the door in the old building where I was speaking, and the others put it out and got into a real fight. I went right on, shouting above it all until I made them listen. I tell you, Harriet, it was tremendous! I don't mean I was—I've outgrown that disease, thank God! But the power of the desire that all men be free. Men were ready to die for it right there. The meeting had the fervor of a revival about it!"

"I'm sure," Harriet said. She started to stir up the fire to heat the coffee.

"Don't bother, Harriet. I'll drink it cold. This tastes wonderful after the food I've eaten in the hostelries of the land. Tell me how you've been. And Marcia. This was the longest time we've been separated since I went to the Wilderness, do you realize that?"

Tonight she minded even the word "Wilderness."

"Marcia's fine. She gained two pounds. I weighed her on the kitchen scales." Had she been wrong? Mark was hers, and he loved only her.

"And you, dear? Were you lonely?"

"Yes, I was very lonely. Some of the women came to call and bring Marcia gifts." Should she tell him what Isabelle had said? "Sydney went to Boston last week and heard you. He tried to see you, but you were surrounded and he couldn't wait. He told me about your success."

"I was only one of the speakers. I wish you could have heard Garrison and Parker. Parker's probably the most powerful speaker I've heard. Do you know that Garrison's been fighting for the cause twenty-five years, and he's still against the use of force! But it seems more and more that there may be no way out except by force. Slavery and freedom are as irreconcilable as love and hate!"

Love and hate, love and hate . . . She wasn't listening to Mark, only looking at him, caught up as he was in his new cause; but she was unmoved by the indignation in his face, his flashing eyes, his fervor. He was still on the platform, speaking, really.

He talked as he ate. "As Wendell Phillips says—the North has its own slavery, in its indifference and timidity"—he was spreading apple butter on his bread—"and callous dollar worship, which keeps us from taking up arms against what we know is wrong." His fork banged down on the table.

She sat on the straight wooden chair against the wall, facing him, her hands in her lap, an audience of one.

"And churches, Harriet, which stand for Christian love for their fellow men, are totally indifferent—mouthing noble sentiments and complacently doing nothing! Look at Calvary! The Church is dead unless it fights against slavery!"

When he stopped, the silence seemed to sound in the room. The words "Christian love" echoed in Harriet's mind. Mark was looking down at the bone lying on the white platter. Her eyes looked at his plate. He hadn't touched his slice of bread and apple butter. Then she felt him looking at her and perversely kept her eyes down.

"Harriet." His voice was different, vibrating to a new note, but just as intense. "Harriet?" He seemed suddenly hesitant. "I came back tonight even though it was so late to tell you that I've made up my mind. I'm not going to take another church, not until we get somewhere with the antislavery movement. . . ."

She made no answer, but she could see that he was anxious about how she would take what he was saying. She fingered her brooch, waiting; he must have looked at Eenisskim this way.

"My decision has nothing to do with the trouble at Calvary, though some of them will think that, of course, but I don't care what they think, only what you think. I can't *not* do this work, feeling as I do. And I'm not the only clergyman who's giving up his pulpit to preach against slavery. Can you understand how I feel, Harriet?"

When she didn't answer at once, he went on, almost hurriedly. "I know it's asking a lot of you, because it means leaving you alone so much. I'll have to be away a good deal, of course, but I'll be working in New England. I won't be away more than a night or two at a time."

His eyes were on hers. He was waiting. But she wouldn't let the eager note in his voice keep her from saying what she had determined to say. She clasped her hands together.

"Yes, I understand."

"Harriet, I knew you . . ." Mark began.

"And this time I can't follow you," Harriet continued. "When you went to the Wilderness I didn't know any better.

Now you have a new lure." Words she hadn't known she was going to speak came to her tongue. "It doesn't seem to matter very much what your lure is, so long as you're drawn by it." She saw his face change and his eyes darken. "Isabelle Cavendish said maybe you'd find a handsome slave girl to convert by—" her voice trembled and her jaw drew down so she could hardly get out her words—"by Christian love." She saw the color come back into his face and flung her question at him as she got up to go. "Is it easier to love the slaves than it was the Indians? Or do you have to single out just one?"

"Harriet, what are you saying!" He came across the room and seized her by the shoulders.

His fingers hurt, and when she tried to pull away he wouldn't let her go. She flung back her head so that she was looking straight up at him. Her jaw was under control now, and she was no longer afraid she might cry. "I'm trying to say what I think, Mark. You were so sure I'd understand about Eenisskim. Well, I do. I think you were bewitched by her. Oh, I see perfectly what happened; you let your vision become a human being—" She remembered the mark of the toes on the cover of his Testament—"with muddy feet, and you were drawn to her as a woman. If it weren't so, why would you have to talk about her all the time? In your very first sermon when you came back, and on Easter Sunday? Why?"

"Harriet, I . . ."

"I hung on every word you preached, and I loved the poetry you quoted, but Eenisskim wouldn't listen to you, wouldn't answer you. She's your mystery and the strangeness you lectured about; you can't get her out of your mind and you never will. You . . . you're obsessed by her!"

Harriet shivered visibly as she got the words out; her head dropped to hide the tears in her eyes. Mark lifted her chin, forcing her to look at him. His voice was gentle.

"Harriet, my poor darling, you've been lonely and imagined all kinds of wild things. . . ."

She jerked away from him. "No, I haven't imagined anything, Mark. I've just been stupid not to see before. You've deceived yourself, just as you did about your call to the mission field. You went out to the Wilderness to—to use it, because you thought preaching to the Indians would make you more eloquent. 'Lure' was the right word, Mark! But just remember that I followed you because I loved you."

She made him wince. His face had that stricken look that had moved her before, but it only showed that he knew she was speaking the truth!

"Oh, I tried to shield you from feeling the failure of your mission, and I defended you to the deacons, but you are guilty, Mark. You've done terrible things to me. I loved you so. I let you imprison me and ravish me—and all the time you were obsessed by that Indian woman, by another man's wife."

"Harriet!"

The shocked outrage in his voice drove her on. "No wonder Aapaaki followed you around; you committed a kind of adultery, too." She caught her breath; then the words came: "Eenisskim should have had her nose chopped off. . . ." She turned away from him.

"Stop it, Harriet!" He grabbed her by the shoulders and swung her around to him. "Are you out of your mind?"

"Do you think I like having my mind filled with such ideas? I feel like a savage. And that's what you've done to me, Mark Ryegate!"

"You're hysterical, Harriet!" He shook her so the gas light danced above the white plate and she had to grit her teeth. "You don't know what you're saying."

"I know exactly what I'm saying. You're the one who gets carried away by words, without even knowing what they mean. You use the word 'love' and don't know what you mean by it. And you think you can control people with words; they give you a kind of power. But you can't move me, Mark, not any more."

He let her go so suddenly she staggered. His face was terrible to see. She looked instead at his long arms hanging at his sides. Oh, she was ugly and jealous and shrewish, and Mark would never love her again, but all she had said was true. They had promised to tell each other what they thought.

"I only want to say this, Harriet, and I want you to listen to me." Mark's voice was as quiet as it could be at the beginning of a sermon. He would work on her now, as though she were sitting in the congregation; the way he must have talked to Eenisskim, but he'd had his arm around her. Harriet looked away from Mark.

"I love only you, Harriet. I never thought of Eenisskim in the way you suggest."

Her eyes came back to his. "No, not consciously, but you were drawn to that woman by something quite different from Christian love—by which I take it you mean love for a human soul because it belongs to God—at least, that's what I told the Deacons. But it wasn't true. My word is right, Mark. You are bewitched by her. Obsessed. Maybe you prefer that." Her voice went on rising. "Oh, I'm tired of words, tired of talking. I'm glad you've found a new cause, mission, lure—whatever! It's a good thing you're going to be gone. I need to find myself again."

He turned away and picked up his plate and put it in the sink so quietly the crockery hardly scraped the soapstone. Some instinctive impulse to do it for him twitched at her nerves, but instead she went out of the room, through the house, up to Marcia's room.

She could feel her heart pounding; her mouth was dry, and when she covered her face with her hands they were cold. She held on to the crib in the dark. The little night lamp was turned so low only an eerie spot of light made a pale glow on the ceiling. She wanted to take Marcia up, to hold her, to nurse her, but Marcia was asleep and she had fed her only two hours ago. Women turned to their children when they had lost their husbands. It was whispered that Sydney Hall's mother had almost smothered him with affection after Armstrong Hall left her for another woman.

*

Mark will come up to see Marcia. He will come in a minute now. She sat on the little sofa to wait.

Now he is coming upstairs. He is going to our room to find me. When he finds I am not there, he will hunt for me here.

He has closed the door.

He doesn't care where I am or how I feel. He is only concerned with himself and his obsession. He knows what I said is true. Except about—hurting Eenisskim. But he is to blame for my ever thinking such a thing.

She fumbled for one of the baby's shawls and covered herself, curling up on the sofa.

It is more comfortable in the study. I might go down there, but I couldn't bear it in Mark's study. Or I might go into the room across the hall from Mark, or the guest room.

Why doesn't he come to see where I am?

She lay wide awake, listening to Marcia's breathing.

There he is, walking in his bare feet. "I love only you," he had said. "Harriet, my poor darling, you've been lonely and imagined all kinds of wild things," Mark had said. That was it. That was the trouble. I'll go and tell him so. I'll get into bed, and he'll take me into his arms.

She opened the door and started down the dark hallway, but after a moment she stopped.

Why had he just turned away at the end? He didn't deny that he was drawn to that woman. Hadn't he sat looking at Eenisskim on the boat when she was asleep? He had been restless ever since they came back from the Wilderness. "You and Mark came back changed," Sydney had said. That was so.

She lay down again on the sofa in Marcia's room.

In the morning, before Harriet was awake, Mark set out on another trip, leaving a note on her dresser.

"I have a meeting in Hartford. Will be back to fill the pulpit at Calvary, Sunday. Mark."

Harriet read and reread it. Mark came out of his way just

to tell me as soon as he'd made up his mind about going into the antislavery work. He came to see Marcia and me—to have the night here. It would have been more sensible for him to have stayed there since he had to go away so soon. But, of course, he needed fresh clothes.

He signed only his name. Not: Love, Mark. But I told him he didn't understand the word, so he wouldn't use it. Yet he could have said something more.

He'll be back tomorrow. I'll tell him I was so worried, that I was frantic with loneliness—that I didn't know what I was saying. But I did.

He said he loved only me, but he didn't deny that he was . . . that he couldn't get Eenisskim out of his mind.

Chapter Eighteen

MARK glanced at the boy beside him on the narrow train seat, crowded into the corner by the window. A man's hat covered the boy's face, and his thin shoulders were lost in the hurriedly procured coat; his boots were too new for the rest of his clothes, and too large, but they were better than none. There wasn't much risk taking him along on the late train, and then he'd be farther on his way to Canada. The conductor had spotted him, but he was no informer. "All right, Reverend," he had said, punching their tickets, giving him a quick look.

Mark took away the hat without waking the boy. Sweat beaded the light-brown face beneath it, and the full moist lips were slightly parted. The closed eyelids lay against his smooth cheek like a child's. He couldn't be more than thirteen or fourteen. Somebody's houseboy, he must have been; he didn't look like a farm worker. Mark glanced at the light palm that lay open on his knee; that was no farm laborer's hand, either. All Mark knew about the boy was that his owner had gone to Boston after him, and the boy had to get to Canada before his master picked up his trail. Joel, his name was.

The sudden jerking of the train wakened him, and he sat bolt upright, his eyes large and bright as those of a frightened colt.

"It's all right. We're almost there," Mark said quietly. "Put your head out the window a minute and get a breath of air."

The boy hesitated and then leaned out over the sill. The beam from the engine light shone back, cutting his profile out of the dark and giving his skin an incandescent glow. Mark found himself staring; no one could help being struck by the boy's beauty. He put his hand on Joel's arm. "Better shuck down now and catch a cat nap." But the other occupants of the train seemed to be asleep. There were only six, and he had looked them over carefully when they got on.

Mark shifted on the too narrow seat and tried to rest his head against the straight back. He hadn't let himself think about Harriet; there hadn't been much time, with two speeches instead of one in Hartford and his sermon for tomorrow, but now he couldn't help himself. Single words and phrases sprang at him out of the darkness in his mind. He saw her face as she stood there in the kitchen. She looked as though she hated him. It was the congregation working on her; all those women coming to call, and that foolish Isabelle Cavendish. . . . But Harriet . . . How could Harriet think, let alone say, such things?

After childbirth, did women sometimes have strange notions and turn against the very person they loved? That he was bewitched! She had looked demented when she taunted him about Aapaaki's following him around—saying that Eenisskim should have . . . His mind boggled at recalling her words, trying not to hear them, yet hearing too clearly the strident, hysterical note in her voice. How could Harriet, who was all gentleness and understanding . . . Mark rubbed his hands over his face, smearing the train soot deeper into the lines of weariness around his mouth and eyes, which gave his thin face a gaunt, grim look.

He hadn't done well in Hartford, hadn't really carried the audiences with him, and the money contributions were disappointing. He'd heard someone in the crowd say the young feller couldn't hold a candle to Higginson, who had been there the week before. But he hadn't been at his best. His mind had felt numb; he wasn't free.

That time when he turned to the group of escaped slaves on the platform, a pitiful enough group to move any decent human being, he had said any Christian heart must stir with compassion and love for these oppressed fugitives. But even as he said it, Harriet's question about whether it was easier to love the Negroes than the Indians sounded in his mind so loudly that he lost his train of thought and stood there like a schoolboy stumbling in his first declamation. He had tried to make his silence seem rhetorical, but he could feel the attention of the audience wavering.

Mark stood up, touching the soot-streaked ceiling of the car to ease his cramped shoulders. Then he sat down again. He had meant to spend this time on his sermon. If he didn't set to work on it, he would make a botch of that, too. But it was hard to put his mind on it.

"I hung on every word you preached," Harriet had said. He had felt that and preached to her rapt attention, but now she listened cynically, not believing him. "You're the one who gets carried away by words, without even knowing what they mean. You use the word 'love' and don't know what you mean by it."

Harriet had twisted and turned the things he had told her, things he would never have told anyone else, and flung them back in his face. That time he had confessed to his fear of liking his power over an audience too much—stripped himself naked in front of her—she had gathered him to her and understood. More than that, she had freed him from his own self-accusation and loathing. Now she taunted him. He should never have told her about his vision. "You let your vision become a human being . . . and you were drawn to her as a woman."

Perhaps she had never believed him when he tried to tell her what that nearness to the Infinite was like.

Did he himself know any more? What *was* it like?

He closed his mind to his own question. He could preach anyway; go through his paces; put on an act if need be. And he had his text: "The man that wandereth out of the way of understanding shall remain in the congregation of the dead." Let Harriet make what she would of it. But he mustn't risk looking at her, sitting in her pew.

The train was coming into the station with its high, shrill whistle and clanging of bells and explosion of steam, terrifying the boy.

"It's all right, Joel. You'll soon be in a comfortable bed, and Mrs. Ryegate will take good care of you." Mark spoke quietly, keeping his hand on the boy's arm. He thought the man across the aisle looked at them too sharply, and took pains to be in no hurry getting off the train.

"Home again, Reverend!" the night station man called out.

Mark called back in a hearty voice anyone could hear, "And glad to be home!"

Then they were free of the lights of the station platform, walking toward the refuge of Elm Street, their feet loud in the night. "Only another block now," Mark said, but he was wondering how Harriet would take the runaway slave boy.

"Is it easier to love the slaves than it was the Indians? Or do you have to single out just one?"

Mark's feet slowed. They were coming to Sydney's house, and he saw that the lights shone through the library windows. Sydney was still up. He would take care of the boy overnight. Hadn't he said that he was there if there was anything he could do? "You can count on me," he had said. It would be better to leave the boy with him tonight.

"Mark! And friend," Sydney added, as he opened the door. "Come in." His look was quizzical but welcoming. "You must have arrived on that late train. You must be starved."

"Sydney, this is Joel. Will you keep him tonight? There's a man I know who would take care of him, and he'll put him on the train for the North in the morning, but he lives on the outskirts of town. I'd rather not take him way over there this late. In fact . . ." His voice sank to a murmur. "And I knew I could count on you."

"Of course." Sydney was helping the boy off with his coat, smiling at him. "You have to preach tomorrow. I'll take care of him and get him off myself; don't have him on your mind."

"Thank you, Sydney. I'm grateful to you. I didn't want to

disturb Harriet tonight. It might worry her. You'll be safe here, Joel. Mr. Hall will take good care of you," he said to the boy.

Mark's own house was dark except for the light in the hall, but when he opened the door he found an envelope with the word "Mark" on the outside, propped against the card tray on the table.

He carried the letter into his study and let it lie on his desk without opening it until he had taken off his coat and vest, his collar and tie. All the time he was listening for the sound of Harriet's feet on the stairs, or her voice calling. But, of course, she didn't want to see him; she had left the letter instead.

He was tired; too tired to think. It seemed too much of an effort to read a letter. Finally, he took out of the envelope the two sheets in Harriet's handwriting.

Mark:

I regret losing control of myself the other night, and I am deeply ashamed of the violence I expressed toward Mrs. Phillips. You could have been no more shocked than I am myself that my mind can think in such terms of jealousy, for I discover that I am jealous that she should possess so much of you, and that I can think in terms not only of jealousy but of savage cruelty. Nor am I less ashamed because I was speaking of an adultery that exists only in the mind and of which I believe Mrs. Phillips to be entirely unaware; that seems, in fact, to be unrecognized by you, although it is no less true, and to me no less a sin.

I realize that, without intending to do so, I have made that wretched Aapaaki a symbol of adultery, as you also, without intending it, have made Eenisskim into a symbol of your heavenly vision, and your love for her a symbol of God's love for mankind! It is curious, is it not? The effect of the Wilderness on two *civilized* people who have thought there was no harm in words or thoughts so long as there was nothing "real"! You might add a new lecture to your series for the Lyceum circuit and call it the effect of the Wilderness on civilized persons who are accustomed to live in the world of words.

But that I could think in such cruel and violent terms makes me realize what "loving" you with complete abandon of mind and body, even of soul, if the soul is separate from the mind, has done to me. I have become another person and one whom I can neither respect nor live with.

Until I can make peace with myself, and until you understand yourself sufficiently to be free of your obsession with Eenisskim and all she means to you, I wish to live my life quite separately, although I will be here whenever you return, and we will converse and take our meals together as usual, sharing in Marcia, who I must always remember was conceived in the Wilderness in our first joy of being together there.

I have made up the bed in the east bedroom for you, and prefer that you use that room.

I sign my name as you signed yours, without using that word which has become so difficult to understand.

Harriet

Mark sat with the letter in front of him, seeing Harriet's clear, delicate handwriting, without a word crossed out, and knew she must have made several attempts before writing this final copy. He felt her struggle to say exactly what she meant, and her difficulty in knowing, in the stilted and formal phrasing. Her tone wasn't taunting as it had been last night, except for that remark about a new lecture. It was hardly hysterical; rather, it was full of self-accusation and guilt—but she blamed her state of mind on her loving him.

He crumpled the letter into a tight ball and threw it across at the fireplace. She had made this all up in her own twisted mind. She was only one step above the mentality of the congregation. She had no faith or trust, no understanding at all. How could she have thought these things?

She admitted that she was jealous. And that amazed him. How could she be? He went over and picked up the letter, smoothing out the sheets on his desk. "I am jealous that she should possess so much of you. . . ." What utter nonsense! ". . . 'loving' you with complete abandon of mind and body, even of soul . . . our first joy of being together there."

He ran up the stairs to their room, calling when he found the door locked. "Harriet! Harriet darling, I have no obsession. You know I love only you. And I've already forgotten those things you said."

He heard her stirring, but she didn't answer.

"Harriet!" Anger and impatience were in his voice. This writing letters and locking him out—like some heroine in a cheap melodrama; he would have no part in it. "Harriet, don't be foolish. Open this door."

"Mark . . ." Her voice was almost toneless. "It isn't as simple as that. I can't forget what I said or thought. You don't seem to see what has happened to me—because of what happened to you."

"Dear," he began patiently, "you're conjuring up all sorts of wild imaginings out of—"

"Please, Mark, I'm so tired of talking, I told you. Just leave me alone. I'm so ashamed."

He leaned wearily against the wall. There were things to say; the words he said so easily to guilt-ridden people at the revival meetings, cleansing, comforting promises—prayers. His head was full of them, but they blurred together in his tired brain. He couldn't seem to get them out.

He saw the light left for him in the east bedroom and went in and closed the door.

Chapter Nineteen

HARRIET had already eaten breakfast and was upstairs with Marcia when Mark came down. He sat alone, and Hannah served him. That was when he saw the bright square of wallpaper where the oil painting used to hang.

"Hannah, what happened to the painting?" he asked when she came in with his egg.

"Mrs. Ryegate said she didn't want it there any more. She said she never liked it."

"Mrs. Ryegate is very tenderhearted; she doesn't like the thought of someone shooting a duck," he said for Hannah's benefit, and added, "She saw too much cruelty in the Wilderness." If Harriet had only known that the painting reminded him frequently that the bird of his vision had been only a duck, she might have left it hanging. He ate hurriedly and left the house without trying to see her.

Even though he could use the time for his sermon, Mark stopped at Sydney's before he went on to the church. He had to be sure that the boy was safely on his way north.

Robert, who ran Sydney's house, opened the door and announced that Mr. Hall was still sleeping.

"I'm on my way to church, but I want to see Mr. Hall, so I think I'll go up and wake him. I'm sure he won't mind, Robert," Mark said, hardly hearing Robert's murmuring that Mr. Hall had left word not to be disturbed. Sydney must have taken the boy across town before daylight, without Robert's knowing it, and come back to bed again.

Mark tapped on the door. So he had stood outside Harriet's door. Sydney's voice sounded sleepy. Mark turned the knob and went in.

The curtains were drawn and only a bar of light reached across the large, high-footed bed, but it struck a bare, boyish shoulder, dark against the white sheet, and a round black head deep in the pillow. Sydney sat up, pulling the covers around himself, reaching at the same time for his dressing gown on the chair beside him.

"Mark! This *is* an early pastoral call. Were you afraid I wouldn't get your boy to the agent? O ye of little faith!" His tone was truculent, amused—defiant. Mark felt such a rush of amazement and rage he was slow in speaking.

"As a matter of fact, I decided to take Joel on up to Canada myself," Sydney said coolly, smiling at Mark. "Then I can make sure there will be no slip."

Mark moved his steady gaze from Sydney. "Joel!" He went over and put his hand on the boy, taking care not to touch the smooth bare shoulder.

Sydney was out of bed, pulling the sash of his dressing gown tightly around him. "Got to cover up the 'unaccommodated man,' " he said dryly. "Look, Mark! There's no sense in this. Joel's perfectly safe here with me; nobody knows he's here. We're going to have breakfast, and I think I can fit him out in some clothes I had as a boy. Nothing is ever discarded in this house. . . ."

The boy was sitting up, wide-eyed. When he saw Mark, he smiled, but his eyes slid away from the sternness in Mark's.

"Joel, get your things on. We have to go at once."

Sydney's face flushed with anger. "Mark, I told you I'd take care of him. Why don't you go along and preach your sermon? I won't be there, so maybe you can make a sermon out of this. But I doubt if you could understand. You're so wrapped up in your preaching, there's a good deal you don't comprehend."

But the boy was scrambling into his clothes, his back turned toward the men.

"Wash your face, Joel, and we'll go," Mark said.

"Don't be a fool, Mark! Joel was half starved last night. He needs a decent breakfast before he goes anywhere. I've planned it all out so there'll be no danger. He's no ordinary slave boy, I've discovered that. He's been taught to read and write, quite well, really. And he's quick to understand," Sydney said while Joel was out of the room.

Every word Sydney said increased Mark's rage. He turned on Sydney. "You told me once that I could count on you. Now I'll have to run the risk of taking the boy over there in daylight."

"Mark, you're so sure of—" Sydney broke off as Joel came back in the coat that was too big and the new boots that were too loose around his thin ankles. "For God's sake, let me give him some decent shoes!"

As though that were the only thing he cared about, Sydney rushed across to a closet and hunted among his shoes.

"Here, Joel boy, sit down and let me try this pair." He knelt on the floor and put on socks of his own and then a shoe of English make that came much closer to fitting.

Mark stood by the door, watching Sydney on his knees and the boy looking down at the shoes.

"There you are. That's more like it." Sydney went over to the chest of drawers, where his watch and chain and money lay spread out, and sweeping up a small heap of the coins he gave them to Joel. "Tuck it away where it's safe."

Mark started to protest that he wouldn't need it. "It's not thirty pieces, Parson!" Sydney sneered. "Of course, you know you couldn't be more conspicuous walking across town with him! I planned to take him in the buggy ten miles north and then—"

"All right, Joel," Mark said. "We'll go."

"Good-bye, Mas'r. Thankya kindly," the boy said, looking back at Sydney, and Mark realized that Joel hadn't spoken a word until then. Mark looked away when Sydney laid his arm around Joel's shoulder.

"Good-bye, Joel. You don't need to call me Master; you can save that for the Reverend, here."

Sydney went downstairs ahead of them and opened the front door. "You're a damn fool to do this, Mark," he murmured.

"I'll manage," Mark said as they stepped out into the bright light. The door closed behind them. It was taking a chance, but he wouldn't leave him with Sydney. For just a minute he thought of taking him to church, but almost instantly decided against it.

"Joel, we've got to hurry for me to get you across town and then get back in time to preach. Can you walk fast?"

"Yessa," the boy said.

"You may have to wait a bit before you get any breakfast. Do you think you can stand it?"

"Yessa. Me an' Mas'r . . . Mistah Sydney, we ate real good fixin's las' night." As he looked up, his bright eyes in his light-brown face reminded Mark sharply of Eenisskim's.

◇ ◇ ◇

I quite understand your going out to Kansas, Mark.

I was afraid you would feel it was foolhardy. But it's the place where the issue of the freedom of the human soul is being fought out.

If you're working for the movement, of course, you want to be in the thick of it. I was interested, by the way, in a remark of Wendell Phillips' that I saw you had underlined in that article you left on the study table. "If we never free a slave, we have at least freed ourselves in our effort"—wasn't that it?

It's hardly fair to take the sentence out of context. "From the blindness of American prejudice, the most cruel the sun looks on; from the narrowness of sect; from parties, from quibbling over words; we have been redeemed into full manhood . . . taught to consecrate life to something worth living for!"

You committed it to memory! I had thought your life was consecrated.

They need men out there desperately, and since the Church has decided on its candidate, I feel I should go.

Of course. You can hardly lounge around the Fort.

You must write me what you think of the new minister. I'll be curious.

I imagine you'll be moving around, so that letters will be hard to get.

Not that hard. You must write me, Harriet!

My letters will make such interesting reading: Marcia has gained. I believe her eyes are going to resemble yours. It has been warm today. Oh, yes, I trust that you are meeting with success in your chosen field.

I will be eager to read anything you write. I am concerned about your being alone so much, Harriet. I realize what I am asking. . . .

So much so that you volunteered to go off to Kansas, but, of course, it's the next thing to the Wilderness you could find. There is no need to worry about me. I shall keep busy.

What will you do?

What will I do? This is the way our courtship began, do you remember? Oh, I shall read and enlarge my mind, I said. And now I have Marcia.

I believe you said "understanding." And I said what will you read? Will it be Lord Byron this time?

No. I think neither Byron nor Donne. I've lost my taste for love poetry. Perhaps I shall go in and select some of your sermons to read to see if your voice comes through them. It will be interesting.

You can find better reading than that.

How modest you are! Sydney Hall reported the speech you gave in Boston and said it was the best of them all. But, of course, that was hardly a sermon.

I'm not interested in what Sydney Hall thinks. That unfaded square of wallpaper looks bad; why don't you hang the painting back there?

I thought I might try to find a gold eagle to put in its place. It would be so patriotic.

If you'll excuse me, Harriet, I must look over my sermon for this evening.

◇ ◇ ◇

Chapter Twenty

Sunday Afternoon.
July 16th.

I have just come up from dinner with Mark. I would not have believed that Mark and I could ever talk to each other as we did. We said nothing, really. I was horrid, but I couldn't help it if I was to get through the meal without bursting into tears. Mark protested that he wanted to hear from me, that he was concerned about my being alone so much, but really he is eager to be off to another Wilderness, and, of course, he is convinced that he is called of God, consecrating his life "to something worth living for." Marcia and I can get along as best we can. Once I was awed by his dedication, but now I see that it is his need to be caught up in some cause.

I should have gone to Church; this was Mark's last sermon at Calvary. But I couldn't trust myself to sit in the pew and listen to him, and remember how I loved to hear him. Instead, I sat on the porch with Marcia and tried to separate myself from Mark and be the person I was before . . . everything, before I knew Mark or ever went to the Wilderness.

Mark waited until all the services of the Sabbath were over, and the half-embarrassed handshakes at the end, the curious glances, the stiff murmured regrets, too mumbled to be articulate, and the God bless yous, before he took leave of his study back of the platform. On his desk was the familiar envelope in which the Church treasurer always sent him his salary, but he let it lie there for now.

He had never written his sermons here; the library at home had become his real study; but he had talked here with the people of his Church. They had told him their troubles and doubts; surely he had been of use to a few. He had sat here before the service always, praying that the words of his mouth and the meditations of his heart be acceptable unto God. He had prayed that before his Easter Sunday sermon.

There were only a few possessions that he wanted to take with him. On the window sill was the old clock he had got to working, a seven-day clock, so he had to wind it every Sunday. The bland face with the crowded Roman numerals seemed to know too many of his thoughts and moods to leave behind.

And he wanted the piece of granite he had found as a boy on Ascutney Mountain and wondered at the intricately fluted shell imprinted on its surface. It always made him think of God's questions to Job: "Where wast thou when I laid the foundations of the earth? . . . Hast thou entered into the springs of the sea? or hast thou walked in search of the depth?"

He repeated them aloud, letting them take him beyond this room and the business of leaving. Nothing gave him more sense of the mystery of creation. He held the rock in his hand a moment before he wrapped it in his handkerchief, so it wouldn't mar the clock, and put both in the valise he had brought.

And there was the Book of Common Prayer his strict Baptist deacons would have wondered at; he wanted that. The volumes of sermons he had bought in the seminary could stay there for his successors. Had he known intuitively that his tenure here wouldn't be long and so had never really moved into this room? Then he remembered his baptismal boots and got them out of the cupboard. It might be muddy in Kansas.

He took up the white envelope and started to put it in his pocket, but he saw it contained a letter along with his stipend, a rather long letter. He sat down at his desk to read it. Was it only last night that he had come home to find the letter from Harriet?

Reverend Marcus Ryegate
Calvary Baptist Church

Dear Reverend Ryegate:

Enclosed you will find the remuneration for your services on the dates listed below. As you will see, this is less than your usual rate of payment, but seems correct as you have spent so much time away between Sabbaths, as well as on several Sabbaths, and your pastoral calls and labors in consequence have been less.

It is with regret that we terminate the connection with Calvary Baptist Church of one who came with such brilliant promise, and in whom we placed such hope. We are not unmindful that the success of the Revival Meeting this spring was the greatest ever experienced in the history of this Church. This gives us reason for hoping that you will return to the pulpit in another ministry and perform a great work.

Furthermore, it is the feeling of the Deacons of this Church that your experience in the Wilderness unsettled you for a time, but your sermons of the last few months lead them to hope that you are moving back to a firmer hold on orthodox religion, and that the unfortunate circumstance of your leaving this your first pastorate has opened your eyes to the danger of that tendency to use sensational, not to say objectionable, material in your sermons.

The prayers of the below named Deacons for your further growth in the Lord go with you.

He noted that all the deacons had signed their names; it must have been a struggle for Goddard and Slocum. He was glad of the money for Harriet, now particularly. He himself wouldn't need much or any on the Kansas trip. Beyond that, he felt empty of emotion.

Mark walked slowly up the street, in no hurry to get home. This was the last time he would walk back from preaching at Calvary. It was finished and over with—his first pastorate. A minister built his reputation with his pastorates, piling them up like blocks, or he made a solid edifice out of one. Well, the rumors of his difficulties at Calvary wouldn't help him any, but they didn't worry him. He had none of the heavy sense of failure he had had as he went down the river in that boat, with Aapaaki running along the shore.

He had let himself go tonight; reached past those faces to the beings inside. He hadn't written an evening sermon—he had spoken the words that came to him. "There must be no rancour between us," he had said, "only a deeper understanding of ourselves and each other." He hardly remembered now what he had said, but it was no act. Perhaps it wasn't anything he had said, just that he was leaving and some of them felt regret, even a little uncertainty, about their asking him to leave. At any rate, they had listened. That was the way it was with preaching, sometimes; something went out from those who listened and charged the most ordinary words, drew words from him that he hadn't written or thought of before. Tonight, at least, he had talked to his people, and they had heard.

Now I must go in and try to talk to Harriet. But will she hear me? Our talk at dinner was a travesty.

What can I say to her except that I love her? And she will say I don't know what the word means.

Nor do I know what she means by "obsessed" or "bewitched," either. How can she be so wildly jealous of an Indian woman who would not even speak to me? Harriet has too much sense. I've always felt her wisdom until now.

Of course, I will never get Eenisskim out of my memory; neither of us will. She was the source of my vision. That fades farther and farther away from me, so that I can hardly believe in it—but she's mixed with my failure out there, too, because I could never reach her. Doesn't Harriet remember all that? She lived through it all with me. I came back to her from those terrible nights on the mountain with Eenisskim, and she took care of me, seeming to understand how I felt. Now she imagines all kinds of things.

Sydney's house is dark. He must have gone away. Did he go because he didn't want to face me? I remember many things now, impressions that merely brushed across my self-centered—once I might have said God-centered—consciousness as an excuse! The night he wanted me to come in after the revival meeting I felt the urgency in his voice, even his loneliness. I knew he wanted to talk, but I went on, bemused with the thought of all men's need to talk, to speak out of their solitude—forming phrases for a sermon! If I had gone back I might have known him better. And that remark of his about my not understanding the ramifications of love—wasn't that the way he put it? Then I took Joel to him.

"You can make a sermon out of this, Parson," Sydney had said, in that sarcastic tone he could use. To myself, for myself. That I am a self-absorbed, blind fool.

That's what Harriet thinks. She sees my joining the movement and going to Kansas as a cause to lose myself in. A lure. A cause and a lure are worlds apart. Is there anything wrong with a cause? How can any Christian minister not be stirred by the need to put down slavery? Not want to throw his whole strength and all his powers into the work? Nothing has ever seemed more vital to me.

Harriet keeps saying I've deceived myself, as she thinks—as I did—about my call to the mission field. But she is wrong. And the experience out there wasn't lost.

Nothing could keep me now from this work. I might not have agreed so readily to go out to the Territory if Reverend May—Brother May, as they say in the Anti-Slavery Society—had asked me before Harriet's outburst and her letter saying she wanted to live her life quite separately; but I would have gone. When May told me how hard it is to get enough ministers to go into the Territory, I couldn't refuse. And I am eager to go; that's the crucial point just now in the whole struggle.

But I wonder if it is a mistake to leave Harriet alone so much? Her state of mind worries me. I shall have to get back frequently, though that may not be possible. But things in Kansas will come to a head. Maybe it is better for us to be apart for a while. Yet I hate to leave her.

As he opened the front door, Harriet called to him from the stairs. "You look as though you were already on your way with that valise!"

She meant . . . But her voice was warm and natural. She was smiling down at him. Some tightness he hadn't known was there went out of his shoulders and his chest, and he let out his breath.

"Just some things from my study," was all he could say, but he was looking up at her, smiling, too. She stood on the landing of the stairs with Marcia in her arms, caught by the light from the hall above and the hanging lamp below so that her hair was bright but shadows crept up her face, touching it with sadness.

"I'd just fed Marcia when I heard you come, and I thought you would want to see her," Harriet said.

Mark dropped his bag and ran up the stairs to take her from Harriet. "I do. Thank you." He was almost afraid to say too much, for fear of spoiling this moment. As she gave the baby to him, he was more aware of Harriet's hands than the liveliness of the child in his arms. Harriet went ahead of him up the stairs.

"You've had your last service at Calvary!"

"Yes." He fished the letter from the deacons out of his pocket and handed it to her. "It makes interesting reading. At least there's some money for you, so I can feel I'm contributing to the support of my wife and child. But you notice I'm carefully docked—it's precious little."

"How small of them," Harriet said as she read it. "The letter is horrid."

"It doesn't matter. They mean well, you know," he said, pleased by her indignant tone.

But when they came back from the baby's room into what had become Harriet's, she said abruptly, "I wonder if you will ever take another church."

"Why do you wonder that? Do you think I shouldn't?"

"I don't know. I'm not sure."

"I feel that this is a more real ministry I am entering upon than accepting a call to any church would be just now."

"Entering upon" had too public a sound when he was talking to her; she minded it.

"Of course, you have convinced yourself of that just as you did about the Wilderness. That's the way you are." Harriet stood in front of her dresser with her back to him. He sat down on the edge of the bed, behind her, but he could see her face in the mirror. It was resentful. They were back where they had been before.

"Harriet, when all the faith and understanding between two people have gone, there is no use trying to talk with each other. They live in a wilderness of their own making. For us the wilderness has shrunk to the space of this house—even smaller than that, to ourselves."

Harriet was taking the pins out of her hair. She glanced at him in the mirror only briefly and tossed her head so her hair came down her back. "It will be a relief, then, for you to leave this wilderness."

"For you to have me gone, too."

She turned swiftly to face him. "I never said that. Do you think I'm going to enjoy being here alone with a helpless child, and people feeling sorry for me; feeling sorry for myself and loathing myself. You don't have to go. You want to. You can't wait to go!"

He started to retort, to take hold of her and make her listen to him. But what was the use? He had tried that the other night. Instead, he said simply, "Don't let us go on like this the last night before I leave. I am sick of words, too. For this night, come to bed with me, Harriet."

*

But how much does it mean? Harriet thought, lying silent and apart in the wide mahogany bed. Why did I agree so easily? I might have been an Indian squaw, I gave myself so readily.

Our bodies have more wisdom than our minds, Mark thought, or our words. She must feel my love for her. Beyond any doubt. And she loves me, but she won't trust her love. She has set herself to believe those things she has imagined. And she resents my going so far away.

Could Mark be like this and care so much about Eenisskim? But maybe he is thinking of her all the time I am in his arms. No. I won't believe that. But neither is he wholly mine. He is glad he is going away.

This morning, I could have dragged Sydney out of bed and beaten him. Now I blame myself. I wonder about poor Joel.

Mark turned back toward Harriet and laid his arm gently over her. She didn't move away. But neither spoke aloud. And after a while they slept.

Chapter Twenty-one

MARK left early this morning. Just at the end, when he stood by the cab, looking back at me, I think it was hard for him to go, but, of course, he has gone just the same. He is intent on what he is going to do; he doesn't think what it is like for me here. I mind it more than when he went away to the Wilderness. Then I didn't understand his "Call." I thought it was beyond me to fathom, nor did I question it. We had been married so short a time, and we hadn't lived together so closely and been one flesh, as the Bible says, so utterly; more than one flesh, one soul. But now I understand this need of Mark's to go off and fight for freedom; it is partly for himself. He must always be caught up in some great Cause, and he must have need for his power to move people by his eloquence. Eenisskim made him feel that he was a failure, and he is driven to prove himself in an odd way that he doesn't understand, but I do.

Marriage does terrible things to you. If you are separated, you are nothing out in the emptiness of the prairie, and there is no place to go but back in your memory; your love is like a burden on your back. Mark said that the Wilderness has shrunk to ourselves. What a terrible thing to say or to think! But I feel I am wandering in that Wilderness now.

Last night we lay together, almost the way we used to

211

back at the Fort, but Mark was so silent, and I couldn't speak until he did. He didn't call me one endearing name, or ever say he loved me, but his hands seemed to speak and his lips—not just on my lips. And once I woke to find his arm over me.

But when he came to go, all my anger and desolation at his going came up in me and I felt myself stiff and solemn and plain, but I couldn't stand it any other way, and I wouldn't cry.

August 10th.

I can't sleep so I shall resort to this Journal again, though I haven't had any desire to write in it since the day Mark left.

The Woollett *Republican* is full of terrible reports of continued violence and bloodshed in Kansas.

One sentence bothers me especially: "The advocates of slavery seem to have resolved that if they cannot intimidate a speaker the bludgeon can be made to accomplish what fair argument could not effect." And Mark would be sure to inflame them; he would never think of his own safety, just get carried away preaching for freedom for the slaves, fighting, really. He says the Church must fight for freedom for all men if it's going to stay alive. Mr. Goddard told me Sunday that he hoped Mark would get over his tendency to exaggerate issues. But Mark will always feel strongly about things.

I have had only two letters from him, scribbled hurriedly with a pencil. In one he wrote, "Believe me, Harriet, I am not using this struggle; it is using me." That was because of what I said. "This is where I should be as a minister of God." But he only signs his name. He does not write "love."

Nor do I. The word seems spoiled for us. I write a letter and then cross out half of it and rewrite it, testing every word, thinking how he will take it. There is so much that I don't tell him. I didn't say I dreamed of Eenisskim again the other night. I feel we can never get free of her, even though we will never see her again. And I don't tell Mark that I miss him, but I told him that when he comes back we will sell this house. He must know that I will go wherever he feels "called" to go.

And I didn't tell him that I hung the painting of the dead duck back on the dining-room wall. Hannah told me he explained to her that I had taken it down because I was so tenderhearted I didn't like to think of killing anything, that I saw too much cruelty in the Wilderness. He said that after what I said about Eenisskim.

I signed my last letter "your faithful wife." I suppose that will mean that I am morally faithful; he will not think that means as much as a wife who does not doubt her husband's love. Faith and faithful seem to be two different things.

August 11th.

Slowly I am beginning to find myself. Mark was too strong a temperament for me, and I lost my own way of thinking and being. I have ordered my life and I spend long afternoons out on the porch reading, with Marcia asleep beside me.

Mark was so moody and so intense it was exhausting living with him. I am thankful to have a chance to be tranquil and serene. (Lovely words that could never be used to describe Mark!) It seems to me that I have not felt this way since I left for the trip to the Wilderness—since I married Mark, really.

August 16th.

This afternoon, I wheeled Marcia way out beyond the last house in Woollett, until we came to open farm land. I left the perambulator by the stone wall and carried Marcia across the meadow. It would be much easier to carry her on my back. When I came to the far edge, so far from the road nobody could see me, I laid her on the ground on a blanket and took off her long dress and petticoats so she could move her legs in the sun the way the Indian babies do. Child of the Wilderness, I told her she was, but I wasn't using the word the way Mark did.

I lay down myself on the hard grassy ground and watched the clouds. When I rolled over and tickled Marcia with the ferny end of a blade of grass, she laughed so clearly I laughed, too, and wished Mark could hear her.

I nursed her there in the meadow with the sun warm on my naked breasts. Way off below me I watched a load of hay go by on the road, and then a buggy. I could just see the parasol of the pram sticking up over the stone wall. It looked so silly and civilized, and I felt very far away from civilization.

And then, for no reason at all, I was crying for Mark. I didn't cry when he left, or at any other time until then. I miss the way Mark could snatch me up out of my seriousness with his teasing, or quote me a poem, or burst out of the study excited over some new idea for a sermon. I feel dull left to myself and have no desire to "enlarge my mind." I would have given anything to be sitting in Church just to hear his voice.

By the time I pushed the pram all the way back to Elm Street I was tired.

Chapter Twenty-two

THE rawhide ropes pulled at the soft flesh of his throat. The old medicine man had cut the gashes too high. Should have been on his breast, where Two Knives' had been. Two Knives had shown him his scars. Now the ropes were tied to the pole of the medicine lodge. His feet seemed rooted to the ground. The din grew louder.

Round and round . . . in spite of the pain. He was dizzy from dancing but he mustn't stop. Round and round. He was going to fall. If he hit the earth hard enough, the flesh would tear free. The ropes jerked. He tried to get his hands up to tear them out—even if it killed him—but his hands were tied.

He tried to pray, but no sound came. His throat . . . He couldn't stand any more. Sun in Heaven . . . No, God in the Sun . . . CRISTICOOM, let this cup pass from me!

His throat caught in a knot, and the pain drew a groan out of him that tore his breast apart.

No passing the cup. Must hold on till the flesh lets you free.

Round and round . . . everything was whirling with him. Let me be caught up on eagle wings, borne up, up. . . .

Someone threw water at him and he could feel it running out of the corners of his mouth, down over his chin. Mark opened his eyes and stared at the face bending over him, the bearded face of a white man. His eyes moved above the man's head to the pole of a tent.

"You've come to. You were in a kind of delirium, but you

couldn't talk. We had to tie you to the cot. You're in the hospital tent we had to rig up, there were so many injured."

Mark stared at the man without understanding what he was saying.

"I think we can untie you now; got you all reefed up here so you wouldn't throw yourself off the cot, you were thrashing around so hard."

Mark lifted his hand up where the pain was and felt the ropes still wrapped around his neck. He tried to move his head, but it began to whirl again.

"Do you remember you were preaching and the Missouri bushwhackers broke up the meeting? They got a rope around your neck and dragged you out of the hall and down the middle of the street, if you can call it a street. Don't know why you weren't choked to death or trampled to death. Somebody said you fought and yelled at 'em all the way till you lost consciousness. Late yesterday afternoon, the storekeeper found you dumped back of his store and dragged you out for dead; scared him out of a year's growth when he found you were alive."

The man was doing things, pulling the thongs tighter. Mark opened his mouth, trying to ease the pain.

"More water? I'll just trickle it in. Your mouth must taste like a last-year's bird nest. Smells like it. Pretty damn sore!"

Mark was beginning to remember. His eyes sought the tent pole. He was fastened to that pole by the ropes tied to the skin of his throat, and he was dancing . . .

The water dribbled from the dipper into his mouth. He jerked his head away; it hurt too much to swallow.

"Just let it lie on your tongue."

The water felt cool on his lips and tongue, running down his chin.

"That rope burned through your skin, so you'll have a hell of a scar the rest of your days, but you're lucky to be alive."

Mark's eyes rested anxiously on the doctor's face. Had the

flesh given way? It had or he wouldn't be here, unless they cut him free because he passed out. That was what they had done—so he had failed. Two Knives. He wanted Two Knives, not this white man.

The white man was giving him something on his tongue. Bitter taste. Sometimes they gave them sage to chew, Two Knives said.

Talk came to him from far away, but he couldn't make out anything. "That'll give him some relief anyway, but he's only half conscious; didn't seem to take in anything I said. I don't know whether he'll ever speak in a normal voice again or not. Too early to tell."

"That would be a terrible thing for a preacher like him."

Preacher-like-him, that wasn't his name. Short-coat, that was it. Black Robe and Short-coat. And the Black Robe loved . . . He slid down into the comfort of the buffalo robe.

By the time Mark could walk to the post office in the town, he found that people on the street seemed to know him, even came up to speak to him. He was conspicuous enough with his neck bandaged and the bruises on his face; his head was still bandaged, too. He hadn't been able to get anything down his throat but gruel, so he was skin and bones. Brother Wolcott had asked him to sit on the platform of the rally last night even though he couldn't speak, and some of these people must have seen him there. Wolcott had turned to him and said all that stuff about the slavers discovering it was as hard to kill Brother Ryegate as it was to kill the power of freedom in the Territory. Mark winced as he remembered Wolcott yelling out, "Stand up, Brother Ryegate! You've become a symbol of invincibility!" and all the crowd stamping and cheering.

He was getting tired of not being able to talk out loud; getting worried. He kept trying, but his voice came out in a hoarse whisper. "Give it time," the doctor kept saying. "You just can't tell yet. Do you good to keep mum for a while. And you better get out of this hellhole, if you'll pardon my language, Parson, and get back home, where you'll have proper care and rest."

He was going; no use in sticking around here if he couldn't use his voice. He didn't think he'd write Harriet about it; no need to worry her. When he remembered the night he'd made a fool of himself raving to her about having to feel his own eloquence and power, the irony of his present state gagged him. He began to wonder if this was a judgment on him, but he moved his mind away from that idea. He'd served the Lord with his voice, tried to, at least, and he'd fought the pride he had in his eloquence, if it was ever eloquence, hadn't he? But what would it be like to live if he could never talk in more than a rasping croak? It would only be half living.

He could write, perhaps. Harriet had said she was going to read his sermons and see if she could hear his voice in them, but she had said it to mock him. Writing could never be like seeing the effect of what you said on the person in front of you; speaking to what you saw in that person's face, many faces; feeling something grow between you.

The postmaster came out from behind his desk to greet him. "Damned Missouri pukes thought they'd killed you, Parson, but by God, they got another think coming!"

There was a thick packet of mail from Harriet that had been there five days. "May I sit down someplace and read my mail here?" he asked the postmaster, hating the way his voice came out in a whisper. "Little tired," he added, grateful for the chair that the postmaster gave him in the back at his own desk.

He undid the packet and found two letters enclosed with one from Harriet. One was from Sydney, postmarked Montreal. He held it a moment, then put it aside to read later. The other, from Illinois, was addressed in a careless flowing hand to Reverend and Mrs. Marcus Ryegate. And in the upper left-hand corner, "Mr. Ephraim Phillips, Esq., Forestdale, Brighton, Illinois." It took him a second to realize that Mr. Ephraim Phillips, Esq., was the Major.

He read Harriet's first.

My dear Mark:

You will be as amazed as was I to read this letter from Major Phillips. How embarrassing it must be for them, with grown children to attend their wedding. But I think more of them for wishing to have their marriage sanctified by a Christian ceremony even at this late date. (Perhaps you made more of an impression on Mrs. Phillips than you thought, since the Major says she is "particularly desirous" that you should perform the ceremony.) I took pains to mention their coming marriage to Deacon Slocum when I saw him—oh, quite in passing—as the fruit of your influence on her.

I am sure you must be gratified and would not think of failing to comply with their request, even though it means interrupting your labors for Freedom. I have been looking at a map and find you are not so far from Illinois as I, but notwithstanding the distance, I also shall attend the ceremony, since we are both invited. (This I mentioned to Isabelle Cavendish. I really wanted to say that I was to be matron of honor!) It will be a considerable trip, but I have had experience before in travelling by myself to the Wilderness, you will remember. You note that the Major says they have made a small Wilderness for themselves there!

Marcia laughs and sits propped up against pillows now. I wish you could see her, and especially hear her.

I attended Church last Sunday, but my mind seems to have stayed at home, for I cannot remember what Reverend Wiley preached about. I met him at the welcoming reception, which I felt I should attend. He is middle-aged and kindly, somewhat unctuous. He spoke of my "dear husband" as one of those he calls "the warrior ministers of God." I refrained from saying that you were now on a war raid.

I trust you are well and not spending yourself too recklessly in the battle. Dispatches in the Woollett *Republican* call the situation outright war, which gives me great concern. Please be careful.

If all goes well, then, I shall arrive at "Forestdale" the morning of the wedding, and have written Mrs. Phillips and the Major to that effect, telling them that I feel confident you will be there.

> Your faithful wife,
> Harriet

Amazed! He was dumbfounded. He could understand that the Major would want to be legally married now that they were living in civilization, but that they should ask him to come out to perform the ceremony both touched and surprised him.

He went back to find Harriet's words: "Perhaps you made more of an impression on Mrs. Phillips than you thought." How did she mean that? Her tone all through the letter nettled him. Was she being humorous? "I took pains to mention their coming marriage to Deacon Slocum . . . oh, quite in passing—as the fruit of your influence." And that remark about Isabelle Cavendish. The slyest kind of humor, her eyes sparkling wickedly as she wrote.

But she was being neither humorous nor light in that remark about the Wilderness. She meant him to remember his saying that last night that they lived in a wilderness of their own making. And "your faithful wife" again. He wished she had said "loving."

"Marcia laughs . . ." was the only clear and simple sentence in the whole letter. "I wish you could see her," she had said, too.

Why would Harriet want to go way out there to see the Major and Mrs. Phillips married? "I have had experience before in travelling by myself to the Wilderness . . ." She meant —she could mean all manner of things. Was it that she didn't want him to be there without her? How could she want to see Eenisskim when she felt as she did about her?

He had never expected to see Eenisskim again. As though his mind had been held from thinking of her and now was let free, her face came before him—laughing as she held the duck over him; asleep on the pile of robes on the boat; riding bareback in the buffalo hunt, her hair streaming out behind. . . . Eagerness stirred in him.

Eenisskim would speak to him this time. Very slowly he would repeat the words of the ceremony and she would say each word of her vow after him. He wanted to hear her speak

English words, words he could understand; to have her answer him.

He had forgotten that he couldn't raise his voice above a whisper. But that was no matter, and no matter, either, that it still hurt him to say more than two sentences at a time. He would marry them even in his husky rasping whisper.

He opened the Major's letter.

My dear Reverend and Mrs. Ryegate:

Mrs. Phillips and I came to the States on the first boat down-river, leaving the Upper Missouri the last day of June, and are now pretty well established in our new home. We have named the latter "Forestdale," since we have a forest of three hundred acres, stocked with wildlife from the plains. We already have deer, antelope, and elk, and a pair of buffalo are expected. We have also plenty of range land for some of the finest horses money can buy. But I trust that you will be viewing Forestdale with your own eyes and see that we have made for ourselves a small Wilderness on the edge of civilization.

But to come to the point of this communication: now that we have retired from the Fur Trade and are taking our place in society, it seems advisable that Mrs. Phillips and I be united in Holy Matrimony by a Christian ceremony. The children are of an age when this is important for them, as well. Mrs. Phillips is especially desirous that you, Reverend, should perform the ceremony. It would please me also.

I am aware of the long and expensive journey involved but will appreciate your effort if you feel that you can undertake this mission, and I shall consider it a privilege to cover the expenses for both of you in the honorarium.

I write in haste to catch the mails.

Hoping to hear from you in the affirmative,

Sincerely yours,
Ephraim Phillips, Esq.

He could see the Major! Now that he had wrested a fortune from the Wilderness, he would become a commanding figure in society. Neither an Indian wife nor an Indian marriage would be any hindrance at all. Eenisskim might even be a help. As Mrs. Ephraim Phillips she should make quite a stir with her beauty and grace. When she presided at the table in the Fort she had been proper and civilized enough for any place, but even then she had always worn braids and moccasins with her dress. He saw her in his mind most often in elkskin dress. Now she would have to speak English as well as understand it. He marvelled again that she wanted him to marry them; it meant a great deal to him, and to see her again when he could talk with her.

Reluctantly, Mark picked up the letter from Sydney.

My dear Mark:

I got off too fast to try to see you. Just as well, perhaps, knowing all you think and your obvious outrage and disgust. You want to watch that, Mark, if you're going to love your fellow man—with Christian love, of course. I had thought your "Journey into Strangeness" had taken you beyond Woollett views.

I followed your boy to Canada on the same train; then I persuaded the agent who met him there to let me take him. Had the devil of a time at first, but Joel's relief and gladness at the thought of going with me helped.

I am going to put Joel with friends here in Montreal, if possible; in good hands, anyway, and I've already found a Jesuit priest as a tutor for him until he can enter a proper school. I'm convinced that he can do it. I shall hope to send him to England to finish his education.

As soon as I have all this arranged to my satisfaction, I shall return, although I hope to see him on his holidays. Educating him is my contribution to the cause you are now engaged in fighting for. When you get the slaves freed, I will have one educated to be a leader, perhaps.

Not, I hasten to add, that I am beyond all you thought, or that I don't find myself drawn to him—even as to you at times, much as that may shock and revolt you—but that night I took into my bed a boy who was scared out of his wits when I started to leave him in a big room by himself. I did not corrupt him. It would have advanced my tentative faith in Christianity and been rather less disillusioning if you could have delayed judgment, or, if indeed the worst you believed were true, if you had viewed even that with the compassion and understanding you preach.

Sincerely yours,

Sydney Remington Hall

Mark sat still so long in the back of the post office that the postmaster came to see if he was all right. The preacher was just sitting there with his face between his hands, so he went back out front without disturbing him. A man that was so near dead he was drug out to be buried, but come alive in the nick of time, had a look about him. He had a right to be let alone.

Part Four

THE WEDDING

Chapter Twenty-three

I N the yellow clapboard mansion with the elaborate jigsaw lace trimming its sharp gables, and the white pillars, too wide for the narrow porch at the top of the broad flight of steps, bottles of champagne chilled in a tub of ice in the pantry; a saddle of venison roasted noisily in the oven; duck simmered in wine sauce; and the tiered wedding cake awaited the first cut the bride would make with her husband's hunting knife.

Buzby, the young reporter from *The Star,* breathed in the fragrant smells and smiled at the lissome daughter of the house who opened the door.

"First, I'll show you the grounds!" she announced, fondling the black curls on her neck.

Buzby noted each astounding fact on his pad: the three hundred acres of wood lot and open land, yet only three miles from town, and stocked with deer, buffalo—buffalo, by God! —two antelope, two elk. . . . Quite like the Ark! A pond made from the river and filled with beaver, muskrat, otter . . . And all brought down-river from the western Wilderness! The Major, he gathered, had had men working on the place for several years, building the impenetrable fence of logs that resembled nothing so much as a stockade, but was scarcely visible in all that forest growth. Better not to go into too much detail about all this wildlife; the good people of Brighton would be up in arms.

Strangest of all, yet not so strange, considering, was the tipi made of skins, set beyond the wide lawn and safely hidden from both house and road. An honest-to-goodness Indian tipi!

"What's this, a kind of summerhouse?" Buzby had been tipped off that it wasn't the thing to stress the Indian race of the bride too heavily.

Mary hesitated. "You won't put it in the paper, will you?"

"Why, is it a secret?"

Mary smiled and shook her head. "Not exactly. You see, my mother is an Indian princess."

"Really!" the young man murmured, not bothering to write down this new piece of information.

"Oh, yes. Her father was a powerful chief whose lands extended for hundreds of miles. Of course, Mother lives like a white woman and she can understand French and English perfectly, but she doesn't care to speak them. . . ." Mary paused for breath.

"Saves a lot of trouble," the young man remarked.

"But sometimes she minds the heat here in summer, so she comes out and stays in this tipi."

"I shouldn't mind having one myself," Buzby said. "Tell me, do you come out here, too?"

Mary dropped her head back and laughed. "Gracious no! I don't like Indian things at all."

"Pity," the young man said.

Mary guided the reporter up the steps into the house. His eyes moved quickly from chandelier to flamboyant tapestry carpet, to the pier glass in the hall, and came to rest on the mural covering the north wall of the long parlor. He went up to it and gave a low whistle.

"That must have cost a pretty penny," he said finally.

"My father is fabulously wealthy," the ripe young thing by his side confided.

"How nice for you." He leaned a little closer and pinched her arm, but she giggled so hard he moved quickly along the wide hall. "And this room is the, er, library, I imagine?"

"Yes, but Reverend Ryegate's in there with my mother.

He's the minister who's come to marry them. He used to be a missionary at the Fort."

Buzby risked one more step in the direction of the library and caught a glimpse of a slender, black-haired woman in a red dress, sitting motionless in a straight wooden chair. The minister sat in front of her, leaning forward in close conversation. But that woman—the way she held her head, the still look of her face, and the warm color of her skin! He couldn't stop staring. The minister seemed to be waiting for her answer. He might have been a suitor, Buzby thought.

Mary pulled at his sleeve, and he turned reluctantly to follow her, hearing the minister speak in a whisper that carried his words out to the hall.

"In the Christian wedding service both husband and wife must repeat their own vows. Now . . ."

"You know," Mary told him, "poor Reverend Ryegate can't talk any louder than that. He got dragged by the neck in a fight in Kansas, when he was preaching against slavery, but, of course, he can marry them all the same."

"You betcha," Buzby agreed. "As tight in a whisper as in a shout." But he was still thinking about that woman. She was . . . God, she was something to look at!

"I'm going to be the bridesmaid and my brother's going to stand up with my father," Mary was saying.

Buzby had intended covering the story from this visit; he really had enough now, if he got the guest list and the details of the bride's gown. But he wanted to see that woman again, so he said, "And I'll be here to describe the wedding party! Till tonight, then, Miss Phillips." He bowed to Mary with exaggerated politeness, his hand on the silver doorknob. A racket like a whole pile of lumber falling just outside the door made him jerk it open in a hurry. He backed quickly out of the way, drawing Mary with him.

A horse reared up above the top step of the porch, his eyes rolling, his open jaws slavering on the bit. The boy riding him looked higher than the frame of the door.

"Raymond, you can't ride that horse in here!" Mary screamed, stamping her foot, but she had to jump back, for the horse and the rider kept coming, the horse's hoofs crossing the threshold with a skittering kind of trot, the boy lying close to the horse's back to get through the doorway. Once in, the boy rode over the tapestry flowers of the carpet, under the crystal chandelier, and up to the long mirror on the rear wall. He sat back heavily, let out an ear-splitting yell, and pulled up the horse's front legs so the hoofs rested on the low marble console beneath the mirror.

The woman must have heard the noise, because she came running out of the other room, followed by the minister.

"Mother, look what Raymond's done!" Mary shrieked.

But when the woman saw the horse steaming the mirror with his wet nose, she just clapped her hands and burst into laughter that seemed to ripple all through her till she bent over to her knees. Nobody Buzby had ever seen laughed like that. The minister's face was funny enough, too; he stood there thunderstruck.

The woman said some Indian words to the boy, waving him to get off.

"Ah, Ma, I'll lead her down," the kid begged, sitting tight.

The woman's eyes flashed, and she said something that sounded like an Indian swearword. Anyhow, it worked. The boy slid down off the horse, and the woman grabbed ahold of the horse's mane and sprang astride in a flash of her red skirt, too fast to see how she got there. Her moccasined feet rubbing down against the horse seemed to calm him, Buzby noticed. Nobody said a word.

As she wheeled the horse around, she reached up and set the crystal pendants on the chandelier clashing against each other, and laughed down at the minister. Then she pulled up the reins and rode straight for the door. She came so close, Buzby got a real look at her. Her eyes were enough to burn you, they were so bright, and she held that small polished head of hers as high as though she wore a checkrein. There was no quiet in her now, by glory!

When he saw what the woman was going to do, the minister rushed up and grabbed ahold of the horse's bridle, whispering in that raspy voice of his that she mustn't risk her life, but the horse kept sawing his head up and down and when the woman dug her moccasins into him he jerked his head so hard the minister had to let go or he'd have been scraped off against the door. The woman lay flat on the horse's neck, sort of off to one side, and they went through the doorway out onto the porch. Buzby thanked his lucky stars he was here; he wouldn't have missed this for all of P. T. Barnum's freak shows rolled into one.

But the horse balked at the steps and reared. For a second it seemed, from the hall, that he might take the whole flight of stairs at one flying jump; you could see him getting ready for it in the way his muscles quivered in his rump.

She was talking to him—at least Buzby saw her lips moving —and her hand was on his neck, and then she walked him along the porch, past the row of rocking chairs, as slow and calm as you please, but his hoofs hammered the boards in the stillness. Buzby and Mary and the boy crowded to the door along with the minister. Was she going to try it?

Buzby felt a hand on his shoulder and the minister was whispering. "Perhaps if we don't watch, it would be better. Perhaps she'll lead him down."

Buzby could see that was a good idea. The woman was showing off, all right; you could tell by the way she'd looked down at the minister when she set those pendants tinkling, and laughed. But Mary and her brother were already on the porch, and he didn't want to miss the show, either, so he stepped over the doorsill after them. Holy smackeroos! There was the Major driving his surrey through the gates! Maybe he could stop her.

She saw him all right. For a minute, she held the horse still, then she turned him away from the steps and walked him the length of the porch again, and Buzby thought she was going down the steps to the porte-cochere. The Major must have thought so, too, because he stopped his buggy in the drive so she'd have room, but she wheeled her horse around again and came back to the front steps. She was going to put on a real performance.

The Major was out of the surrey and charging up the walk. "Nisskim," he yelled. "Don't be a fool. The horse can't go down those steps. You'll break his neck and yours, too!"

The woman didn't look like she heard him; she just leaned down close to the horse's head, with one hand in his mane, talking to him.

"Nisskim, God damnit, do you want to kill yourself on your wedding day!"

The Major was halfway up the steps, reaching for the bridle, just like the preacher had, but the horse tossed his head and the Major's wife was holding the reins high and tight in her hand. She was going down! All the Major could do was to get out of the way.

There wasn't a sound but the horse's hoofs on the steps, the front ones kind of dainty and scared, one at a time, and the back hoofs dragged together afterward. The horse had his head down, and his rear stuck up so much higher, Buzby couldn't see the Major, but he could hear him saying, "Whoa boy, steady. You're coming, Nisskim." The minister stood right next to Buzby now, breathing hard.

"I believe she's going to make it!" the minister whispered. "Thank Heaven!"

The horse's black tail was hardly moving. The hoofs seemed to hesitate; the head lifted. A hideous animal squeal split the stillness. Buzby couldn't see at first what had happened, but he heard the horse come down the stairs with a crash of wood and a thud that shook the whole porch. He must have tried to jump the last step or . . .

"Caught his near hind foot in that damn foot scraper; front leg's broken," the Major snapped out.

Mrs. Phillips was all right. She'd slid off and over the railing of the steps onto the ground, but the horse lay there, kicking and trying to get up and falling back, squealing all the time. Mary threw herself on Buzby's shoulder weeping, and the boy let out a yell and began to beat his head against the pillar of the porch. The Major swore at him to shut up as he came past into the house, went right past his wife, too, who was standing there without a sign of any expression on her face.

The minister pushed out and went down the steps to her, but she stood there, looking at the horse, not saying a word.

Quicker than scat, the Major was back with a pistol. "Get out of the way, Nisskim, everybody!" He stood on the steps and killed the poor beast with one shot right through the head. Buzby felt sick, seeing the animal jerk, but he noticed Mrs. Phillips' face didn't move a muscle. She came up those steps with a rustle of silk and disappeared inside the house.

Buzby disengaged himself from Mary. "That was a darned shame," he murmured. He patted her shoulder and went quickly down to the driveway, stepping around the dead beast.

If that wasn't the goldarndest, wildest performance he'd ever seen in his life! But it might take away from the story of the wedding if he put it in the paper; might bring the Major down on the paper, too. And if he had all that gold stashed away in the cellar, and all the Fur Company stock people said, or even half as much, better not. The wedding ought to make a ripsnorter of a story by itself. As for that woman—she was a dazzler.

Chapter Twenty-four

WHY had she come? Harriet had asked herself all the
long way from Woollett, hanging the question on the dusty
lamps that swung a little from the ceiling of the jerking,
rumbling train; posed it to the red plush headrests, and the
passing farmhouses, and the country that was growing flatter
now. She had asked the question of the big bedroom of the
hotel where she had had to put up in Chicago, and again as
she tried not to look at the cuspidors that glittered in sickening array down the aisle of the train, from Chicago to this
place.

The aching weight of her breasts, bound tight underneath
her travelling suit, pressed the question, and her guilt at leaving Marcia twisted it in her mind.

"It would be better to take the baby with you, if you're
bound and determined to go," Hannah had said, "though it's
the foolishest notion I ever heard of, and I know the Reverend
won't approve of it!"

"But I couldn't carry her. I need one hand free," she had
answered, and known it sounded ridiculous, "to hang on to
railings—and then I'll have a bag, a heavy bag. Reverend
Ryegate doesn't have his best suit. . . ." She had had a feeling of needing to grasp, to hold.

Now that she was actually here at Brighton, Illinois, sitting
on the bench outside the station, her hands were folded in her
lap.

"The Major was down this morning," the station agent told

her. "But when the train didn't come in on time, and I couldn't rightly tell him how late it was going to be, he thought he ought to go back. Said he'd come again soon as he attended to a few things. I guess he has plenty on his mind." The agent grinned. "His wedding ain't but three hours away. A handsome-looking bridegroom he'll make, too! Yessir, a fine looking man he is, an' he's built hisself a mansion out there! Come back from the Wilderness with a fortune, I guess, an' goin' to settle down here with his bride and, uh, his children." The agent looked sharply at this proper young woman, waiting for her to give some sign that she knew about the Indian wife.

Had the Major come to meet the train alone? But she couldn't ask that. Instead, Harriet looked out across the low buildings of the town to the grassy open land, straw-colored in the hot afternoon sun beating down on it, like the land around the Fort, except that here there were more trees, and no faraway mountains. Grasshoppers jumped out of the dry grass here, too. Then she saw the heart-shaped, butter-yellow leaf on the boardwalk in front of the station, and went over to pick it up. Cottonwood, it was, like the few scraggly trees along the river; too big to be an aspen leaf.

Didn't Mark want to see her? Was that why he had let the Major come to meet her? He had never written to say whether he was coming to the wedding or not. What if he couldn't get away? But he would be here. Nothing would keep him from coming!

The agent watched her. "Yessir, made the town sit up and take notice, the Major and his wife did!" Then he gave up and went back into the station.

The air quivered in the heat above the shining tracks, or was it the heat quivering in the air? The quivering, blurring movement made her feel unreal. If the train had been much later, if she had missed the train in Chicago, she would have been too late for the wedding. But it wasn't really the wedding she had come for, or not just the wedding.

Now she must answer her question, before anyone came to

meet her; before she saw Mark. She must say it plainly to herself. I came to see Eenisskim, and I shall call her Eenisskim once, to her face. I want to find out that I don't hate her, that I am not even jealous of her, so I can live with myself again. I want to see Mark with her and know he is free from her. If he loved her only with Christian love, her being married in a Christian ceremony ought to satisfy him. But she had always known that wasn't it.

The curiosity of the station agent brought him back out to stand in the doorway, picking his teeth with a quill pick.

"You know the Major and his, er, wife a long time?"

"Yes, quite a while." But she hadn't really; why did she say that?

"I guess he was quite a figger in the fur trade up-river! Well, that's the place to make money, if you can keep your scalp on your head. I guess he earned his money. I wouldn't want to go off up in the Wilderness, myself. Pretty dangerous."

"Yes. Yes, it is. I mean, I imagine it must be."

"Course his wife musta been a help."

"Yes. I'm sure she was." Harriet took off her gloves and wiped her hot face. The station agent observed her carefully. A real refined-lookin' woman. Must be friends of the Major before he went west.

"You could step inside, but it ain't any cooler. This has been an awful hot September in Illinois. But I've got a fan. I'll go get it." He brought out a battered palm-leaf fan and gave it to her. "Passenger left it one time."

"Thank you." The fan made a sound like the leaves of the aspens down by the tipis as she waved it back and forth, back and forth, fanning the heat against her face.

She was glad to sit and catch her breath before she saw Mark. When she didn't hear from him, she had just started off—the way she had the other time. Maybe Mark had minded what she said in her letter about going to the Wilderness again.

"Several folks come from away for the wedding," the agent came back to say. "Not many folks from town was invited, but, of course, the Phillipses ain't been here long enough to get to know many. An' the preacher, he's from away; come last night, from Kansas, where they're havin' all the fightin'. I guess he got beat up pretty bad hisself. Couldn't talk any louder than a whisper."

The movement of the fan stopped. But Mark couldn't be really hurt if he had come for the wedding. He must have been hoarse from shouting above the noise of the crowd, as he had the time they set the hall on fire and he went right on and made them listen to him. That must be all it was. She began to fan again.

"There's the Major's rig! Well, you didn't have to wait long. You go ahead. I'll bring your bag for you."

A buggy, shining in its paint, drawn by two high-stepping bays, came down the road. That was Mark! Mark was driving. Harriet picked up her handbag and jacket, pulling on her gloves, finger by finger, and stepped out in the sudden cold stillness of the day, waiting. Her hands were so full she didn't try to wave, but Mark was waving. He pulled up at the end of the platform by the hitching post. Like that other time . . . She would know whether he was glad she had come. Or had he wanted to be alone here? He seemed taller; no, he was thinner, and ghastly pale. He had been working too hard. . . . But, of course, he loved it—loved throwing himself into his cause.

"Mark!"

"Harriet," he whispered, kissing her. His arm was around her, and she felt how thin he had grown.

The heat of the day came rushing back to her, and the sounds of the horses, and the agent bringing her bag, saying something-nothing, and their own voices saying each other's name.

"Your voice, Mark. I've never known you to be so hoarse."

He was smiling down at her, but his face hurt her, it was so haggard; his eyes seemed darker in his thin face.

"I'll have to marry them in a whisper. Are you all right,

Harriet? All that long way alone . . ." He was remembering; he meant . . . "I half hoped you would bring Marcia. I tried to imagine her laughing."

She made answers, hardly knowing what she said, still uncertain how he felt about her coming.

Mark was helping her into the buggy. "I'm sorry you had to wait. Couldn't tell about the train. The Major came this morning while I was going over the service with Mrs. Phillips."

Why would he have to do it just then? Couldn't he wait, when his wife was coming?

"How are they? The Major and Mrs. Phillips?"

"The Major seems as much in his element here as at the Fort. I'm not so sure about Mrs. Phillips. It is very different here, of course. . . . That she cared about consecrating their union in this wedding is . . ."

Did it hurt Mark to talk, or did he go off into his own thoughts?

"The Major said it was for the children, and now that they are living in the States, of course . . ." She knew the Major's letter by heart.

"But they could have been married by a judge. . . . No, I think it's significant that she wanted a Christian ceremony."

Or did he mean because the Major said Mrs. Phillips wanted Mark to come and marry them? She looked away, watching a grasshopper rise out of the grass and disappear into it again; Mark was silent so long.

"I was surprised that you wanted to come, Harriet. It must have been such a hard trip." His eyes, sunken in his gaunt face, seemed to search her mind. His asking in a whisper made it impossible not to speak the truth.

"I wanted to see Mrs. Phillips again." Should she go on and tell him that she wanted to find out that she didn't hate her? More than that; that he was free from her, that they both were. She had come to be obsessed by her, too, in a way.

But before she could speak, Mark said, "She seems different

in these surroundings—almost like a child one moment, yet the next, very dignified and very much the Major's lady."

But she had always been like that. Mark was more concerned with Eenisskim than in hearing why she had come all this way. He didn't really care. Hadn't he ever worried about how she had felt all these months? Whether she *loved* him?

"What is the place like, Mark? The station agent said it is a mansion."

"It is a mansion. No expense has been spared downstairs, but it's not quite finished; upstairs, that is. The wedding guests will all sleep at the hotel in town here. Oh, it's perfectly comfortable." Mark reached over elaborately to take the whip out of the socket and flip it lightly over the horses, who hardly needed it. "The Major has had to be away a good deal, and I think Mrs. Phillips just suddenly lost interest. Furnishing a whole house would be new to her, of course."

He seemed to be absorbed in Mrs. Phillips. Puzzling about her. "You'd never know Marcia!" Harriet said abruptly, holding her up before him, blocking out Mrs. Phillips, making the baby laugh for him, bringing him back within the safe circle of his family.

The drive out of town in a shining buggy, drawn by two fancy horses, of a late September afternoon, was nothing like, and yet it was like, riding horseback across the plain to the Fort. This country, smelling of sweet clover, with cornfields and fences, hardly resembled that bare dry ground, dotted with prickly pear and sage, pockmarked with gopher holes; nor did the newly built mansion, looming up ahead, suggest the adobe Fort inside the stockade; but she felt as though she were going to the Fort. She swallowed against her sudden nervousness.

The Major came to hand her out of the buggy under the porte-cochere. He was as handsome as the agent had said. She had remembered him in his buckskins or in his blue frock coat

with the gold buttons, but now he was dressed like any gentleman, and there was no least embarrassment in his manner as
he welcomed his wedding guests.

"We appreciate your coming all this way, Mrs. Ryegate,
'specially when you had to make the trip alone. Just as you
did the last time you came to see us, if I remember correctly,"
he said, smiling and bowing over her hand, as he had then.
Mary came running and flung herself on Harriet, a strange new
creature in a flounced and furbelowed rose-colored dress, and
with long black curls. And Raymond, incredibly changed into
a young man; but his eyes still moved uneasily away from
Harriet's, and he tossed his hair back in a quick, self-conscious
nod that passed for a bow.

"My bride is waiting on the porch to greet you!" the Major
said in high humor.

Harriet looked up and saw Eenisskim standing there under
the elaborate fan-shaped window that crowned the doorway,
watching them. She seemed too still, too solemn for a bride, in
her brown satin gown, but regal, too. The late sun caught the
lustre of her greased black hair and the black velvet bands on
her skirt, and drew a sparkle from the gold cross—on a chain
instead of a thong, Harriet noticed—and long jet earrings
that swung as she moved her head. Even her hands were covered with black net mitts, dotted with bits of sparkle.

"Mrs. Phillips!" Harriet cried out, hurrying up the long
flight of stairs, one hand lifting her skirt, the other moving
swiftly over the white railing that had been patched roughly
with unpainted wood. Had she expected to see Mrs. Phillips
in white, with a bridal veil? Not that, but she seemed . . . elegant. Elegant and unapproachable.

When she stood beside her, Mrs. Phillips' mouth relaxed
rather than smiled. She shook hands with a quick chopping
motion of her arm and nodded her head with an odd indrawn
breath Harriet remembered. But her eyes held no light, no
hint of secret amusement in them as they often used to do.
Harriet felt uncomfortable under her gaze and her silence,

but she was more beautiful than she remembered. Mark must feel that.

"I'm so glad to see you again, Mrs. Phillips, and it is lovely to find you settled in your handsome new home." How unutterably silly she sounded, as though she were speaking to someone in Woollett!

Mrs. Phillips led the way into the house without any acknowledgment of her remark.

Harriet wasn't prepared for the wide hall with its glittering chandelier and long pier glass, a little smeared in one spot; or for the flowered carpet that was already marked with odd rings. Mrs. Phillips stopped to look at the rings, tracing one with the toe of her satin slipper, as though it were some Indian sign. When she lifted her eyes to Harriet, they had that old look of some secret merriment. But Harriet could think of nothing to say. She wondered if Mrs. Phillips was laughing at her.

Mr. Ferrière came from the parlor to greet Harriet in his courtly way. "We little thought, Mrs. Ryegate, that we would meet on such a happy occasion," he said. She remembered his telling her on the boat that Mrs. Phillips was a fascinating woman. "Fascinating," he had repeated.

And how unbelievable that Pierre should be here! He looked uncomfortable in his dress-up clothes and high collar. But she remembered his saying her hair was the color of yellow willows in the spring. The world of the Fort came back to her, almost too fast. She was glad to follow Mary upstairs to change for the wedding.

"You could dress in Mother's room, but mine's nicer." Mary wrinkled her nose. "Mother's has skins on the floor and the old red blankets we had at the Fort. I don't know why Mother didn't get the guest rooms ready in time. I was shocked when I got here, and Papa was mad about it, but he went down and took the whole upstairs of the hotel for all of you." Of a sudden, Mary sounded like a proper matron, complaining about the negligence of a housekeeper.

"Thank you, I'd like to use your room," she told Mary, passing quickly by the Phillips' room, remembering how covertly she had glanced in when she went by their open door at the Fort.

"Oh, you know, the most terrible thing happened this morning!" Mary began excitedly, patting her hair with careful fingers. "Mother isn't over it yet. Raymond rode her horse right up the steps into the hall and over the carpet, and then Mother made him get off and she rode the horse back down the steps, only he caught his leg and fell and Papa had to come out and shoot him. Reverend Ryegate tried to stop Mother; he even grabbed the reins. But nobody could stop her. After that, she went up to her room and wouldn't come down. First she told Papa she wasn't going to be married, and then she said she was going to wear just what she had on. And Reverend Ryegate talked to her, and finally Papa had to really yell at her to make her get dressed."

"She looks very lovely," Harriet said. Why hadn't Mark told her about Eenisskim's crazy prank? All the time they were riding back he must have been thinking about her. Like a child at times, was all he had said.

"But she won't carry her wedding bouquet Papa got for her with mine. She went out and picked some old yellow weeds. I better go tell Reverend Ryegate where to come," Mary said.

Mark was so long in coming, Harriet was almost dressed. "You're just in time to hook me up," she said lightly, drawing him back again into domesticity. "I brought your things for you, your best suit, and Hannah did up your shirt so carefully. I even brought your cologne. Doesn't Mrs. Phillips look charming!"

"Yes," Mark said, "but she's still badly upset because of an accident to her horse this morning. He had to be shot."

"How dreadful!" But why did he feel he must protect her so from his wife? Why didn't he say it was Eenisskim's fault, that she was a crazy Indian woman?

"She was very different last night, and this morning, before it happened, I felt quite sure as I talked to her that she would repeat the words of her vows after me in English. Think how wonderful that would be, Harriet, even if the words themselves sound strange!"

"Why, Mark? Why does her saying the words in English matter that much, if she understands?"

"I suppose I've wanted her to speak to me for so long . . ." He broke off with a laugh that was caught in his throat.

"Get dressed, Mark. We ought to go down." She busied herself packing the clothes she had taken off.

"You think I'm obsessed with her." His words in a whisper seemed to come out of her own mind, as though their minds came together. "It's only that I want to feel my preaching in the Wilderness, my being there, wakened that much response. More than ever, after not seeing her for so long, that whole struggle comes back."

But didn't he see? It wasn't just his struggle out there, it was theirs after they came back home. And it wasn't just Eenisskim's response to his preaching that he cared about, though his preaching was such a part of Mark, of course. She looked over at him. He had taken off his shirt and she saw the angry red line of puckered flesh ringing his neck.

"Mark, you were really hurt! I thought you were just hoarse from having to shout."

"It's an ugly-looking thing, but it's healing all right. And I can whisper now without its killing me, but I'm beginning to doubt whether I'll ever do any more than that." He seemed intent on the buttons of his shirt when he said, without looking up, "Do you think you can live with a croaking frog voice like this, if it doesn't get any better?"

"It isn't froglike!" she said quickly. "It sounds quite interesting and confidential. All the way out from the station I felt you were whispering delicious things to me. Mark, what happened? That scar—did they try to choke you to death?"

"I think that was their idea. A mob tried to break up the meeting where I was speaking and I kept right on, so sure I could subdue them if I talked long enough and loud enough and eloquently enough—you know, the great orator!" He stopped to swallow. "But these ruffians weren't swayed. They got a rope around my neck and dragged me out. You won't have to worry any more about my being . . . intoxicated with the power of my own . . . eloquence." The last whispered word came out with a hissing sound. "That's—" he stopped again to swallow—"one slight advantage." Either the edge of bitterness that came through his whisper or the quick grimace he made as he swallowed kept her from answering. He looked over at her with an attempt at a grin. "I thought you'd appreciate the irony of it, anyway."

"Mark, how can you say that, or even think it? That's cruel! As cruel as anything I ever said."

"I didn't mean it to be cruel. It *is* ironic. Samson shorn of his strength and blinded because he was so blind in the head."

"You know I loved your voice, and the way you put things!"

"Only," he whispered, taking her word, "I loved it too—loved using it too much for my own satisfaction, and loved words, as you said, whether I understood them or not."

But there wasn't time to go on. They could hear the fiddler tuning up. Mary rapped on the door. "We're going to start as soon as you're ready, Reverend Ryegate."

Chapter Twenty-five

WHEN Buzby returned that evening a little before seven, the Phillips mansion was lit up like a new saloon. You could see it half a mile away. Plenty of carriages from town driving slowly past the place, but outside the fence you couldn't see anything but the lights, and the top of the fancy roof with the lightning rods pricking the stars. Nor did he see more than a couple of carriages in the driveway, inside the fence.

There weren't many guests gathered in the long parlor, sitting on the tasselled red-velvet furniture, waiting for the wedding. He got Mary to sit beside him at the back of the room and tell him about each one who'd come from away, while the three-piece orchestra played in the alcove under the stairs.

The fashionably dressed Frenchman was Louis Ferdinand Ferrière, no less, from St. Louis, a big nabob in the fur company the Major was mixed up with; and the French Canuck had been the Major's clerk out in the Wilderness. "Sweet on me, too," Mary had told him with a giggle. "He only has an Indian squaw for a wife." What did she think she was? But being the daughter of an Indian princess lifted you out of the squaw class, maybe. It sure wouldn't matter to him what that wonderful woman the Major was getting married to was! The preacher, Marcus Ryegate, and his wife came all the way from Woollett, Massachusetts, just to perform the ceremony; looked like New Englanders, too. Buzby jotted down the hair-raising bit about his being dragged through the street in Kansas and hurting his vocal cords, so the poor devil was going to have to whisper like that all his life. Just lucky to get out alive. The two of them didn't look like his idea of missionaries, but that was how they'd come to know the Major and his bride. He wondered if the Reverend converted Mrs. Phillips to the Christian faith and hung that cross on her, and that was why she wanted him to come way out here to marry them.

Buzby glanced again at the preacher's wife; a pretty woman in that blue dress, blue to match her eyes, with her high color and all that blond hair piled up on her head. Hard to imagine her in that rough country out there. A wonder some redskin didn't want that gold hair of hers! He wondered what she was thinking; didn't appear to be missing a trick, but a little too serious for him. Maybe she was still worried about her husband.

"See you after the wedding," Mary twittered in his ear.

"Right!" He might just give her a little whirl; she was asking for it. Then he turned to noting the local guests.

From town there were only Waley, the banker, and his wife, and a fat-faced daughter who looked dull as a squash beside Mary. But all the female contingent suffered next to the bride!

And Dan Campbell, "our congressman." Folks said he was buttering up the Major for political reasons.

And that was every last one of them. Maybe the Phillipses hadn't got to know folks well enough to invite them, or maybe an afterthought wedding like this, you didn't want many people at it.

But it was all as proper and elegant as anybody could ask for, with uniformed maids floating around back there, and a three-piece orchestra, and cases of champagne he'd seen with his own eyes. Hard to believe that Mrs. Phillips had jumped on a horse bareback and ridden him down the front steps only a few hours ago. He couldn't wait to see her as a bride—carrying a bunch of goldenrod. Mary had been so indignant at her throwing away the wedding bouquet that came from town and running out to pick some wild flowers—Mary with her own proper bouquet trimmed in lace paper. This story got better and better. Not the story so much as that woman.

He guessed at a likely headline and wrote it down.

INDIAN PRINCESS MARRIES FUR TRADE MAGNATE
COUPLE ATTENDED BY TWO CHILDREN OF PAIR

That would give the good people of the town a pretty morsel to chew on.

The orchestra struck into the wedding march. Then he saw her, coming down the stairs by herself, every inch a princess, not looking at anybody. Sure enough, she was carrying goldenrod; tied with grass, it looked like.

The Major was waiting for her at the foot of the stairs. Nobody was going to give this bride away. Her Indian chief father must have done that the other time. She laid her hand on the Major's arm and the two walked into the parlor together. Buzby sighed.

Harriet watched Mark take his stand in the bow window at the front end of the parlor. His face, gaunt in the sidewise light from the bracket lamp, showed too plainly how tense he was. She looked away at Eenisskim coming in on the Major's arm, staring straight ahead, as she had walked that day at Robert's funeral. Raymond and Mary walked together to stand, self-consciously, beside their parents. They were so clearly a family that they made the opening words of the ceremony Mark was pronouncing sound like lines spoken on a stage; not even that, lines whispered by the prompter.

Weren't vows meaningless if you already knew how your life together would be? You had to plight them not knowing how you would stand all those things; not you, your love. How your love would stand adversity and illness, whether you would cherish this one person all your life, or be drawn—bewitched, in spite of yourself—by someone else; whether you would grow suspicious and jealous, even cruel and savage. Harriet glanced at Mr. Ferrière and Pierre and the others. They were listening with indulgent looks on their faces, as people watch a play they have seen before, a children's play, perhaps.

But Mark was as intent as though he had never performed a marriage before. He might have been speaking just to Eenisskim, but, of course, that was exactly what he was doing, looking so earnestly at her, making each whispered word distinct, trying to give each one expression and meaning. She almost wished she hadn't come. But no, she might as well be here and see how he cared. . . . Did his throat hurt when he swallowed like that and waited a minute before he went on? This must have been the way he tried to talk to Eenisskim that night on the mountain. Only then his voice would have been deep and . . . and tender.

He paused. He was waiting for Eenisskim to speak. He said again, "If you will just say after me in your husband's tongue, which is also your tongue now, 'I do.' "

Eenisskim was staring out the window. The Major turned to look at her. Mary's bouquet jerked impatiently. Raymond shifted his weight from one foot to the other. Mr. Ferrière stirred in his chair.

Then into the uneasy silence fell a single syllable, uttered in a low, oddly distinct tone. "Ah."

The Major's voice, full, resonant, sure, was a relief after Mark's whispering and Eenisskim's one syllable.

"I, Ephraim, take thee, Eenisskim, to my wedded wife . . . and thereto I plight thee my troth."

Mark turned to Eenisskim, and it seemed to Harriet that his eyes pleaded with her. "Please repeat after me, 'I, Eenisskim, take thee, Ephraim . . .' " The silence lengthened. Mr. Ferrière coughed. Mary's hand nudged her mother's arm, but the figure in brown showed not the least response.

Then, just as the silence grew unbearable, Mark began, "Eenisskim takes thee, Ephraim, to her wedded husband . . ." Very slowly, in his rasping whisper, he continued, "to have and to hold from this day forward . . . and thereto she gives thee her troth, and as sign of this her assent."

Would she know the meaning of the word "assent"? Then Harriet remembered that Mark had been over all this with her already. That was why the Major came to the station first. But again there was silence. The Major turned to her. "Can't you tell them you'll have me, Nisskim?"

"Ah."

At a look from Mark, the Major took a ring out of his waist-coat pocket and put it on Eenisskim's finger.

"With this ring I thee wed," Mark whispered and the Major repeated in his deep voice, "With this ring I thee wed—again." "And with all my wordly goods I thee endow," Mark said. The Major's hearty voice echoed his words.

Then Mark was pronouncing them husband and wife. "And what God hath joined together, let no man put asunder."

Or woman either, Harriet thought. She could feel the disappointment in Mark's voice as he prayed, so low that the words were barely audible, for the Holy Spirit's blessing on their continued lives together. Why did he care so much about this woman? Eenisskim didn't care about him. Asking Mark to come must have been the Major's idea, in spite of what he had written. It was so clear that Eenisskim wanted no part in this ceremony.

Everyone crowded around the newly married couple to offer good wishes in voices made more hearty by the release of the embarrassing tension of the ceremony. The wife of the banker, recognizing in Harriet another properly married woman, murmured to her with a complacent laugh that she declared she hardly knew what to say to them, but since the woman didn't speak a word of English, and as far as she could see didn't understand much that was said, either, it didn't really matter. She raised her eyebrows.

Pierre called out to Harriet as he would have at the Fort, "Well, Missus Ryegate, it's a pleasure to see you lookin' so fine. You was mighty peaked when you took off from up-river that day!"

Harriet was the last to shake hands with the bride and

groom. "Congratulations, Major Phillips. May you be very happy here, as happy as you were at the Fort," she said, as he bowed with a flourish. She had meant to wish Eenisskim happiness, but she found herself saying, instead, watching her face, "Mrs. Phillips, your asking my husband to marry you meant a great deal to him."

Eenisskim's eyes were swamp-black, dull. Harriet wondered if she had understood. Suddenly she was enveloped by the too sharp sense of having stood beside this woman like this before, not knowing what to say next, feeling some deep hostility, or, perhaps, indifference; held in the same vise of silence.

"Here you are!" The Major came back to them, carrying a bottle of champagne, with a maid bringing glasses. The cork popped, and the champagne bubbled over on the carpet as he poured it. He raised his glass to Eenisskim. "To Mrs. Phillips, my new and old wife!" There were clapping and laughter, but Eenisskim in her brown dress stood silent as a slender tree, around which the others spread their merriment. Her face showed no expression, and she drank the champagne without stopping.

Was she angry? Harriet followed her gaze across the room, where Mary was beaming up at a young man with a moustache, but then she saw that Eenisskim was looking beyond Mary at the painting that covered the long wall.

"That's just the time of year we left the Fort, just as those trees by the river were turning yellow," she ventured. "And that's you on your horse up on the bluff."

Eenisskim moved closer toward the mural, studying it for several minutes. Harriet followed her. Abruptly, Eenisskim dropped her stalks of goldenrod over the back of a velvet chair and set her empty glass on the chair arm. Holding her left hand out in front of her, with the thumb up, she brought her right hand, flat as a knife, across her fingers, as though she were cutting them off. All the time her eyes held Harriet's.

Harriet shook her head. "I can't understand. Can't you say it?"

Eenisskim repeated her gestures more rapidly. Then her hands doubled into fists, one resting across the other at the wrist an instant, only to fly apart the next. Her lips moved, forming strange syllables that seemed run together, "Nitaaa-kaxkyaapoo."

"Oh, I don't know what you mean, Eenisskim. Tell me in English!" Her desperation got into her voice.

Eenisskim pointed with her thumb at the black-velvet button on her bodice just above the gold cross; then, tightening her right hand into a fist, pointing upward close to her forehead, she turned it left in a circle.

Did she mean she was going crazy? Harriet looked helplessly around the room for the Major or Mary. She saw Pierre, but she didn't want to call him.

Eenisskim barely touched Harriet's sleeve to bring her eyes back. Looking right at her, she made a sudden sweeping gesture that took in the whole room. She drew herself up straight and spoke, giving each word the same intonation. "I go back home."

Almost before Harriet had realized that the syllables Eenisskim had uttered were words, words she could understand, the Major stood beside them.

"Reverend Ryegate needs us to sign the certificate, Nisskim."

Mark pushed aside the ledgers and papers on the cluttered desk to make a space. He spread out the wedding certificate, decorated with angels holding garlands above the spaces to be filled in. But the velvet covering of the desk was too soft to write on, and he laid the certificate on one of the Fur Company ledgers. He had brought with him his own pen and ink case, the special pen that made deep strokes and flourishes on the letters. The sound of his writing scratched at the stillness of the room like the claws of a magpie trying to walk on the posts of the stockade.

He wrote his name carefully opposite the printed word

"Clergyman," and blotted the signature; then he sat waiting for the bride and groom. The music at a little distance made this room with the closed door seem remote.

They hadn't got around to furnishing it yet, so it was more like a room at the Fort. He glanced with a kind of satisfaction at the bookless shelves, the buckskin jacket on a chair, the boots, left as they were kicked off, the bare floor. Above the mantel hung a stuffed eagle, powerful wings extended, cruel beak hooked. . . . But the eyes were wrong. They were dull, bead eyes. Like Eenisskim's during the ceremony. He went over and stroked the feathers with the back of his fingers, listening to the silken sound they made.

Why hadn't she repeated the words after him? Or if it was shyness in front of so many people, couldn't she have managed just two words, just "I do," in English? Why did she want him to come to marry them if this was all the response she was going to give?

"Here we are, Reverend."

Mark went back to the desk without looking at Eenisskim, but he was acutely aware of her standing there while the Major leaned over to write his name in his bold flowing hand, with large capitals.

"Now Mrs. Phillips." Mark pointed to the space for her name. "If you just make a mark on this line, that will be enough."

Eenisskim seated herself in the chair and took the pen the Major handed her, dipping it in the ink. She held the pen above the well, letting a drop fall off the pen, then dipped it again.

"This does it, Nisskim," the Major said. "It's like a treaty, holding us together."

Eenisskim nodded; she seemed to know all this, to need no explanation. Then she bent over the paper, taking time to study the angels and the garlands of flowers and the signatures already there. The music and the sound of voices and laughter drifted in under the door, but the three of them were as removed as though, Mark thought, they were indeed gathered in the chief's tipi to sign an important treaty.

Eenisskim's pen scratched on the page. Then she laid it down and looked up at Mark with an amused smile that he was unprepared for, as she had looked at him that night at dinner over the cooked duck.

He picked up the certificate and saw, written in a cramped but clear hand, "Eenisskim Phillips." It was difficult to conceal his amazement that she could write her name. He shook her hand and the Major's. "God bless your marriage!" he said.

"I guess He's done that already, Reverend," the Major said. He looked at the certificate with satisfaction. "We'll frame this, by God, and hang it where every guest we have can see it! Now we can go to dinner."

Chapter Twenty-six

THE Major and his lady sat together at the head of the big oval table, which was resplendent with cut glass and heavy plated silver. The guests had seated themselves where they would. Harriet found herself next to Pierre, as she had sat so often at the Fort. "Well, Missus Ryegate, we'll have a little fancier fare tonight than we did at the Fort!" he told her, beaming in anticipation.

Mark had taken the chair between the banker and his wife. Mary had brought her reporter to the table. Raymond sat beside Lydia, the banker's daughter, and boasted of riding his horse right up the steps into the hall, offering to point out the hoof marks on the carpet if she didn't believe it. Lydia's round, china-blue eyes doubted but were dazzled. To give the tale an added flourish, Raymond told her his mother had ridden the horse back down and broke his leg. Lydia transferred her gaze wonderingly to the strange woman who had just been married, a fullblood Indian squaw who couldn't speak a word of English. The woman was staring right at her; Lydia hurriedly dropped her eyes.

But the Major's lady was eating and drinking too heartily to pay any attention to the plump, pale-faced girl beside Raymond, or care how the guests fared. The number of toasts made the champagne go fast, and when it came round again, the Major reached over and turned down her glass. But she laughed at him and held the glass out for the waitress to refill.

Well, let her have what she wanted tonight; she felt so bad over her horse he hadn't been sure she'd go through with the wedding. As for himself, he hadn't been a happier bridegroom that day when he gave the nine finest horses he could buy to her brother in exchange for Eenisskim. But the next day the brother sent nine other horses back to him. Eenisskim was a princess and not to be bought like any ordinary squaw. He'd always liked that.

And he was just where he had planned to be when he went up-river twenty-seven years ago; he had made his pile and come back to live like a gentleman. Next week he was going down to Washington to meet some of the bigwigs Dan Campbell told him he ought to know if he wanted to get into politics, and he thought he did. But he didn't know how Nisskim was going to take to this life.

Dan said having an Indian wife and half-breed kids might go against him, but he'd risk it. He'd told him—and it was the truth—he wouldn't have made his fortune without Nisskim. Wouldn't have had the good life he'd had out there, either. The Wilderness rubbed out half the men who came there, or they ran home with their tails between their legs, or crawled back, done for; but with Nisskim he'd come off all right. His eyes filled suddenly in tenderness deepened by champagne, and he reached over and took her hand, lying dark on the tablecloth. Bothered him she hadn't said a word since he made her get into her wedding dress, 'cept a couple of "ahs." But she'd had a laugh at Ryegate when he looked so surprised she could write her name, good as anyone. She'd come round.

"The wedding's all right, isn't it, Nisskim? We're married right and proper as anyone!"

She didn't answer. Better to leave her alone when she was like that. You didn't treat Nisskim like any ordinary squaw that needed to be beaten up now and then. Hadn't she always had her moods, times when she didn't come to bed all night and went outside the stockade to the Indian camp? He'd never asked her where she went; it wasn't to meet any young buck, he knew that. She was the kind who could be a sacred Sun woman if she hadn't married him.

He took another swallow of champagne; then he set it down so suddenly it splashed over the rim of the glass. His eyes had lighted on the Reverend's wife. Maybe she kept Nisskim glum. Nisskim always made fun of poor Missus Ryegate. But she liked the Reverend; that's why he'd got him out here to marry them. She'd laughed when he suggested it, and clapped her hands. The Major's eyes squinted with humor. Must be a relief to Reverend Ryegate that he'd got them properly married now. He had an idea Ryegate used to worry about it.

The dinner was long drawn out. Buzby of the *Star* had had all he could eat or drink, and he needed to get back to the paper with his story. He leaned over to tell Mary he had to leave.

"Sure, you can go. I will, too," Mary said.

Buzby glanced up at the head of the table and found the Major's wife looking right at him. Gave him an uncomfortable turn—could she know what he'd been thinking? Sitting there in that tall-backed chair she seemed to have shrunk since she came down the stairway. She wasn't talking to anybody, not even her bridegroom. Buzby hadn't been introduced to her, and he supposed he might go up and say something about the write-up of the wedding and thank her for the dinner, but since she didn't speak English it might be kind of awkward standing there.

"All right, let's go," he said to Mary, but at the door he looked back. Mrs. Phillips was still staring at him with eyes that were black pits. Could be snakes in those pits! He bowed to her, but she didn't move a muscle, just kept her eyes on him. He ducked his head and slipped out through the portieres after Mary.

The banker's wife saw Lydia sliding out with that half-breed boy. Even if Dan did think the Major was going to be an important man, she didn't want Lydia with the boy. She'd see where they were just as soon as she could decently leave this dull dinner. The minister next to her was a regular old sobersides for such a young man; he talked so little and then in a tiresome whisper so she could hardly hear him; she'd hardly heard the marriage ceremony, for that matter. The Major should have got a minister from town, or had one out to give the prayer, at least.

Mark was listening to the banker on his other side tell Mr. Ferrière that the Major had made quite a splash in the town, state, too. "Well, you can see for yourself what a spread he's got here. He's spent money right and left; a good sight too much for a man living on his capital and his investments, if you ask me!"

Mr. Ferrière's sharp eyes studied the black walnut moulding against the ceiling as he nodded, his lips pursed appraisingly. His eyes came back to the banker. "I have an idea he knows what he is doing. Very shrewd man, Phillips, and the best man in the fur trade, I'll tell you that. Certainly, his wife was a great help to him, too."

"She won't be down here. We had them to dinner one night with some important folks I wanted the Major to meet, and she never said a mortal word, not a word! My wife was fit to be tied."

Mark looked up the table and met Eenisskim's eyes, but they stared without any least glimmer of recognition. As he watched, her eyelids drooped, then opened with a jerk. She had had too much to drink, but that wasn't like her. In all the time at the Fort, he had only seen her take a small glass of grog at the two or three balls the Major had given.

The light was too bright. He liked the dim light from the lamps with the smoked chimneys on the table at the Fort. Eenisskim's face would be half-shadowed and dusky, and her smile would flash out as she understood something that was said. Tonight, of all nights, her face was blank.

Last night when he arrived, her eyes and her face welcomed him, even though she didn't speak. And this morning, sitting facing her as he went over the service, he had expected her to say something at any moment. He had wanted to say so many things to her as soon as they had finished, but the incredible business with the horse put an end to that. She had disappeared, and he hadn't seen her again until Harriet and he came back from the station. And then the disappointment of her silence at the wedding. Only after she signed her name on the certificate had he seen any flash of life in her eyes. The minute this wretched meal was over he had to try to talk to her once more.

"Will you be going back up-river in the spring, Pierre?" Harriet asked.

"I hate to confess, Missus Ryegate, Pierre is enough fool to sign up again! I go back up this fall as far as Union, but I get on up before spring."

Harriet hardly listened to Pierre; she was watching Eenisskim lay down her fork and push her plate away from her. With her fingers she picked up a tidbit and sucked it noisily into her mouth, licking her lips with her tongue afterward. She wasn't listening to anything anybody said.

Would Eenisskim have said something more if the Major hadn't come just then? She must have made up her mind at that very moment. When she couldn't make herself understood by sign language, she grew so vehement—angry, really—that her anger seemed to force her into using English words in spite of herself. With a sense of wonder, Harriet shaped them silently on her lips. "I go back home." The first English words she had ever heard her speak.

But why should Eenisskim care whether she understood or not? Unless she had to confide in someone, and she didn't believe Eenisskim ever had to confide in anyone. It was more than that. Eenisskim had hardly bothered to look at her until they were standing in front of the painting together, quite apart from the others, even apart from this house. She herself had had a curious sense of being back there, and Eenisskim must have felt it, too—the yellow leaves on that tree above the river where she had floated on Eenisskim's arms, the pale-gray rimrock and the clay banks, and the tipis, and all that endless land and sky. It wasn't until then that Eenisskim tried to tell her.

Eenisskim wasn't happy here. She was different from the way she had been at the Fort, different from the woman she and Mark had each made her in their minds. But even harder to understand. In all the time she had known her, she had never seen her eat like that at the table. When she made that circle by her forehead, did she mean that she was going crazy, or that the wedding was crazy when she had thought of herself as married all these years?

Eenisskim slid out of her chair, without pushing it back, not looking at anyone. The Major went on talking to Mr. Ferrière, but Harriet saw his eyes follow her. Was she sick from so much champagne? Mark was watching Eenisskim, too. Of course, he could never take his eyes away from her; but then neither could she, tonight. Eenisskim was so separate in the midst of all this showy expense, separate from all of them. Even her fashionable wedding gown seemed wrong on her now; yet when she stood in the doorway, she had been beautiful. Some change had come over her; after she spoke those words in English, perhaps.

The wedding cake was brought in triumphantly on a silver tray, the third and fourth tiers tipping a little, and set before the Major. "What a pity Mrs. Phillips isn't here," Mrs. Waley said to the minister. "Somebody ought to call her back to cut it. She's supposed to cut the first slice with her husband!" But old sobersides didn't seem to hear well, either.

"Well, now," the Major said. "In my bride's absence I guess

I'll have to do the honors here." He held up the horn-handled knife, scoured for the occasion until it looked like silver. "I never thought when I used this on a buffler that I'd ever slice my own wedding cake with it."

The wedges of heavy cake were passed around the table. "We need more champagne to wash this down," the Major told the waitress. When she murmured something to him, he said irritably, "Bring brandy then, bring something."

Harriet nodded to Mrs. Waley and both ladies rose, leaving the gentlemen to their brandy and cigars. It might have been any dinner party instead of a wedding supper. On her way out, Harriet met Mark's glance. She nodded to him, knowing he wanted her to see if Eenisskim was all right. Of course, that was what she was going to do.

Excusing herself to Mrs. Waley, who seemed to have her own concerns, Harriet went upstairs, wondering if Eenisskim would want her to come. The heat was stifling on the second floor. One lamp barely lighted the long, uncarpeted hall, but threw distorted shadows from the buffalo skull mounted on the wall. The door of the big front chamber that was Eenisskim's and the Major's stood open, but the room was empty. The flame in the lamp on the dresser had been turned too high and it flared against the blackened chimney.

Harriet crossed the room to turn down the wick. She noticed that the heavy red curtains were caught up over their poles to let in any least breath of air—or to let a person climb through the open window onto the porch roof. She peered into the summer dark, which resounded with the intermittent chorus of cicadas. Maybe Eenisskim was somewhere close by, watching her! She drew back, glancing uneasily around the room.

Spread out on the high bed was the waist of the handsome brown satin wedding dress; the skirt, half supported by its cagelike hoop, stood on the floor where Eenisskim must have stepped out of it in a hurry. Beside the skirt lay one black satin wedding slipper, the other halfway across the floor.

The room had an odd smell, yet it was somehow familiar. Her eyes moved from the buffalo robe that was the only rug on the unpainted wood floor, to the skin pouch ornamented with beads and porcupine quills that hung from a knob on Eenisskim's dresser drawer. On one wall hung the buffalo skin, decorated with paintings of warriors and buffalo hunters, that she had studied on the wall of the Fort. Elkskin clothes were piled in a heap on the one chair in the room, and a pair of the Major's moccasins protruded from under the bed.

Harriet stooped down beside the buffalo robe on the floor, laying her hand on the coarse thick fur that yet felt cool. She lifted one edge to bring it closer, and then droppd it so quickly the dust rose from the floor. The touch of the fur and the faint scent of the robe on their bed at the Fort came back too sharply. The rank smell of the raw skins piled in bales in the storeroom of the Fort came back to her, too, and she remembered how it made her eyes sting and her stomach turn.

The lamp flared up again, seeming to assert a life of its own. Harriet turned down the ragged wick and blew out the flame, but the dark made the room more alien and the heat oppressive. She hurried from it, pulling the door behind her to shut in more than the wild smell—some sudden fear, some sharp memory from that other time. But the door was swollen and refused to stay shut, and the wild smell seemed to go with her.

Chapter Twenty-seven

MARK stood with Harriet at the top of the flight of steps leading down from the Major's mansion. The chant of the cicadas with their jargon of unintelligible syllables warred against the music drifting out from the house.

"You're sure, Harriet, that she spoke in English? It's hard to believe after . . ."

"I heard her distinctly, Mark. She said, 'I go back home,' just as plainly as that. She'd tried so hard to make me understand every other way first that she was pushed into it, I think."

"And that's all she said?" he asked again.

"She didn't have time to say anything more. I told you, the Major came to take her to you to sign the certificate."

"And you think she meant she was going back to the Wilderness?"

"To her own people, I think. You saw how she was at dinner, and ate with her fingers, and didn't listen to anybody. As though she was through with civilized living. When she tried to make me understand by sign language, she held her hand out straight and brought the other one down on it as if she were cutting it off. There was something final about it."

"But they've been getting this place ready for several years. She's had plenty of time to make up her mind."

"She left her wedding clothes up in her room, and I think she's in an elkskin dress by now. Perhaps she started right out." Mark was silent so long that she said, "Pierre's going as far as Fort Union this fall; perhaps she'll go back with him."

Mark shook his head. "No. I can't believe she would go off and leave the Major. I think she's just gone out to the tipi she put up herself on the edge of their woods. The Major says she goes there and stays several days at a time in this heat."

His whispered words were almost lost under the brassy blare of the cicadas. Harriet came closer to him. "But would she want you to follow her, then? If you could have heard her . . ." She was sorry she had said that. Mark must mind that Eenisskim had spoken to her in English when she had never even tried to speak to him; he had wanted it so much. Perhaps—she hadn't thought of it before—but perhaps Eenisskim had never forgiven Mark for coming after her in her vigil on the mountain. It might have seemed to her that he had no right.

"If I'd heard her I would have told her she mustn't make a farce out of this wedding, Harriet!" Mark burst out more hoarsely because of the intensity of his feeling.

"Mark, you always think you can talk to people! Even if the Major hadn't come just then, she wouldn't have heard you. There was something . . . wild and desperate in the way she spoke. I can't explain what she was like when she talked in sign language. Anyway, their *marriage* hasn't been a farce all these years, whatever she does now. I'm sure she agreed to this wedding for the Major and the children, not because she wanted it. Now she wants to go back to her own world."

"That would break the Major's heart if she did."

She minded the trite phrase. It was like the things Mark used to say sometimes in his public voice, so she ignored it and said, "The Major must know her after all these years, and love her as she is. Remember how he let her go off to the mountain alone when Robert died? I think he'll leave her free to do what she wants." She had loved Mark and left him free to do what he wanted, she thought, but she had blamed him for being the way he was.

Mark didn't answer right away. He must be remembering

how he had gone to the mountain after Eenisskim. He was fingering his throat in a way that had become a habit, as though it was still sore. They stood in a curious quiet out here on the porch, shut off from the others by the music that streamed through the windows.

And Mark would go after Eenisskim again, Harriet thought, and try to talk with her, but this time he could speak only in a whisper, and Eenisskim wouldn't listen to him, especially after today. It would be just as useless as before, and he would come back just as upset. The whole thing would be the same —it was almost funny, except that Mark cared so much.

"Perhaps she won't want me to come, and I know she may even be sick from the champagne, or asleep, but I'm going out to the tipi and try to talk with her. There won't be any time in the morning."

"It isn't because of Eenisskim, Mark. I don't feel the way I did any more, but I hate to have you go through the same thing again. I think you should learn something from the Major."

Mark, who appeared not to have heard her, went on. "When I was in the hospital I was in a kind of delirium, from the pain and the medicine they gave me, I guess; and I thought I was back there in the Wilderness, going through the medicine dance torture to get back my vision. It was so real to me that even after my mind was clear, lying on that cot in the hospital tent, I kept thinking about it. I thought about Eenisskim and tried to figure out why I could never reach her. Then I realized I should have told her about my vision, and that it was through her that I had it. She might have listened. Indians believe in their dreams and visions. Perhaps that would have been a way to break through her silence. I felt so bad that I'd never tried to tell her. And, of course, I didn't supppose then that I would ever see her again."

His words, which sounded like a whispered confidence, came to an end. "Reach her," "break through her silence," this was so important to him. Not to grasp or hold . . .

"Harriet, I know you think I'm crazy, but believe me, I'm

not bewitched! It's just that I feel I've left something unfinished. If she would talk to me once, so I knew she had understood me, and I understood her, in ever so small a way, I could be content."

"I believe you could be," Harriet said. But was communicating with a person really that important? He wasn't even trying to bring her any great spiritual truth any longer; did he realize that? He only wanted to speak with her and have her speak to him. Oh, yes, he was still bewitched—by her very silence. But the word didn't mean to her what it had before. She had felt something of the kind herself, when Eenisskim was talking her sign language and she wanted so desperately to understand her.

"Go and see if you can find her, Mark. Tell her about your vision right away. Don't wait for her to answer you." Perhaps she might listen to him if he talked about the river and her catching the duck. . . . She hoped Eenisskim would speak to him. "I'll ride back to town with the Waleys. I think we should go so the Major could be free from guests." She was halfway through the door, but then came back to him. "And Mark," she said lightly, "don't get lost in the Wilderness!"

Mark turned quickly. "Bless you, Harriet. I won't."

Harriet watched him go down the steps into the midst of the babel of sound and walk across the smooth lawn into the darkness. She sat on the top step, not ready yet to go in.

At least he had gone alone, she thought, still hearing the word "Wilderness" in her head. She had learned that much. How stupid she had been, insisting that they must talk everything out, always say what they meant, when they themselves couldn't always know. She had tried to possess him, body and soul, and he had to be free to have his bewitchment. "Ah," she said softly.

Chapter Twenty-eight

A faint breath of coolness came to him from the edge of the dark woods, and the rasp of the cicadas retreated farther off into the heat. There was a kind of path; he could feel it with his feet. It seemed to run close to a high wall. He reached out and felt the bark surface of logs, set tight together like a stockade. That must fence in the wildlife. There was no danger of getting lost.

It would be natural for Eenisskim to slip away out here if she was sick or upset. The Major must have known where she would go, so he wasn't worried about her when she disappeared. He hadn't understood how the Major could go through dinner being jovial when he saw her leave the table, or how he could sit in there talking with Waley and Ferrière and the others.

Of course, if Eenisskim was sick or sleeping, he might not be able to talk to her at all, Mark reminded himself. But he couldn't leave without trying. He had come for that as much as the wedding, though he knew it sounded foolish to Harriet.

He saw the tipi ahead of him, white and improbable in the dark, and much closer than he had expected. He had forgotten how tipis looked at night. He walked faster, stumbling once and saving himself from sprawling on the ground only by catching hold of the fence that held in the Major's little wilderness. Eenisskim must have heard him, but he waited a minute to calm his sudden excitement. He wet his lips before he called her name in his miserable, rasping whisper, which might have scared anyone else.

"Eenisskim!"

When he came to the front of the tipi, he saw that the flap was caught back; so he was right, she had taken refuge here. He went almost to the opening and sat down on the ground in front of the dark interior.

"Eenisskim, I came to see you. I cannot go away before I tell you about a gift you gave me, without knowing it—the gift of a vision."

There was no answer, but he heard a movement inside the tipi, and made out a darker shadow in the back. Don't wait for her to answer you, Harriet had said.

"Eenisskim, do you remember the time you held the duck over my face, my first week at the Fort?" There was no answer, but he heard a rustling sound in the tipi.

He tried to whisper slowly, to repeat, as Two Knives did when he told a story. "I was asleep on the bank above the river, and when you held the duck over my face, a drop of water fell on my face and wakened me." As he paused between each short statement, he felt sure that she was listening. Once he tried to hear her breathing. "I opened my eyes and looked up into wings—wings that seemed as large and strong as eagle wings. . . ." He broke off, thinking that she might laugh at the idea, listening to hear that little giggle of hers.

"Eenisskim, can you hear me? Only say 'Ah' so I will know." His whispering gave a clandestine sound to his words.

When there was no answer he moved closer to the opening. "May I enter?" he whispered, feeling her presence in the familiar smell of sage and other dried herbs and smoked skins. He went inside, touching the dark shadow gently, but it was a blanket lying in a heap, wrapping nothing. The tipi was empty. He heard again the rustling sound he had thought Eenisskim had made, and knew it for the movement of some small animal.

Mark backed out, turned around, and sat squat on the ground, his thoughts stopped by his flat sense of disappointment. Then he saw himself, heard himself; now that he had lost his voice he had come to whispering a children's story to nobody in the dark! A sound came from his throat, a sudden involuntary laugh, that had more of disgust in it than mirth, and hurt the lining of his throat.

Only say "Ah," he had begged! And if she had, he would have taken even that as somehow renewing his tattered old vision! The vision had given him his moment, but he had hung on to it, turning it into a holy relic that must keep on working —magic, not holiness. He might better pack it in an Indian medicine bundle!

If she had spoken in English, if she had said "I hear" or "I understand" or "I remember"—what had he wanted her to say?—he would have been lifted and taken it for a sign.

That was what he wanted. He hadn't come out here for her sake. He had come like a boy running to a fortune teller's tent for a sign. Like Thomas, the doubter. Well, he hadn't got one.

He lay back on the ground, holding his throat to ease the rawness. From out here the faraway gibberish of the cicadas merged into a hissing whisper; small feet rustled through the leaves, and somewhere in the woods behind him an animal, transplanted from the faraway Wilderness, stamped on the fenced-in ground. He couldn't hear the music at the house. Perhaps it had stopped. Once he thought he heard horses' hoofs and the sound of wheels. He turned his face away, feeling the earth cooler than the night.

Eenisskim had often understood him; he had known that from the quick lighting up of her face, sometimes from her closing it to what he was saying. Was it so important that she speak words in his tongue? He *had* made her into a symbol— Harriet was right—a symbol by which he could prove something for himself. And it was true that he had been obsessed with her because of it. It seemed to him now that he had tried to use her, as interpreter, so his mission would succeed. Even when he had followed her to the butte to comfort her in her grief, hadn't he wanted to prove to himself that he hadn't failed utterly if he could reach one suffering soul? And he had taken her wanting him to marry them in a Christian ceremony as the result of his influence, as Harriet had said! He turned restlessly on the ground, trying to get away from his own thoughts. Eenisskim understood him well enough! No wonder she had laughed at him from her horse this morning, and set the glass prisms tinkling against each other. The moment of feeling love for her in her filth and grief and misery, when he put his arm around her, seemed to him now the only time he hadn't tried to use her. At least there had been that.

Mark wiped his face with his hands and brushed the leaves out of his hair. Without looking at the Indian tipi, he went back up the path.

When he came out of the dark of the woods, the tall lighted house loomed up, more fantastic and unreal to him than the tipi. There was no sound from within, and the carriages had gone from the driveway. Through the open door and windows, the newly furnished rooms stood exposed and strangely empty. Had the Major gone to find Eenisskim?

Then Mark caught the heavy odor of a dead cigar, and heard the creak of a rocker.

"Reverend." The Major spoke out of the shadow behind the pillar. "She's gone. Nisskim's gone." His usually confident, hearty voice broke like an old man's.

Mark came quickly up the steps. "But she'll come back," he whispered in a voice that was as different from his own as the Major's had been.

"No. She don't like it here, and she's had enough. I've seen the signs. I thought the wedding might help to hold her, but I should have known better." He was in command of his voice again.

"I'm afraid the wedding was hard for her." Mark sat down beside him.

"The wedding didn't mean anything to her after she lost her horse. Almost wouldn't go through with it. She did it just

for me and the children, anyway." After a long silence, the
Major added, not looking at Mark, "All day she's showed me
she was going back, but I wouldn't notice. You saw her at
dinner tonight, eating as though she was already back in an
Indian lodge."

"But you'll make a trip back in the spring. Surely she could
wait till then."

The Major didn't answer; perhaps he hadn't heard Mark's
whisper, which trailed off into silence. His jaws moved on the
dead cigar.

Mark had never seen the Major sit still so long, or so
slumped in his chair. He wondered where Mary and Raymond
were, but he hesitated to ask. Had they gone, too? The cicadas'
rasp had a hollow sound in the emptiness.

"I went out to the tipi to see if she was there," Mark said.

"She used it for a while, but she made fun of it in the end.
And she didn't like the animals fenced in. Three hundred
acres were nothing to her. Only thing she liked was the horses,
and that painting . . . the mirror in the hall, maybe," the
Major said.

"But Mrs. Phillips wouldn't leave without telling you. Has
she actually *said* she was going?" Or had she only told Harriet?

The Major shook his head. "She knew I'd know. She told
me plain enough. She don't have to use words."

"But she can't go all the way up the river, or even overland
this time of year," Mark burst out, with relief at the thought.

"Oh, yes. Nisskim could do it," the Major said wearily.
"Take time, but she could do it. We've done it plenty times
together. And Pierre's going up to Union."

"But he wouldn't let her go with him, when he knows how
you feel about it."

"Pierre wouldn't argue with Nisskim. She goes where she
wants."

There was something impenetrable and exasperating about
the Major's acceptance of her going. Perhaps she *wanted* him

to come after her. Except for the one time when she went to the butte alone, and a couple of trips to take supplies to some camp, she seemed always to be with the Major. And surely she loved him. Didn't that mean anything?

He leaned over to the Major. "She will come back in her own time, as she came back down from the butte, and be here again with you." He saw her so clearly, appearing silently on moccasined feet, that he felt he was speaking the truth.

The Major took the cigar stub out of his mouth and threw it off into the shrubbery. "No, Reverend, she won't come back. I tried to hold her with all this, but she don't want it. I was the one who wanted it. I wanted to come back and live in the States like a gentleman, and spend my money, but I wanted— Nisskim, too." His voice thickened over "Nisskim" so he could hardly get the name out.

When the cicadas ceased for an interval, the hot night pressed more heavily on the stillness; then the mocking chorus began again. The Major sat lost in his own desolation. He seemed to have forgotten that Mark was there. After a while, Mark wondered if he had fallen asleep. His head was bowed and his chin rested on his chest.

Mark went down the steps without speaking, lest he wake him, but he heard the rocker creak as the Major shifted his weight. When Mark looked back at the end of the drive, he saw that massive head against the lighted window of the bay where they had stood this evening for the service.

Chapter Twenty-nine

IT was a relief to move; even more so to take off his hot broadcloth coat and his waistcoat and tie, and wrench off his collar. They had almost grown on him, but he had been so eager to find Eenisskim in the tipi that he hadn't thought about them. A comical enough figure he must have been, crawling around in a tipi in the dark, and lying on the ground in his ministerial clothes. Comical enough anyway, whispering to thin air. He bundled his coat and vest under his arm, stuffed his collar in his back pocket, and set out on the dusty road for town, his step keeping pace with the headlong stride of his thoughts.

How long ago was it that he tried to tell Eenisskim, who wasn't there, about his vision? If he were to have any vision now, it would be of an eagle in its gyre and swoop before its destruction of life. He had just left the Major in his loneliness, with his marriage destroyed; and his own mad spin out of civilization into the Wilderness had ended in enough destruction. The carrion of his own life—a fine phrase, a fitting one— the carrion of his own life smelled in his nostrils. He had lured —that was the word—lured Harriet in the eagerness and innocence of her love for him out to the Wilderness, and let her suffer his inadequacies and doubts and obsessions. He had changed her faith in him into distrust, almost hate. She was right in saying that was his fault. He had been so wrapped up in himself that he had been as blind about her as about Sydney.

The bright promise of his own career was dead enough; that had a particular stench of its own. He stepped on the skirt of his coat and stopped to make a tighter bundle of it.

What a posturing, yapping, humorless fool he had been, lost in the forest of his own trite verbiage. Trying to ape the great, sonorous phrases and images of the Bible—calling a duck an eagle and his stumbling attempts in the Wilderness a "Journey into Strangeness"!

And then that other wilderness. No trouble there being understood, or heating men's blood by his phrases! Feeling his power as never before in a cause he knew was right. But coming out of it with that power—yes, power—destroyed.

Sudden giggling laughter broke in on his thoughts, and he stood still in the road, looking in the graying darkness for Eenisskim. She must have seen him go to the tipi and followed him, and waited while he talked with the Major. She was laughing at him now from behind some tree. The laughter came again, but it was ahead of him. If he could find her . . . He ran toward the sound.

The door of a cheap tavern opened and in the streak of light he made out a barmaid with some yokel, standing at the corner of the building. A loud voice called from the tavern, and the woman ran, giggling, back inside. How could he have thought that was Eenisskim's laugh; it was nothing like it.

Mark went on down the road; his breathlessness hurt his throat. If Eenisskim had come this way, it must have been hours ago. The houses of the town were beginning now, dark and sleeping. Nobody walked here but himself. The town was silent, and even the chant of the cicadas was missing. He wondered when it had stopped.

He had been lost in the Wilderness before Harriet's warning, and so had Harriet, waiting at the hotel at the end of this street. And Eenisskim had been lost outside her Wilderness world, he supposed, and was trying to make her way back to it as hard as they had struggled to find their way out.

But it would always be with them, and Eenisskim could

never lose some trace of civilization, either. He wondered about the Major, knowing both worlds; or would he find himself a stranger, after all, in the world of Waley and his kind?

Oh, he saw them all very clearly, himself the clearest of all; and if he had his voice, he could translate some truths into fine ringing phrases for a congregation, phrases they wouldn't soon forget. But he didn't have.

The night clerk at the hotel refused to let him in at first. Mark was a sorry sight; his shirt stuck to his back with sweat, the boiled front buckled and gaped. His collar dangled from his back pocket, and his trousers were gray with dust. His shoes were almost white and looked like work boots. But it was his face that bothered the night clerk most. It had that clear, shiny look that some drunks got when they'd had so much to drink that nothing bothered 'em, but they hadn't passed out yet. The gent must have been in a fight, 'cause he had a scar around his neck that was just barely healed, and raw enough to make you puke to look at it. He whispered instead of talking out loud so you could hear him.

"I'm Reverend Marcus Ryegate," Mark said hoarsely.

The clerk looked at him. "In a pig's eye you are! You look like you just came out of the backwoods."

"I have," Mark told him. "The dark woods. But I have a room here, number sixteen, on the front. My wife is asleep up there."

The clerk wasn't going to swallow that either, but finally he went with the man, keeping the key in his own hand. He thought he might have to apologize to the lady for waking her, but she answered right off.

"Mark?" She called so quick she couldn't have been asleep, and the gent answered in that whisper of his, calling her Harriet.

She unlocked the door before the clerk could get his key in the lock, but she stared at her husband as though she couldn't make him out, poor lady. He must have looked some changed from the way she was used to seeing him; but she let him in, staring all the while at his face. Then they closed the door. Well, they'd have to fight it out; it wasn't any of his worry.